MW01167171

the WEDDING & DISASTER of
felONAMABEL

the WEDDING & DISASTER of
felONAMABel

KeNN BIVINS

INVISIBLENNK
Invisible Ennk Press, LLC
P.O. Box 69, Avondale Estates, GA 30002

First printing, 2015.

Published by Invisible Ennk Press

This is a work of fiction All names, characters, places and
incidents are the product of the author's imagination.
Any resemblance to real events or person's living or dead,
is entirely coincidental.

Paperback ISBN-10: 0985370726
          ISBN-13: 978-0-9853707-2-5

E-book   ISBN-10: 0985370734
          ISBN-13: 978-0-9853707-3-2

felonamabel.com   .

Cover illustration by Kenn Bivins
Book design by Kenn Bivins

for Mom

contents

*"I never learned to count my blessings.
I choose instead to dwell in my disasters."*

– Ray LaMontagne from 'Empty'

1

Ethnically Coalesced

Defined by coils of red hair, freckles, and a faint, circular tattoo on the soft part of her neck, Felona Mabel is undaunted by the menace before her.

Damon Hayes shifts in the seat across from her. The metal cuffs that bind him clang loudly against the steel table. He closes the folder in front of him and slides it back to Felona.

He sits back, returning to his menacing grimace. His thick eyebrows shroud the slightest hint of remorse and he shrugs, "Why're you showing me this? What does this have to do with her?"

A two-way glass mirror runs the length of the wall facing him, adorning the otherwise gray, lifeless room reserved for interrogation.

Felona clasps her hands together in front of her, gingerly smiling. Her pastel green pantsuit and tan blazer offers sharp contrast to the orange-clad Damon.

"It's been a few years. I wanted to put a fresh image in your head to remind you of her, when she was a baby...an innocent child in all of this."

He lowers his chin and scowls, snorting air from his nose

as a bull before charging.

Felona calmly continues, "This has everything to do with her because my next question has been on the minds of millions of people that saw you convicted for torturing and brutally murdering eight innocent people. Why would you take your infant daughter with you while you strategically stalked and murdered your victims? Is childcare so difficult to find?"

Fifteen years ago, circumstantial evidence indicated Damon Hayes as the prime suspect in connection with the murder of eight medical professionals over a period of six months. Forensic evidence not only overwhelmingly confirmed that he was responsible, but also that his two-year old daughter was present during at least five of the killings. The media labeled Damon as the Babysitting Butcher, but investigators never fully knew his motive.

He shifts in his seat again, clenching his fists and tightening his jaw, glaring at Felona in grim silence.

An unarmed officer stands behind her with a stone glare fixated on Damon while the overhead hum of fluorescent light bulbs fill the void of tense silence.

Damon's face softens briefly and he quietly says, "I'm her father. I'm all that she had. And those people were far from innocent."

Felona scoffs. "They weren't innocent? You eviscerated them of their sexual organs. Evidence shows that most of their wounds were sustained while still alive. What did they do that warranted such inhumane torture by you, Damon?"

"They deserved it. All of them. They killed an innocent woman who trusted them," he mumbles.

"They killed...who, Damon? Who did they kill?"

He looks up from the floor and a cruelty returns to his face.

"They murdered Ainoa's mom. They murdered my wife!" he snarls.

"Who made you judge, jury and executioner?" Felona returns abruptly.

"I tried to get justice," he shouts, slamming his fists and chains on the table. "For a year I tried to get legal and civil help to bring those monsters to justice. No one did anything about it. I had no choice. I had to avenge my wife all the while protecting my daughter!"

Felona exhales deeply and leans back in her chair. She looks past Damon's shoulder at a large camera perched atop a tripod where her partner, Guy Greatstorm, holds a boom microphone a few feet above the table. They exchange brief glances full of some meaning and Guy nods his head slightly.

She leans forward, returning her focus to Damon.

"But you knew you would get caught. You staged those last two crime scenes to make a statement. You knew you would get caught, Damon. How were you protecting Ainoa? How were you planning to be there for her after you got caught? If you're all that she had, how would you be there for her when you went to prison? Who would she have then? You sacrificed Ainoa, but for what?"

"Her legacy," he growls. "While your pretty little head may not get it, my fate was sealed the moment they murdered my wife. The most I could do was perpetuate justice and make sure that Ainoa was taken care of. I staged the last theater of justice because I knew that it would gain enough national publicity that she would be relegated to the best possible care. I'm not crazy, mad or obsessed, as I have been labeled. I'm a parent who loved his child enough to make a tough decision that most people wouldn't have the guts to consider."

Felona chuckles, mockingly. She looks over her shoulder at the officer and then back to Guy.

"A loving parent, huh?"

"Yes!" he hisses as he leans forward, yanking his cuffs toward him.

Felona leans in so that her face is mere inches away from Damon's.

"Loving parents don't leave their children to chance fate," she sneers. "The greatest legacy a parent can leave their child tomorrow is to be present in their lives today."

"Bad ass interview, Felo," Guy says, smirking, as he unloads a dolly full of camera equipment into the back of the news van that's parked in the loading dock of Siddim Valley State Prison.

"Um...thanks?" she says, standing near, as she scribbles on a clipboard.

"I'm not fuckin' with you. We're onto some Emmy material here. But toward the end, I thought you were gonna punch Damon in the face."

"Guy, if I don't lead with aggression, I'm not taken

seriously and all people will see is a pretty face."

"That's definitely what I see. A pretty face that will bite your head off if you cross her or say the wrong thing."

He laughs as he heaves a large battery pack into the van.

Felona stops writing to peer at Guy who fails to notice as he continues, "But we got some good footage. It was probably good that you showed bias and emotion in there. That'll amp the ratings and your fan base."

For the past six years, Felona has worked as a news reporter and special assignment anchor with WADM, one of the most visible news markets in the nation.

Despite her attractiveness, public appeal and soft appearance, she's proven to be tenacious, intelligent and stubborn when pursuing a story.

Because of her attractiveness, she's received some privilege that many of her male counterparts don't enjoy without much persuasion, such as the opportunity to interview one of the most talked about criminals in the last decade.

She returns the clipboard to the prison guard standing near. He flips through a few sheets of paper, glancing at them, before smiling and saying, "Thank you, beautiful. I hope you got everything you needed. Maybe you can interview me next time, huh?"

Felona smiles back politely and says, "Thank you for your hospitality."

"Or not," he mumbles, returning to the security booth to open the gates for them to exit.

She returns to Guy who is leaning against the news van,

smoking.

"We good?" she asks.

"Golden good," he smiles before exhaling a cloud of odorless smoke.

She opens the passenger side door and removes her blazer, slinging it and her handbag onto the seat before returning to join Guy.

He has been her cameraman, producer and sidekick since she started. They've won several industry awards as a team. During that time, their professional relationship evolved into a friendship peppered with sarcasm, insults, eye rolling and irreverent banter that would typically be exchanged between bar room buddies.

"I thought you were trying to quit. You smoke those fake cigarettes more than you smoked the Marly Reds last year."

Guy removes the cigarette from his mouth and studies it. With his other hand, he strokes the long braided stream of hair that hangs from his chin, contradicting an otherwise hairless face.

"I did quit," he finally responds. "But I like the flavor of nicotine without the harmful side effects of carcinogens."

Felona scoffs. "You sound like a commercial."

"I'm a fan. Plus, it makes me look classy," he says with a lisp, posing with his hands on his hip.

"Seek help, dude."

They both laugh, but the laughter trails off. Felona leans against the van, looking at the ground thoughtfully with her arms crossed.

"You alright?" Guy asks in a concerned tone.

"Yeah, sure. Why?"

"You've been acting kind of strange."

"Strange?"

"Yeah. Weird. You've been acting like... like a girl."

Felona shifts from her leaned position to turn to Guy. She holds her hand to mouth, simulating that she's holding a microphone, with her other hand to her ear as if she listening with an earpiece.

"This just in. It's been reported by a burly, fake cigarette-smoking source that Felona Mabel, the freckle-faced, roving reporter for WADM, is a woman. That's right. A woman! Please lock your doors and keep your children and small pets secured until further notice. We'll keep you posted as this story develops."

"Hardy fuckin' har. You know what I mean. You're usually unfazed by shit, but lately you've been all...feely."

"Feely?"

"Yeah. Feely."

"Is that even a word, dude?"

"You know what I mean. Like the interview that we just wrapped. I think those were real feelings in there and not you just trying to get a rise out of butcher boy. Basically, I think you've been losing your edge ever since..."

"Don't you fucking say it, Guy!"

"Somebody has to say it, Felo. Your edge is what people love about you and you've kind of gotten soft ever since you got engaged."

Felona fakes laughter and shrugs. "I'm not agreeing with you, but if I'm different in any way, it's got nothing to do with getting engaged. Maybe it's just coincidental. Who the fuck knows? But since I got engaged, I've been thinking more about where I'm going and what I really want in life... beyond right now."

"I thought you already knew what you wanted...to be anchor, make a difference and run shit."

"Me running shit? Well, we know that's not likely anytime soon. Your girlfriend, Ms. Dashley, pilfered the anchor spot from under me by sleeping with every exec that was within influence of promoting her."

"My girlfriend? Ha! I wish. I'd love to go home to that sweet, little blond ass every night."

"Puh–lease. You're better off with your self-respect and dick intact than messing around with that walking petri-dish-cum-bag."

"See? In a confusing instant, you go from being Oprah to exercising the vernacular of a bad ass barfly who fails to understand the finer and subtler wiles of sensitivity."

"And meanwhile, you're consistently and evermore my asshole producer."

"Ha! I just keeps it real," he says in an exaggerated manner. "But you know that thing with Danielle isn't about you, right? I mean, even though our exposure is buried on weekends, our ratings are still relatively good. Plus, we got three Emmys. She ain't won jack shit. I'm scratching my ass over how she got promoted over you when her viewership isn't even close."

"You already know what that's about, Guy. In this industry, blond hair and blue eyes trump ethnically coalesced all day long."

—————

Towering frames of metal and concrete jut from the commotion and busyness of Admah City, stretching toward a calm, orange sky where pink-tinted clouds drift slowly.

While Felona is drawn to the metropolitan lifestyle, which includes varied cultures, diverse music and food and a litany of things to do, she chooses not to be consumed by the perpetual traffic, crime and noise. Her job is chaotic and demanding on its own.

Instead she salvages a modicum of peace in her loft, located fifteen miles southwest of Admah City in an industrial live-work community called North Wells.

North Wells was once a sprawling acreage of manufacturing plants, but those businesses eventually succumbed to a declining national economy and work being shipped overseas. The abandoned area was neglected for almost two decades before development was proposed by private investors to convert it into retail, office and residential spaces.

North Wells was once teeming with tractor-trailers, dump trucks and blue-collar workers, but now, during business hours, it's bustling with German cars, delivery couriers and Fioravanti-clad professionals.

The smell of tar and pine straw still lingers in the air, bearing evidence of a relatively new development. Unique architecture of weathered brick and stone is married with tinted glass, floating facets and other modern design elements throughout this highly coveted and exclusive span of lofts, condos and boutique businesses.

The jingling sound of keys, as she unlocks her front door, marks the official end of Felona's workday of filming and editing.

She lightly taps a panel on the wall in her foyer and light overwhelms the shadows that were previously waiting for her to return home.

She tosses her handbag and keys on a chaise near the entryway, kicking off her shoes before walking across the cool, hardwood floor toward the kitchen.

Finally! Home sweet home, she thinks.

Felona exhales as she collapses onto her couch.

She breathes deeply and lies still.

Long, peaceful moments pass until a thump comes from outside the front door, followed by a rattle of the doorknob and keys jangling on the other side.

The door opens. "Bella?"

Felona stirs from her repose, irritated by the sudden interruption. Her irritation dims as she sits up to see her fiancé.

"Vin. Hey," she says sleepily.

The door slams closed as Vincenzo Ricci, or Vin as Felona calls him, is already towering over her.

"Bella, come give your man a hug."

Felona, still seated, looks up at his statuesque, six foot five figure. She reaches up toward him, gesturing him to come closer.

"Why don't you come get it?"

"Ugh! You're so stubborn sometimes!" she surrenders, sighing before standing to hug him. "What're you doing out so late?"

He engulfs her slender, five foot, seven frame in a tight embrace, momentarily lifting her from the floor.

"I just wanted to wrap my arms around this tiny waist and stare into these hazel eyes. Is that a crime?"

"No. Not at all," she purrs, reciprocating his blue-eyed gaze before tiptoeing to kiss him.

He relaxes his grip from their temporal embrace and turns his attention to the kitchen, brushing past Felona.

"I just finished another late night and was headed home. I wanted to grab some of that gnocci that I made the other night. Anymore left?"

She collapses back onto the couch, sighing.

"Whatever you cooked is still there. I've been pretty much living at the studio trying to finish everything up this week."

Vin rifles through the refrigerator while Felona asks, "Did you want to go with me to meet with the photographer tomorrow?"

The clatter of dishes from the kitchen is all that answers her.

"Vin?" she whines loudly after a few moments of continued noise.

"What?" he eventually returns from behind a mouthful.

Felona sits up and looks toward the kitchen in surprise. "Are you eating that cold?"

He nods his head as he stuffs another forkful into his mouth.

"It's perfectly vested with flavor after it sits for a day or so. Heating any kind of pasta at this stage ruins the integrity of the dish."

"If you say so, Mr. Chef. Do you want to meet the photographer with me tomorrow?"

"I can't." He smacks loudly. "Besides, she just needs a check. I got the merger meeting with Brisbane Properties coming up and a full day of meetings before that. You may be looking at the next VP if all goes well."

"That's exciting. A big merger before our big merger."

He slurps from a glass before slamming it down on the counter and sucking his teeth while chuckling.

"Cute, bella."

He returns his attention to Felona on the couch, leaning in and kissing her on the neck with intensity.

"Really?" she says with some resistance. "With your garlic, wine breath and everything?"

Vin peels his jacket off while advancing down her neck to her breasts, fumbling with her belt buckle.

Felona relents. With one hand, she runs her fingers through his brunette hair, pulling him closer, while with the other, she unbuttons her own blouse.

Vin finally answers, "Really."

2
Inconvenient

The dim room and spirited conversation is no indication that it's early morning as Felona and Guy sit slouched in front of several computer monitors.

A majority of their work is done in editing rooms like this, away from the prestige of the cameras and the inherent danger of the streets. Instead, they're camped in a modest, darkened, soundproof suite with two or three large plasma screens mounted on a wall, a couch in the background, random snacks and the consequential glow of any supporting equipment.

"So you're telling me that you don't want this shot here?" Guy says with a side-eyed glance toward Felona.

"Yes, Guy. That's what I'm saying. Actually, I don't think the shot works at all. It changes the tone. It looks like something that would be in an outtakes reel."

"But it's funny as shit to throw it in for random sake."

"We're putting together a documentary, dude. Not some fucking, half-scripted, desperate-attempt-at-ratings, reality show. Can we move past this, please? I'm not trying to spend all day here."

"Geezus! I'm just kidding. What crawled up your ass this

morning? Fine. Done."

He leans back in his chair and takes a drag from his electronic cigarette, before exhaling a thick cloud of steam.

Felona sighs. "I'm sorry, dude. I'm just ready to be done with this. I didn't want this shit assignment anyway. It just feels like busy work since I was denied promotion. Plus, I'm out of here in a couple of days. You shouldn't have to suffer alone."

Guy leans forward, stroking his goatee and with a melodramatic tone says, "I hear you, Felo. And I want to believe that your heart longs for my well-being while you're on your honeymoon, but we both know you're full of shit."

"Full of shit? How so?"

He smirks.

"Don't act baffled. You know you're full of shit. And here I thought you were making such progress going to those CFA meetings last year."

She scowls, confused.

"CFA meetings? Guy, what the hell are you talking about?"

"CFA. Control Freaks Anonymous."

"Boy if you don't get out of here."

She shoves his chair away from her and he nearly falls out of it as they both laugh.

The ringtone of a cell phone from inside Felona's handbag on the couch interrupts their brief merriment.

She jumps up from her chair and across the room to retrieve her phone as if she's expecting a call.

"Hello?" she answers as she holds up a finger to silence

Guy who is still laughing hysterically. "Hold on a second," she says as she steps out of the editing room

---

"Ms. Mabel?" a gravely voice asks on the other end.

"Yes? This is she. Who is this?"

"Ms. Mabel, this is the office of Dr. Oscar Amos of the respiratory unit at Swan Providence Medical Center in Nathaniel. Dr. Amos needs to speak with you in person about an urgent and time-sensitive matter regarding a Dianne Mabel, who is a patient here."

"A patient there? She's still in the hospital?"

More than a month ago, Felona received a voicemail from Tobias Coles, a childhood friend, who informed her that her estranged mother had collapsed while at the grocery store and was rushed to the emergency room. What the voicemail didn't go further into detail about was that it was discovered that she'd suffered internal hemorrhaging. Tests revealed that both of her lungs had become infected. Shortly after being admitted, her condition worsened and she never regained consciousness.

For most of her life, Dianne Mabel has had lupus, a condition where inflammation and tissue damage occur due to the immune system attacking the body's cells. It was further complicating matters.

Felona never returned Tobias' call and, given the fact that she and her mother hadn't been on speaking terms for eight years, she gave little regard to the realization that her mother's accident could have serious consequences.

"Yes, Ms. Mabel. Your mother is hospitalized here. She has appointed you as her power of attorney and, given her declining condition, it's imperative that you get here as soon as possible. I'm sorry to have to tell you this, but it appears that she doesn't have much time at all."

Felona drops her arms and leans against the hallway wall. She sighs.

Felona paces the hallway before making a call to Kinaya Odoyo, or Ny, who is her best friend and also an obstetrician.

"Ny, hey. Good morning. Do you have a moment?"

"Hey, sweetie. I'm waiting for a patient to dilate right now. I got a couple of minutes. What's up, girlie?"

"What do you know about lupus?"

"Ummmm….? Why?" she asks with a concerned tone.

"I just got a call about my mother. She's got it. Well, she's always had it, but now she's in a coma and they said the lupus is working against her."

"Coma? Oh no! Sweetie, when did this… what happened?"

"I don't know the details, really. I haven't talked to her in years. But the hospital said that I needed to go there immediately and I just wanted to get your perspective as a doctor."

"Well, I don't have enough information to tell you anything

professionally, but as your best friend, I can tell you that you should go as soon as you're physically able. Now, even."

"I can't just leave now, Ny. I have some major work to finish today."

"If she's as bad off as you say, you won't get this chance again. Lupus coupled with a coma, that has been aggravated by who-knows-what, is a critical issue. You don't want to live with the regret of delay. You and her may not be close, but you need to go."

Felona sighs.

"And then I have the wedding coming up."

"Felo, sickness and death are always inconvenient, but this is your mom we're talking about. You need to go. You asked for my advice. There it is. Go."

"Shit!" Felona mumbles.

"Hey, girlie, I'm getting paged. I have to run, but I'm going to call you back in a few and check on you. Know that I'm here for you. You're not by yourself with this."

"Guy, I just got a call about my mother," Felona says when she returns to the editing room.

"I guess it would be inappropriate for me to insert a momma joke here right now, huh?" he returns, with his back to her.

Felona's silence causes him to spin around to see that she is standing in the middle of the room and wearing a sullen expression.

His smirk turns to concern.

"What's wrong?"

"She's in a coma. She's dying."

"Oh, shit. I'm sorry, Felo."

Felona shakes her head, dismissing any sign of emotion.

"I need to drive to Nathaniel today or tonight or whenever the fuck soon. The hospital needs me to be there… as soon as possible, they said."

Guy stands.

"Hey, do what you need. You know I got this."

He steps forward and hugs Felona, lightly patting her on the back while looking away.

"I appreciate that," she says, pulling from the awkward embrace and patting him on the chest. She looks at him with sincerity. "You're a good dude. I'm sorry to leave you like this."

"Hey, it's not your fault. We see stuff like this all the time. Sickness and death don't make appointments. They just show up, eat all your food, break your shit and then leave."

3
Comatose

Several hours of duty, delay and daylight passes before Felona finally relents.

A sudden and torrential downpour does little to soothe her lingering reluctance while her SUV barrels through the rain and darkness.

She tightly grips the steering wheel that dwarfs her petite frame while leaning forward, straining to focus past thick sheets of rain crashing into the windshield.

With one hand over her nose and mouth, she groans to herself. "I feel nauseous again. Ugh... I really don't want to have to pull over a third time. I just want this to be over."

She purses her lips tightly as the remnant taste of vomit lingers between her tongue and the roof of her mouth. It was only thirty minutes ago that dinner erupted from her stomach and the bile and stomach lining that remains is threatening to spew forth as well.

The headlights of oncoming cars passing in the opposing lane intermittently hinder Felona's vision as she winces to see, rocking back and forth, trying to ignore the increasing queasiness.

"10:45," she mumbles, glancing at the clock nestled among the dashboard instruments that emit a green glow, illuminating her soft features.

"Left turn ahead," announces a monotone female voice from the navigation system. Felona slows her Range Rover to a stop as the turn signal dings.

"Left turn ahead," she mocks aloud. "I wonder if the voice of the nav system has a husband who appreciates her with that boring voice. If he does, I hope her bedroom voice is a little more seductive than the drone she delivers directions with."

Felona chuckles at the ridiculous and random thought, though it does little to distract her.

She exhales sharply.

The windshield wipers thump wildly back and forth, in sync with her increasing heartbeat as it pounds against the wall of her chest. Adrenalin and frenzied thoughts suddenly race through her mind at the realization of where she is now. Home. Or what was once home. The city of Nathaniel.

Nathaniel is two hours away or ninety-five miles south of Admah City. Her aversion to her hometown hasn't diminished since she's been away.

As far as she's concerned, Nathaniel is desolate and unforgiving of anyone who is different. It's either black or white here. No room for freckle-faced, mixed kids born to apprehensive and hateful mothers.

Without taking her eyes from the road, she presses a small button, which is marked with an illustrated icon of a person talking, on the left side of the steering wheel.

"Vincenzo Ricci," she articulates slowly. A rapid succession of beeps respond to her voice followed by a ring tone through the speakers, which were previously playing an allegretto of Chopin in the background.

The line clicks.

"Hey, bella. It started raining here as soon as you left. Did you make it there okay?"

"Vin, hey. Yeah, I'm here. The rain caught me and stayed with me most of the way, but I made it safely." She exhales loudly, "And now for the hard part."

"It'll be okay, bella. I wish I could be there with you, but I have to be physically present at this merger meeting in the morning."

"Vin...you don't have to justify not coming with me. That meeting is important. I understand. Believe me, if I didn't have to be here, I wouldn't be. But I'm her only child so the responsibility falls on me. I haven't been here nor talked to her in years so coming back here feels strange under the circumstances. Perhaps there is some kind of closure that..."

She abruptly stops talking as hateful, out-of-context words from her childhood shove their way to the forefront of her thoughts... *Not good enough. Fake white girl. Accidental baby. Dirty face. Bitch.*

Suddenly muted, Felona gazes straight ahead and abstract memories ebb and then fade.

Vin's voice interrupts her fog of thought. "Bella? Hello? Felona, are you still there?"

She shakes her head from side to side as if to empty it of

all negative clutter.

"Oh. Yes. S–sorry about that. Traffic distracted me. I was saying, maybe this is a necessary thing… for closure."

"Closure? Closure of what?"

"Closure of wanting the relationship that I'll never have with my mother."

A pregnant silence follows as Felona waits for Vin to say something in response. He says nothing.

She finally says, "Get some sleep. I'll let you know how things go once I find out more in the morning. I'm thinking that I should be on my way back home as soon as I make the arrangements. It probably won't be until late tomorrow though."

"So, you've already decided what you're going to do?"

"There's nothing to decide. I'm simply talking to the doctor and signing whatever legal documents necessary. She's been on a ventilator for five weeks from what I understand and not improving, but getting worse. I'm not playing God nor claiming any real responsibility here. I'm just taking part in a legal procedure that has my name on it… that's all."

"Okay okay. Calm down. Look, I know that you and your mom aren't close. Until now, I've never known that you desired a relationship with her based on how angry you get whenever I ask about her. And you know, maybe you're right. This will be closure for you. Bella, I'm here for you even though I can't be there with you. Okay? Let me know how it goes as soon you find out anything."

"I will. Good night."

"Good night. Love you, Bella."

She responds with, "I love you too," but the line goes dead before he can hear her.

The city of Nathaniel has bad cell phone reception in certain areas. A declining population has led the local government and mobile carriers to be reticent to build new towers to support the current subscribers.

Chopin resumes over the speakers.

She glances over to her phone where it lies in the center console and sees that the reception indicator shows no service.

"No bars. Bad reception. Great. I see this town is still this town. Welcome back to Nathaniel, Felona," she sarcastically mumbles to herself as she guides her vehicle onto a street that reads, "HOSPITAL ENTRANCE."

The rain subsides and she comes to a fork in the road with a sign bearing, "Right EMERGENCY. Left MAIN HOSPITAL ENTRANCE."

She tilts the rearview mirror down toward her face and checks her eyes for any debris, misplaced makeup or reason to turn back and head home. A soft, bluish glow reflects on her freckled face from a nearby caged light bulb, overlooking a public telephone on a wall that is marked POLICE EMERGENCY near the parking deck elevators.

She gazes in the mirror, her mind absent of any real thought at this point. She tilts her head down slightly and to the side, pulling at taut, red ringlets of hair that are cropped close to her head. They recoil from the grasp of her tan fingers, returning to the organized chaos of curls that are tamed only by two jade barrettes that are atop either side of her head.

Her breathing has calmed and her heart is no longer pounding in her chest. But she seems to be in no hurry to go inside the hospital to confront neither her unconscious mother nor the role she will play in her inevitable fate.

She returns the rearview mirror to its original position and grips her handbag close to her, sharply exhaling as she opens the car door, tugging and smoothing out her plaid, pencil skirt, which has become wrinkled from the long drive.

"I can do this. I can do this." she assures herself as she walks toward the hospital entrance. The slow clicking of her heels reveals her reluctance.

Thirty-two years and some odd months ago, Felona was born here at Swan Providence Medical Center. While most parents would hail the birth of their healthy, seven and a half pound daughter as a miracle from the heavens, her parents were not as privileged to possess those feelings of pride and jubilation.

Her mother, Dianne Mabel, was too distracted with the lament and shame of giving birth to the product of rape... while her father-by-fate, Ignazio Bernardi, was forty miles away in a prison, unaware that his seed had been born into a world that would not trumpet her arrival.

Felona's footsteps become more deliberate and quicken,

as does her heartbeat, as she gets closer to the automatic sliding door that opens into the hospital where her mother awaits.

4

Mother's Day

1994

At age eleven, Felona's growing fixation was to garner her mother's approval. For almost a week, she'd planned and prepared for Mother's Day, her perfect opportunity to win adoration.

She loved to paint and make pretty things so she decided to make her mother a bouquet of flowers from felt, colored paper and pipe cleaners. She wanted her mother to have flowers that would last forever and not die like those bought from a flower shop or plucked from a garden.

Yellow, pink, and white flowers with green stems and leaves were crafted into a bouquet and she'd planned to give them to her mother right before church. She didn't want her to see them before it was time so she tucked them behind her back and under the waistband of her dress. Since the flowers were made of felt, they easily flattened from detection along with the card that she'd made for her as well.

On the front of the card, she'd drawn a picture of her mother wearing a green and yellow sundress, wedges and a big smile while little hearts floated around her. Her mom was also pictured with a bouquet of flowers that looked like the ones that she would receive. At the top of the picture, bubbly letters read, "Happy Mother's Day to the best mom ever."

Inside the card, were more hearts and she'd written, "Dear Mom, I hope you have the best day ever and I hope I don't make you mad today. I love you."

Scribbly, cursive writing that was supposed to be Felona's signature, followed. She went through a phase where she wanted to be a doctor. According to her eleven-year old mind, since doctors scribble their names on prescriptions and important letters, she needed advance practice so she'd started signing her name with what looked so illegible that it had to be important.

"Mom, I have a surprise for you," Felona announced as soon as her mother parked the car. The parking lot was full on that particular Sunday as it was Mother's Day, a well-attended event, second only to Easter.

Felona was adorned in a lacy, white dress covered in patterns of yellow and white flowers with pink, puffy short sleeves and she had on pink socks with patent leather, white shoes. Her mother took pride in Felona's appearance despite her tomboyish behavior.

She would often lecture her on how girls were supposed to act although Felona acted like she wanted to be a boy. She often warned her that if she continued in such behavior, boys would not like her and she would grow up to become a lesbian.

At the time, Felona didn't know what a lesbian was so her

mother's warnings did little to change her rough, unladylike ways.

While her mother prepped her makeup in the visor mirror, Felona opened the car door and ran to the driver's side to greet her with her present. She stood at the car door with her surprise hidden behind her back, waiting for her mother to get out, her eyes fixated on her.

When her mother finally opened the door to get out, she looked down at Felona's legs and exclaimed, "Felona! What've you gotten into?"

"I have a surprise for you," she innocently said as she revealed what was behind her back.

Her mother's expression melted from concern to shock to disgust.

Felona followed her mother's widened eyes and looked down at what she was seeing. A stream of blood had run down her leg and stained the top of her white socks.

Felona looked up at her mom and in a terrified voice whimpered, "Mommy, what –?"

Her mother's expression turned into a scowl just as she grabbed her by the arm and jerked her around.

The card and flowers, intended to win her mother's favor, fell to the ground.

The yellow and white flowers on the lower back of her dress were dotted with specks of blood.

"Felona Mabel, you've made a disaster of a mess! What in the devil has gotten into you? Why didn't you tell me?"

Felona started to cry because she didn't know 'what in the

devil had gotten into her.'

Blame it on too much television, but she associated blood with bad things. To her, blood meant something horrible had happened and she was going to bleed to death due to some disease that little girls get when their mothers are unhappy with them.

Her mother got a garbage bag out of the trunk and emptied it of the clothes that she had planned to donate to Goodwill. She made Felona step into the garbage bag and hold it above her waist before she got back in the car to sit.

"I'm sorry, mom," she pleaded, searching her mother's face for some hint of compassion or forgiveness. But she found no forgiveness in her display.

"Be quiet, Felona, 'fore I give you something to cry about. You just ruined your new dress and now we're going to miss church because of this foolishness. You should have told me something. Now just shut up that crying right now. I mean it!" was all she said as she drove back home.

Felona continued to cry.

The card and flowers that she'd made to earn her love were no more than trash to her, thrown in the garbage bag that Felona now sat in, stained with blood.

She'd discarded them just as Felona felt that she'd been discarded.

Dianne Mabel didn't talk to her daughter as a mother should when she first gets her period. She didn't put an arm around her and explain to Felona that this was her entry into early womanhood and there was no reason to be afraid. She didn't make her feel safe at all. She simply condemned her with silence for reasons an eleven-year old couldn't begin to understand.

When they got home, her mother made Felona sit in a bathtub full of warm water while she continued to weep, afraid. She sat in the water until it turned as cold as her mother who told her that she needed to be careful around boys because now she could get pregnant.

Later that day, Felona sat outside on the front porch, ashamed and unsure of what was happening to her. She'd started to feel cramps, which made her all the more fearful. She'd never had that feeling before and she was bent over clutching her stomach, wanting her mother to hug her and tell her that everything was going to be okay.

Tobias, her best friend and next-door-neighbor, was outside tossing a football in the air before he noticed her sitting on the porch.

He was a handsome and charismatic child that would initiate conversation with anyone. He seemed more comfortable exchanging with adults than children his own age, but he was fond of Felona.

She wanted to call him over, but she remembered what her mother had said about being careful around boys so she remained silent and watched him until he visited on his own.

As was normal between them, he playfully punched her

in the side of the arm before sitting beside her.

"What up, Curlytop?"

She felt a nervousness that she'd never felt before, more akin to fear.

"You can't sit next to me now," she informed him.

"Why?'

"You just can't."

She shifts, putting distance between them.

"Why? Are you mad at me?"

"No."

Tobias stood and looked at her sadly.

"I don't understand," he shrugged.

She lowered her head to look away from his disappointed eyes. They'd been best friends until that moment, but Felona was abandoning him in the same way that her mother had done to her. But she didn't want to be like her mother. She didn't want Tobias to experience the same rejection she felt.

"I was bleeding today," she volunteered. "And now I hurt."

He sat down beside her, judging a comfortable distance.

"Bleeding? Where? I don't see. What hurts?"

She looked up and searched his eyes. Her friend was still there. He didn't abandon her. He was the only one that she felt she could trust so she revealed to him her shame.

"At church, I was bleeding where I pee. I had blood all over my clothes. And now my stomach hurts really bad. My mom said that I can get pregnant being around boys now so I can't be your friend anymore."

"Oh."

Tobias laughed heartily.

"Why are you laughing? That's not funny."

"You're silly. You can't get pregnant from just being around me or sitting next to me."

"My mom said I could."

"That's not true. You just got your period. That's all."

"My period?"

"Yeah. Duh! Don't you know anything? It's when a girl bleeds down there." He pointed at her groin. "Like...three times a year or something. The egg inside her drops and breaks and that makes her bleed."

"I don't have eggs inside me," she protested as she punched him in the arm.

"When you become a teenager, you do."

"I'm just eleven. I'm not a teenager yet. Duh! Don't you know anything?"

"Vivian, this girl in my homeroom who is only eleven, got her period last month. She was wearing white pants and everything. Everybody was laughing at her and she didn't even know. It was crazy."

Felona lowered her head, reliving the shame.

"I was wearing my new dress and shoes. My mom was so mad. That's when she said that I could get pregnant being around boys."

"Maybe she was just kidding around. You know. Playing a joke on you or something."

"My mom doesn't tell jokes."

Felona was more confused than ever at that point. She was

of the opinion that Tobias knew everything because he talked about a lot of different things with authority. He certainly knew more about periods than she did or that her mother shared with her.

"How do you know about periods?" she asked. "You're not a girl."

"I'm not a girl? Whoah. All this time I thought I was? Who knew?" he joked.

She laughed.

"No really. How do you know?"

"My mom makes me walk to the store sometimes to get lady stuff for her. She told me what it was for. And they talk about it in health class too."

"We don't talk about that in my health class. We just do a lot of running around in the gym. So your mom tells you a lot, huh?

"Yeah. She told me about the birds and the bees too."

Felona proudly said, "I know about birds. I don't like bugs though."

Tobias laughed and playfully punched her on the side of her arm before he jumped up.

"Do you want to play, Curlytop?" he asked as he smacked the football between his palms.

She swung at him still clutching her stomach, but failed to connect from her seated position.

"My stomach hurts, Smartypants."

"Oh. Okay."

Felona and Tobias had nicknames for each other that no

one else could call them. Hers was Curlytop because of her big, curly hair, while his was Smartypants because he seemed to have an answer for everything.

He turned to leave, but she asked, "Where're you going?"

"You said you couldn't play."

"I didn't say I couldn't play. I said my stomach hurts. But even with a stomach ache, I can still run the ball and fake you out before I make a touchdown."

"Yeah, right. We'll see."

"Just don't hit so hard."

Even as womanhood had reared its head in blood, Felona still persisted to act as a tomboy. She and Tobias played despite the fact that she moved awkward with a pad between her legs and stomach cramps that were getting increasingly worse. He was her best friend and she would learn many more things from him...including the birds and the bees.

5
Reunion

"Pardon me," Felona announces to a woman, seated behind a large desk that is clearly marked INFORMATION. The woman is fixated on a computer monitor in front of her and doesn't stir from her concentration or give any indication that she's heard her.

"Excuse me?" Felona says loudly and with a bit of attitude while leaning her five foot seven frame over the desk.

The woman peers over narrow glasses that rest on the tip of her nose while continuing to peck on a keyboard in front of her. "How may I help you, ma'am?" she drones.

My name is Felona Mabel and I'm here to speak with Dr. Amos about my mother who is a patient here."

"What is your mother's name?"

"Dianne Mabel."

"Dr. Huffman is on call for Dr. Amos. If you don't mind waiting in your mother's room for a few moments, I'll page him to come speak with you."

"Where is her room?"

"Excuse me?"

"My mother! What room is she in?"

"Your mother is in the same room she's been in since being released from ICU. I thought you said ..." Valerie frowns slightly and sighs, "She's on the fourth floor in Room 433," and returns her attention to the monitor, shaking her head.

Felona stares at Valerie, who doesn't look up or acknowledge her presence further, before she finally turns and walks away.

An elevator ride and several uncertain hallway explorations later, Felona opens the door to Room 433.

Darkness greets her, but as she moves beyond the entranceway, her eyes slowly adjust to the dimness. She's able to focus on a bed that is tucked in the corner of the room where her shadowy figure of a mother lies. A single night-light above the bed creates an ominous collection of shadows, which are made more menacing by the repetitive beeps and hissing of machines that are nearby.

She tiptoes on the balls of her feet so that her heels won't make a sound on the linoleum floor as she stalks toward the bed.

Holding her handbag close to her chest with both hands, she moves closer, staring at her mother in the muted light.

A clear mask covers her nose and mouth obscuring features that were once all too common to Felona. Now she's unsure if her mother's present appearance is due to the consequence of years of aging. Or if what remains of the woman she once knew is lying lifeless and mummified due to the past few weeks of deteriorating health in a coma.

A tube runs from the mask alongside the bed to a large machine that emits a hiss and a click, synonymous to and responsible for her breathing.

With eerie stillness, her chest movement underneath the covers is barely visible.

She looks frail and helpless, unlike the last time I saw her, but I refuse to feel sympathy or compassion for her, Felona vows to herself.

No, I won't fall for the trap of feeling sorry for her. Not when this woman has been more my nemesis than my mother. She's been the author of many hateful words and deeds.

Felona's jaw tightens as familiar and hateful phrases echo in her head.

Not good enough. Fake white girl. Accidental baby. Dirty face. Bitch.

Startled by the sound of running water and a flushing toilet, she glances to her left and sees light coming from underneath a closed door, just before it swings open.

A tall, dark-skinned man steps out and looks up from wiping his hands on his clothes just as their eyes meet. A wide smile that bares white, perfect teeth spreads across his face.

"Felona! My god, girl, you made it! Come over here."

He steps forward, pulling her into an unsolicited hug.

With her arms to her side, Felona's body is stiff as he engulfs her in a bear hug. She stares straight ahead for a moment before finally returning the hug... albeit with a little less enthusiasm. "Hey, Tobias."

People are usually captivated by Tobias' charm and engaging smile. Armed with symmetrical features that are consistent with someone who models and eyes that seem to be continuously smiling, he has no trouble warming strangers to him.

Women, especially, were drawn to his attention, thoughtfulness and unmistakable confidence that were a few inches shy of pretentiousness.

As children, he and Felona were inseparable playmates. That is until puberty and circumstance tore them apart.

After high school, he enlisted in the Army while she escaped Nathaniel to go to college in Admah City.

"Sit down here. Take a load off," he says to her, as he gathers up an armful of magazines and a blanket from the chair near her mother's bed.

Felona brushes the seat of the chair before gingerly sitting on the edge of it.

Evidenced by the empty coffee cups, scattered crumbs and crumpled fast food bags on the floor, Tobias had been lodging there for, at the least, a couple of days.

He pulls up a chair from across the room and sits, still smiling at her. His face is clean-shaven and his hair is cropped so close to his head that, in the dim lighting, he appears bald.

"Wow, Felona, you look great. How long has it been?

Ten years? You haven't aged a bit, girl. How's the big city treating you? I thought about moving out there after I got back from my last tour, but I don't know what to do about my mom's house. The economy being what it is, selling isn't really an option although I don't know if I would sell it anyway. I feel like I would be leaving your mom all alone. So how long have you been..."

"Tobias! Shhhhh," she says with her eyes closed and her hands held up, already frustrated with his talkativeness and enthusiasm. "Can you pull it into the slow lane for a few? I just got here. I'm the one who should be asking questions."

"I'm sorry. I'm sorry. You're right. I'm just excited to see you. It's just been a long time."

A few moments of silence fall between them as he looks at her while she is looking away.

He breaks the silence with, "I get that it's late and you probably need to rest from your drive. And you also probably want to know what's going on with your mom and all. I can help if you tell me what you need. Do you need me to page the doctor so that you can talk to him yourself?"

Felona turns to glare at Tobias.

"Oh...sorry," he says sheepishly. "I'm just trying to help."

"I already talked to someone on the phone and I was told that my mother's condition has gotten worse over the last couple of weeks. Dr. Amos doesn't expect her to survive on her own without..."

Felona glances over to where her mother is lying and continues in a whisper, as if her mother could hear her before,

"... without the respirator and every day that she's on the machine, her body gets weaker and her chances get smaller. At this stage, it's best to let her die with dignity and terminate the machine support."

Tobias blares, "Terminate the machine support? You mean terminate her! That's not right. You're going to give up on your mother and pull the plug just like that, Felona? You'd talk like this about your own mom as if she's dirty bath water that's gonna leave a ring in the tub?"

She leans in closer to him, still whispering, "You would talk like this to me about my mother? This is my mother! You have no right to judge neither my decision nor me. I'm trying to do what's best."

Tobias scoffs and says in a lowered voice, "I'm not trying to argue with you about your mom, I'm just saying you should think this through. You don't want to struggle later on with whether you made the right decision or not. That'll haunt you for the rest of your life. I know. While I was away on duty, my mom died. I feel like I wasn't here for her like I should have been. I've felt guilty ever since. I've kind of adopted your mom as my own, but you're right. This is your decision. Your mom."

Felona studies Tobias, waiting for more words from him, but he drops his gaze to the floor and says nothing.

"Yeah, she is my mother. Not a placebo for your guilt," she asserts, "and I don't want her to continue to suffer."

Tobias looks up from the floor with a scowl on his face.

"Suffer? How do you know she's in any pain at all? She's in a coma, Felona."

"How do you know she isn't? Her brain is still able to transmit pain."

Tobias moves in closer and puts one hand on her shoulder.

"Felona, you just got here. Please don't make a hasty decision before God can intervene."

"God? I'm thinking if God hasn't intervened yet, he's probably washed his hands of the whole matter with that dirty bath water you mentioned. We should probably let that bath water out now!"

"You don't mean that," he dismisses, shaking his head.

She shrugs his hand from her shoulder.

"Don't tell me what I don't mean."

Tobias throws both of his hands up, as if in surrender.

"I'm sorry. Again. Apparently, I'm overstepping boundaries that I didn't know existed. We once were so close, I didn't think...."

"No. You didn't."

He sighs.

"Wow. Okay. How about you sleep on it? You're tired and your mind isn't as clear as it will be in the morning. Just give your mom one more day of consideration, at least. Miracles do happen. They happen all the time and your mom may be due one. She may have been waiting for you to return home all this time."

"Home?" Felona scoffs.

"If you could just give her a little more consideration... Felona? Please?"

She exhales sharply and rolls her eyes, thinking to herself,

I really don't want to drag this out, but I'm too exhausted to put up a fight at this point. Plus, I don't want to appear to be the murderous, hateful, bad guy here.

She says aloud, "Okay, fine. I'll...."

A light tap on the door, preceded by a shadowed figure entering, interrupts Felona's words. He's wearing a white lab coat and a laminate ID badge hangs from one of the coat's pockets.

"Hello?" his voice questions through the darkness. "I'm Dr. Huffman. I got a page. I'm substituting for Dr. Amos. Are you Ms. Mabel's daughter?"

She stands up and extends her hand, stepping forward.

"Yes, I'm her daughter. My name is Felona Mabel. I was told that I needed to come sign some papers regarding my mother's condition."

Dr. Huffman looks past Felona at her mother's bed.

"Let's speak outside," he directs as he steps back and opens the door into the hallway.

Tobias stands from his seat as well, but Felona gestures for him to sit back down while she follows the doctor into the hallway.

Dr. Huffman turns to face Felona as she closes the door behind her.

"Ms. Mabel, is it?"

"Yes."

"Have you talked to Dr. Amos at length?"

"Yes. I mean... not him directly or at length, but... why?"

"Well, I think it's best that you talk to him directly. It doesn't indicate on your mother's chart that you've initiated the health care directive, which may be good news. He might want to talk to you about your mother's options."

"Options? I was told that options were the one thing my mother didn't have. I was told that the respirator was creating a dependency and weakening her chances of recovering from the coma."

"Ms. Mabel, in evaluating your mother's condition, I think that even a glimmer of hope is a glimmer. While her directive is to not be resuscitated, there may be some less than orthodox options to consider that might give her a chance of recovery."

Felona's eyes widen.

Recovery? she panics to herself.

She falls back to lean against the wall, covering her face.

"Oh my god, I just want to..."

"Ms. Mabel, I know this is stressful. Maybe you should get some rest tonight and Dr. Amos can address your concerns tomorrow. While I'm attending to his patient in his stead, I can't speak for him or his intentions."

She sighs as she looks up with her arms crossed.

"What time will Dr. Amos be in tomorrow?"

"He will be here making his rounds around 7AM."

The door swings open and Tobias steps out. Felona glances in his direction before saying to the doctor, "Okay, I'll just wait to talk to him in the morning before I decide what to do next. Thank you, Dr. Huffman."

"You're welcome." He nods to Tobias and turns to walk toward the nurses' station at the end of the hall.

Without acknowledging Tobias's presence, Felona turns to walk in the opposite direction toward the elevators.

"Where are you going?" he calls out to her.

She doesn't bother to turn around.

"Your assessment was right. I'm tired. I'm going to go get some sleep. I'll be back in the morning."

Felona quietly pulls out of the parking deck, winding around the hospital, until she comes to a stop at the intersection that leads back to the highway. Though the rain has stopped, the wet ground mirrors how the darkness shrouds visibility.

She rubs her tired eyes and then her temples. The stillness that accompanies post-midnight embraces her and she dwells in her head, absent of any real thought in the moment.

She sighs and then looks longingly at the right turn that leads back to Admah City before making a left turn that will lead to a place to stay for the night.

For a few minutes, she drives in silence staring into the blackness before her.

But suddenly her mind wanders from the warmth of loneliness back to the shadowed room with the clicks, the hisses, the beeps, and the still shell of a mother. The vision of her lying there in that bed... lifeless, weakened and near death... is all that she can now see before her, emblazoned over the traffic lights and intermittent, passing cars.

This was not the larger-than-life woman who she swore she would never speak to again. This was not the same giant of a woman who constantly lacerated her sense of esteem with razor-sharp words of judgment and hate. Those lithe hands that have several tubes running from them cannot be the same strong hands that shoved her from a car in the parking lot of an abortion clinic when she needed the compassion and protection of a mother instead. This woman that she saw lying before her was frail... and human.

Suddenly, a car horn blares as it whizzes past, startling Felona into the awareness that she's slowed almost to a stop in the middle of the road. A few cars accelerate past as she gradually resumes her speed. Her hands are tight around the steering wheel as oncoming cars scatter light across her windshield from the drizzle of rain that has begun to fall again.

The drizzle, unexpectedly, turns into a downpour, forcing her to pull over into a subdivision to park until the storm passes and she can see better.

I hate driving at night. I hate driving in the rain. And I hate that the sight of seeing my mother so frail and helpless has me feeling anything similar to sorrow for her. She doesn't deserve my sorrow or sympathy.

Felona turns her headlights off and looks around, squinting past the darkness and rain to collect her bearings.

"This house... this neighborhood... looks almost identical to where I grew up on Babaro Way," she mumbles to herself.

But it isn't. I'm not sure where I am, but I know I don't want to be here in the midst of this mess when I should be home anticipating my wedding and starting over. This place, this town is full of bad memories, which is why I stayed away. So many memories. Some of them may even be good ones... but I can't seem to remember any of those.

Felona's left eye stings just before its first tear escapes. She blinks and then another tear joins the race down her freckled face.

She leans forward and wraps her arms around the steering wheel with her head down and her body shakes with regret and fear. She whimpers, feeling empty and inconsolable.

6

Denial

Hints of morning squint past the thick, embroidered curtains into Felona's otherwise darkened hotel room. She burrows further into the pillows to hide from the impending brightness.

"Turn the light off," she mumbles aloud as if there is someone else in the room with her.

She lifts her head from the pillow and looks around.

What time is it? The sun is up? I just fell asleep, like twenty minutes ago.

"10:45? I overslept!"

She slings the covers off of her and rolls from the bed into a yawning stretch.

"Blech! This room smells like an orgy of Fritos, ass, and cigarette smoke. And they call this their executive suite. If this is their best presentation of a luxury suite, the standards in this town have fallen far from grace. If I'm infected with some contagion of lice, bed bugs or leprosy from spending a night here, the red rain of litigation will fall on this place so fast."

Her puffy eyes find the bathroom mirror, which confirms that she has been crying all night.

"Looks like it's a concealer day today," she resolves before splashing cold water over her face.

As she studies her appearance, Felona traces the tattoo on the front of her neck with her fingertips.

Fifteen years ago, tragedy led her to find significance with this symbol that is known as ouroboros, an ancient symbol that is indicative of recreating one's self and, also, of wholeness. In the center of the circular mark is a dot that looks like a heart turned sideways.

"I don't know if I've truly felt whole or good enough. Maybe not so much before now, but death can lead to life, right? Maybe now. I hope."

Her cell phone rings.

Sitting on the edge of the bed, Felona answers, "Ny! Hey, girl."

"Felo! How's my favorite girlie doing in the great metropolis of Nathaniel?"

"The great metropolis of Nathaniel? Really? If I had a toke of whatever it is that you're smoking, things would be going much better right about now."

"How are you holding it together, love? Any word on your mom?"

"I just woke up," she says through a yawn. "I'm on my way to the hospital as soon as I get dressed. I briefly saw her last night. I don't know how to feel other than numb. I know I'm probably supposed to be longing for her to wake up, but I don't. I don't want to linger in this confused and helpless place. I just want this feeling to be over." Her voice quivers,

"Does that make me a horrible person, Ny?"

"No, love, it doesn't. It makes you very human. Most people would be speaking platitudes that they think are profound, all the while hiding what they really feel. You're braver than that. It takes courage to be honest in moments of grief like this."

"Brave? I'm not being brave. All I know to speak is the truth and that truth is that I didn't have a good relationship with my mother. Hell, we haven't even been on speaking terms since I've known you. It's like she and I don't exist to one another. I wasn't exactly her favorite daughter."

"Whatever you call it, it speaks to some degree of maturity that you can say out loud how you feel. Or not feel, for that matter. And as far as being her favorite daughter, you're her only daughter, love."

Unbeknown to Ny, Felona is not her mother's only daughter. She once had a sister named Iris, but Iris, while riding her bike, was struck by a car. She was six and Felona was two.

Dianne Mabel seemed fonder of the memory of Iris than she was of her surviving daughter, probably because Iris was conceived of love and not of a violent crime as Felona was.

Meanwhile, Felona spent the rest of her childhood being compared to a dead sister who was forever immortalized as the perfect and blameless child that she could only hope to be.

"I guess," Felona answers, not bothering to correct her.

"Don't be so hard on yourself and what you think you're supposed to do. Right now, just be. That's all and the most that you can do. Even though she may not have shown it, your mom loves you and some part of her knows that you're there. For her."

Ny is the product of a loving household and she speaks from the position of a woman who has been nurtured and nurturing all of her life. That's the primary reason why Felona was drawn to her friendship five years ago. She has an ability to find the sunny side of any situation.

Ny's optimism in Felona's situation was not only born of her upbringing, but it also springs from her preoccupation with motherhood. For the past two years, she and her husband, Mosi, have been trying to have a baby to no avail.

Ny continues, "My shift will be over at nine this evening. I'll be on call, but I can come be with you so you don't feel like you're in this alone. Because you're not. I know if that were my mom, I would be a basket case. I know you would be there for me."

"Of course I would and I appreciate you. Let's... let's just see what happens today and I'll let you know. I'm not sure how long this sort of thing takes."

"Felo, I love you and I know you're ready for this to be over. But if you were the family member of one of my patients, I would advise that you prepare yourself emotionally and otherwise for what will likely follow. From X-rays to room transfers to the final sedatives that will need to be administered, the medical staff can't legally do much without your approval granted by the health care directive that you said your mother left. You're more likely to be there for at least a week."

"A week?" Felona exclaims.

"Yes. If your mom doesn't have any type of post-death directive, like a will, you could eliminate some of that time and start making funeral and burial arrangements."

"Funeral arrangements before she's dead?"

"Some families make arrangements in advance of a loved one's death if their time of expiration is inevitable and soon. There's less of an emotional burden and the family has a better opportunity to grieve and move towards closure, without all of the inconvenient business associated with death."

Tears begin to swell in Felona's eyes.

Her voice cracks, "Funeral arrangements? W–what about my wedding? I was only planning to be here a day. I told Vin I would be back tonight."

"Oh, sweetie. You're trying to carry too much right now. You just worry about what you have there. Vin is a big boy. He'll be by your side and I'll help with any loose ends regarding your wedding. We'll get through this and you'll be happily ever after soon enough."

"This isn't fair! I'm not supposed to be here. I'm supposed to be getting married. Why is this happening now?"

"I don't know, sweetie. Like I said, sickness and death aren't known to be polite nor considerate companions. A lot of things happen for reasons that we don't understand at the time. You and your mom weren't close. That happened. But it seems like you're stuck on that chapter. Before you start your life with Vin, I suggest you bring closure to this lingering thing that's causing you so much sadness. And then... turn the page."

Felona nods her head as if Ny can see her affirmation.

"I'll check on you a little later, okay?"

"O–okay."

"Love you, sweetie. Talk to you soon."

"Love you too."

Slouched on the edge of the bed, Felona clasps the phone in her hands as the dampened drone of traffic and life outside accompanies her silence.

After a few still moments, she stands, wiping the residue of tears from her face, and slings the curtains open. Light floods in, exposing every water stain, cigarette burn and imperfection littering the room.

As she looks out at the barren cityscape of Nathaniel, she sighs. "This city is still this city."

Standing at a height of six foot, five inches with a broad frame, it's difficult for Vincenzo Ricci to slip out of a crowded board meeting unnoticed, especially being so far away from the exit.

"Excuse me. I have to take this," he mouths, holding his cell phone in front of him, before he lumbers past several people out of the conference room.

"Why are you calling me?" he whispers into the phone as he walks to the other end of the hallway.

"Why are you ignoring me?" responds a woman's voice

on the other end.

"Look, you can't be calling me anymore. I'm about to get married, okay?"

"Can I see you tonight?"

"What? Didn't you hear what I just said?"

"I know. I know I promised, but I need to see you. Tonight. At our place."

Vin bites his lip in frustration, saying nothing in response.

"Come on. Please? I just need to see you tonight."

He exhales, "Fine. If everything with this meeting goes according..."

Vin's phone beeps, notifying him that he has another incoming call. He glances at the screen and sees that it's Felona calling him. He doesn't switch over to answer.

"Look, I'll call you after my meeting. I have to go."

"Wait! Don't hang up yet. Do you miss me?"

"Danielle, I..."

"Come on," she whines. "Tell me. Do you miss me?"

A pregnant silence precedes Vin before he finally answers with, "I have to go."

He ends the call and returns to the conference room.

7
Acceptance

Suspended just above the horizon of Nathaniel is a picturesque scene. The sky is a deep, velvety, cerulean blue and there isn't so much as a hint of a cloud present, giving the long-awaited sun free reign to roam about and shine its glory down on the lush green below.

Although, in all of its afternoon glory, the sun can do very little to redeem the staggered and trite landscape of Nathaniel.

Sprawling green-space is interrupted by poorly planned voids of dirt and concrete where progress was attempted and prematurely halted.

From the dawdling pace to the unrefined people to the sparse development, this city might appear somewhat disheartening to an outsider seeking a more progressive and thriving place to visit.

The drive from the hotel to the hospital is short distance-wise, but mid-afternoon traffic coupled with the unhurried driving of the Nathaniel natives transforms a ten-minute trip into a frustrating, forty-five minute obstacle course.

"This town is a useless, dull-bladed reminder of everything I'd rather forget," Felona mumbles to herself.

When she finally arrives at the hospital at 12:45, her mother's condition is found unchanged since last night. Tobias has left and taken all personal effects and evidence of his presence with him. The afternoon sun bleaches the room with light where the curtains have been pulled back.

Last night, shadows and dim lighting obscured Dianne Mabel's appearance. But now, in the natural light, Felona sees a colorless and withdrawn face while the sun exposes every wrinkle and blemish. She appears emaciated and dead, but the machines that are hissing, clicking and breathing for her move her chest up and down underneath the covers.

On her left forearm is fresh, white gauze previously unnoticed with a tube protruding from it and disappearing into the gathering of wires and tubes that spill out of the machines that surround the bed. She lies in the exact same position that she was in last night.

As Felona stands watching, she thinks, *If her eyes were open, they would be judging me right now – telling me that my hair is too short or my dress is too plain or the dimple on my chin is too defined and makes me look like a man – or the first disparaging and negative thing that comes to her mind.*

Suddenly uneasy standing so close to her mother and before she realizes it, Felona is quietly backing out of the room as if her mother is a bomb that is about to detonate at any moment. Once to the door, she turns and hastens her departure into the hallway to attempt locate Dr. Amos.

It doesn't take Felona long to track down Dr. Amos, who is wearing a white lab coat, wrinkles and bad posture. Thick eyebrows spray over the top rims of his glasses as he speaks slowly with deliberation.

He ushers her to a row of offices that culminate into a conference room at the end of a quiet hall on the fourth floor. As she sits down at a long table in the center of the room, he hands a folder of documents to her.

"This includes the Advance Health Care Directive on top," he says. "Please take a look at it and I'll be back with a couple of people that can best answer any legal questions you might have."

Felona studies the document as Dr. Amos closes the door behind him.

It read, "If the extension of my life would result in an existence devoid of cognitive function with no reasonable hope for normal and independent functioning, then I do not desire any form of life-sustaining procedures, including nutrition and hydration, unless necessary for my comfort or alleviation of pain."

What follows is a long list of the life-sustaining items that her mother wishes to preclude. She scans through those things and then quickly down to the bottom of the page where her mother's signature is scribbled.

"My agent, Felona Mabel, shall consent to and arrange for the administration of any type of pain relief, even though its use may lead to permanent damage, addiction or even hasten the moment of, but not intentionally cause, my death."

To read those words, a sobering reading of her mother's contemplation of her mortality. Felona can't help but wonder about her own.

Will I die as young as my mother who's only 58? she wonders.

As a teenager, Felona romanticized a fairytale exit from an unkind world that she felt didn't want her. She can recall many tear-stained nights, lying in her bed, unable to fall asleep, envisioning herself lying in a colorful field of flowers in full bloom. Velvet ribbons would flow from her wrists that were spread about her side as she lay on her back looking up at a deep, blue sky that would slowly bleach into a bright light. And then some gentle, bearded fellow would lift her into the air as if gravity no longer had any influence over her and they'd float into the white void that smelled of gardenias and fresh strawberries.

Once upon a time, I wanted to run away from all that was my life, even if it meant running away from – life. I didn't care what happened to me. But these days, I'm feeling more in control. My life is starting to feel like my own. Or at least, I'm grasping at more tangible hope these days.

It's taken eight years for me to deafen the echoes that my mother... that Dianne... left me with. Her destructive words, her abusive fists, her disapproving glare... her emotional abandonment... I'm not even sure what I should be feeling in regards to her dying. I just want to accept it and be at peace, but there is this nagging, faint voice that is nudging me to feel something akin to sadness.

Felona is suddenly startled from her thoughts as she hears a small commotion of approaching voices outside the door that swings open and Dr. Amos leads one familiar man and a woman, in behind him.

She stands to greet them.

"Ms. Mabel, I'd like to introduce you to Dr. Huffman and Dr. Fischer."

"We've already met," Dr. Huffman reminds Felona as he shakes her hand.

"Just last night," she returns, forcing a smile.

Dr. Amos continues, "So you probably know that Dr. Huffman is a resident here and assists me with some of my patients. Dr. Fischer is a social worker here. Her job is to enhance the interaction between the patient, her family and us, the healthcare givers. She will help you with the difficult transition that is before you and answer any questions you might have."

As they sit, their attention and eyes are directed toward Felona.

"Ms. Mabel," Dr. Amos starts. "Your mother's condition is quickly deteriorating and the measures that were keeping her stable now seem to be weakening her. While it is my responsibility as a medical professional to sustain and prolong life, it was her wish to not be resuscitated if she found herself in this circumstance. I can understand that if your mother never disclosed this wish to you then this whole matter is unsettling and difficult. Let me ease your mind and say that even if this directive didn't legally restrain me, any further attempts at treatment such as surgery or experimental medicines would only prolong her life for a short time."

"So if my mother has already set the legal course of what you can and can't do, why do you need me to advise anything?"

Dr. Amos leans forward, pointing at a specific area of the document.

"As you see from the advanced health care directive, your mother appointed you as the primary person to consult with during this state that she is in. At this stage, we'll be transferring your mother to what is known as palliative care."

Felona studies the document and frowns before asking, "What's that?"

Dr. Huffman interjects, "Palliative care means that we will no longer try to diagnose or treat your mother's condition. Instead we will let her die at her own pace. At the most, we can administer painkillers to allow her to be as comfortable as possible. That is where you come in as her agent. We are to consult with you on how often we can administer these meds, if at all."

"So you're telling me that this meeting is simply to inform me that my mother is dying, there's nothing you can do, and even if you could, you can't? Oh, and I have been endowed with the almighty power of attorney to give her Tylenol? Got it."

Dr. Fischer speaks up, "Ms. Mabel, you were asked to be here because of this emergency provision. We want to assist you in helping your mother be as comfortable as she can before she expires, since her quality of life is in question at this stage. We have her clothes and belongings in a locker. Perhaps you can retrieve her house keys and go to her home to get some comfortable clothes and familiar items that will make her surroundings feel more natural. It is our belief that even though your mother is comatose, some of her brain facilities may still be active and operational. She may even sense when loved ones are near."

"Okay. I can do that."

"Very good. You might also want to consult with a funeral director for burial planning. Planning a funeral can be a difficult and highly stressful process for yourself and your family. Some advance guidance will alleviate what could otherwise be an overwhelming process during this difficult time. I can also refer to you an excellent grief counselor that will help you during this time and the days that will follow."

"Do you have any further questions, Ms. Mabel? About any of this?" Dr. Amos asks her, in an almost-grandfatherly tone.

"How long?"

Dr. Amos returns a puzzled look.

"How long does my mother have?" she clarifies.

"It's really hard to say at this point. We won't know how strong her lungs are until we remove her from the respirator. She may expire shortly after or she may linger on her own for a few days."

Dr. Fischer interjects, "We can only make sure that she's comfortable."

She slides yet another document across the table to Felona and places a pen atop.

"We'll need you to sign this consent form in order to move

forward. This acknowledges that you will act as your mother's agent according to the health care directive's request."

Felona picks up the pen and reads the document that is two brief paragraphs of legal jargon that concludes with two signature lines. One line is already accompanied with the scribbled handwriting of Dr. Amos.

Why me? she thinks. *Why is my name here and not Brent's? He was married to her. She's not my responsibility. Especially since we aren't even on speaking terms.*

Brent and Dianne Mabel divorced twenty-eight years ago. When Brent remarried shortly after their divorce, he disappeared from their lives. Felona only knew of him via her mother's narrative.

Felona stares at the blank line awaiting her signature as her hand begins to tremble, hovering over the paper and suddenly doubt lingers in a place where she simply wanted this scenario to be quickly over.

What if she were under some kind of duress when she signed this? What if she simply were having one of her estrogen-laced flare-ups where she was the victim again? My mother is known for her temperamental words and actions, but this time, her volatile resolute has been suspended in time in the form of a legal document that will impact her eternal fate. What if she doesn't want to die now? What if her mind has changed since some time ago and she forgot to change things?

Why me? I'm the one that's not good enough, the fake white girl, the accidental baby, the dirty face and the bitch.

Felona closes her eyes and a strange peace washes over her.

When my mother dies, all of the hateful feelings and memories die too. This chapter will be over. And then I can turn the page.
She opens her eyes and exhales before signing her name and resigning to her mother's inevitable fate.

8
Muerte and Revolutionaries

Four or five songs from the radio have played a soundtrack to her procrastination and it takes longer than it should for Felona to move from the driver's seat of her parked car to the door of her mother's house.

She fumbles through her handbag for the keys to the front door. They're still cold to the touch, apparently from the hospital storage locker from where they were retrieved.

She studies the keychain and all of the articles that accompany the house key. There's the obligatory car key amidst the mass of random keys that open doors to elsewhere. Then there are the miniature slivers of discount or membership cards from the grocery store, the pharmacy, the library, a fitness club and a warehouse club store.

It's been noted that one can glean a lot about a woman from the contents on her keychain, but there is little truth exposed with this arrangement. One might assume that Dianne Mabel is your typical healthy, red-blooded American woman instead of the abusive, ungrateful, schizophrenic, hateful woman that Felona accuses her of being.

A few more moments of familiar procrastination pass and

Felona finds herself standing on the porch with the key seated in the lock, waiting for the door to open from the inside.

But it doesn't. Her mother isn't inside. She's at the hospital, dying.

"I feel like I'm trespassing," Felona whispers. "Even though I grew up here."

She puts her weight on the door and pushes it open. Hot air, carrying the putrid stench of ammonia and rotten meat, rushes out to greet her. It's mid-April and seventy-three degrees outside, but inside it feels like it's well past ninety degrees.

She holds her breath as she moves from the living room to the kitchen where she's met by the weak, gargled mewing of one of her mother's cats – SoJo. She looks emaciated like a stray cat that hasn't eaten in five weeks.

In that moment, it suddenly dawns on Felona that everything here is a snapshot of her mother's life minutes before she went to the store five weeks ago and collapsed.

There is garbage littered across the floor from an overturned trashcan. Sitting atop the stove there are uncovered casserole dishes and pots with little food left inside. Evidently, this was how the cats have survived on their own since, underneath the kitchen table; their food bowls are absent of food and water.

"SoJo, where is Freddy?" she asks as the solid gray, green-eyed cat follows her down the hallway, continuing to mew weakly. The stench of rotten meat gets more offensive as she gets closer to her mother's bedroom.

The thermostat is set to eighty-five.

She turns it off.

She pauses at the closed door where her bedroom once was, wondering of what's on the other side.

Is it now a study or a place where all of Dianne's regretful purchases are gathered? Do the walls have new sights to behold to make them forget the common sight of a little freckle-faced girl sprawled across her bed crying, wishing someone loved her? I wonder if it's still adorned with things from my childhood.

Her trembling hand hovers like an apparition over the doorknob. When she touches it, she jerks her hand back as if she has accidentally touched a hot stove. She doesn't open the door, but continues to the end of the hall.

As she runs her fingers along the wall, they discover a smooth area. She faintly recalls that this was due to a repair from a fire.

Her mother would have crying episodes that culminated in her burning things like rolled up pieces of paper in the bathroom sink. One of those times, the fire escaped the sink and got out of control, gutting the hallway before firefighters put it out.

Felona enters her mother's room and it's just as she always remembered it to be. Not an article of stray clothing is lying about and her bed is made. The perfume bottles, jewelry box, and other ornaments atop her dresser and chest of drawers are as neat as staged pieces in a catalog picture shoot. Sprawled across her bed is Freddy, who appears to be taking a nap.

Her mother named all of her pets after black revolutionaries from the 1800s. There was Nat Turn, the dog who came and went during her childhood; DuBois, the goldfish; and BookerT and FrederickDouglass, the cats who seem to have been around for as long as she can remember. BookerT died while she was a teenager and the cute kitten that would earn the name SojournerTruth, or SoJo, replaced her.

FrederickDouglass or Freddy, as she called him, was the one of whom she was most fond.

He was mostly white, but speckled with dots of orange and black, especially about his face and neck.

"Freddy? Freddy Mabel?" she calls as she approaches him.

As she gets closer, she discovers that the source of the stench is coming from Freddy, who has died.

She covers her mouth and abruptly turns to race down the hallway to the front door, stumbling over SoJo in the process.

Once outside on the porch, she leans forward, one hand on her knee and another against the banister, gasping for fresh air. She retches several times, but nothing comes forth so she spits to expel the sensation of vomiting.

Nausea lingers as she stares down at the cobblestone walkway seeing memories in the place of stone.

When she was little, she imagined that each stone was a hopscotch block. She would complete the forward round with no issue, but whenever she would start jumping backwards, she would trip on one of the stones that were raised. Somehow this, more often than not, resulted in her skinning her knees which led to her mother constantly reminding her that she was clumsy and lacked grace.

She would inform Felona of how Iris was graceful and never fell nor skinned her knees. She would tell her how a young lady needed to conduct herself in such a way that she would always have smooth and unscarred legs, so that when she grew into a woman, she would be flawless.

But in all of her grace and alleged perfection, Iris never grew up. She died.

And Felona lived to see her scars clear up... the physical ones, anyway.

Felona's nausea passes and she resolves to finish the task of going inside to retrieve her mother's belonging. She reminds herself that this is the least she can do at this point to usher her into eternal peace.

She briskly walks into the kitchen to fill SoJo's bowls with cat food and water.

Cats are known for gingerly eating their food, but SoJo scarfs most of hers down before Felona can turn away to open a window to air out the house.

She begins putting the trash from the floor into a new trash bag. As she's rushing through the process of tidying up the kitchen, something snares her attention. The front and side of the refrigerator is canvassed with photos, novelty magnets and greeting cards – surprisingly inconsistent with her mother's tendency for neatness.

Beyond all of the faces in the many photos that she doesn't know, she sees a much younger version of herself. Before the tattoo; before the abortion; before the secret that she kept from Tobias; before she started to believe that she wasn't good enough, there she was, looking happy in a moment.

Creamy almond skin with freckles dotted in random places; curly, red hair tamed by two plastic green barrettes on top of her head; and a big, toothy smile. She doesn't remember when this picture was taken, but she appears to be about eight or nine.

She skims over the collage of assorted memories. Several more photos of her from various stages of childhood are among them.

Felona leans in to closely inspect one in particular that is especially interesting – an infant version of her being held by her mother who is seated in a lawn chair while Iris, with her arms crossed behind her, is in the foreground, wearing a Girl Scout Daisy uniform. And it's not framed.

My mother always framed pictures of Iris. Maybe this one isn't as sacred because I'm in it. But Dianne looks so happy here, holding her bundle of joy begotten of rape while her beautiful and living Iris stands near.

She returns to her mother's room holding one hand over her nose and mouth, resilient to finish the task. She walks over to the bed where Freddy's body lies.

She didn't notice before, but he has bloody tufts of fur

near his stomach.

Did he and SoJo fight before he died? Is that how he died?

She turns to see SoJo seated by the doorway, licking her paws, satisfied from her long-awaited meal.

She lowers her hand from her mouth to look back at Freddy and then to SoJo.

"SoJo?"

SoJo stops licking herself to look up at Felona.

"Did you try to eat Freddy?"

She lets out a weak meow before she resumes her cleaning ritual.

Felona shakes her head to clear the horrid thought as she folds the blanket from the bed around Freddy's body.

He deserves a more proper burial than being cannibalized by the surviving house pet.

She then places the makeshift padded coffin in the dumpster outside.

I'm not sure what would piss Dianne off more – that I'm tossing her dead cat in the dumpster or that I'm throwing away one of her expensive blankets, Felona smirks to herself.

Upon returning to the bedroom, Felona hastens her cause as she rifles through the closet looking for clothing that her mother's comatose state would deem appropriate for wear.

"I have no idea which one of these is her favorite."

She stands back and looks at the mass of clothing. Seeing that the dominant colors are shades of purple and pink, she files through the dresses for two that seem comfortable for the season. She lays them across the bed and then looks for underwear and jewelry to complete the ensembles.

Felona has always known her mother to be extremely particular about her appearance. She had to be adorned in jewelry and makeup for any task that involved leaving the house.

She never did like the fact that I wasn't a girly girl, Felona recalls. *As a matter of fact, she didn't like much about me at all. Being here in Nathaniel only reminds me of that.*

She abused me from my very beginning, naming me after the act in which I was conceived. Felona. Felona the felony.

And she has the gall to try to cover up her abuse by telling me some cockamamie story about my name's origin being from a song by an Italian progressive rock band from the seventies.

For so long, I just wanted her to accept me and to not be regarded as the horrible thing that happened to her. But now she's dying and that'll never happen. I should be sad about it, but I'm not. I'm kind of... anxious of what will follow.

I'm actually kind of... giddy.

9
Giddy

While the differences between love and hate can be blurred and difficult to decipher at times, the dichotomy of denial and acceptance are much more distinct. One is halting and aggressively rejects all truth, while the other is more passive and at peace – welcoming whatever truth is in waiting, whether fortunate or tragic.

Driving back to the hospital, Felona happens upon Schnell & Sons Funeral Home. Compulsion leads her to stop to consult about burial services so she would have an idea of what to expect after her mother dies.

Funeral home. I wonder why they call it that, she ponders. *It's neither a funeral nor is it a home.*

A smiling man and the sound of a chime greet her at the door as soon as she enters. The man is short, pale-skinned and portly while his hairstyle is reminiscent of a tanned and plastic Ken doll.

"Hello. Welcome to Schnell & Sons Funeral Home," he says with a distinct lisp. "My name is Jacob Schnell and I'm happy that you stopped in today."

He chuckles nervously while clasping his hands together

and leaning forward as if in mid bow.

He continues, "Something tells me that you're not here under happy circumstances, though. How can I be of assistance?"

Felona nervously smiles back.

"Hi, Jacob. My name is Felona Mabel and my mother is very ill. The doctors don't expect her to make it past this week. I wanted to see if..."

"I'm so sorry to hear that," he interrupts.

"I wanted to see if you could tell me, in advance, what services you offer so that I can better plan –"

"Her home going," he completes her sentence.

Felona shakes her head, mildly annoyed with being interrupted.

He continues, "Here at Schnell & Sons Funeral Home, we're committed to giving you the highest level of service during your time of need. We offer full service so we will take care of everything. Comfort, quality, and care are the three attributes we maintain during our service to you and your loved ones. We've been serving the community since 1973. May I give you a quick tour of the facilities while I tell you about what we have to offer?"

"Sure."

"Okay, good."

He waves his arms widely as a magician would before introducing his grandest act.

"Well, this area you're standing in is where all of our waiting guests relax. You see we have comfortable seating, lots of reading material, snacks, coffee, and a flat screen television."

Felona frowns, thinking, *Why would I want to relax in a*

funeral home? Unless I'm dead, relaxing isn't really optional.

"You look concerned. Don't be. A lot of people think that the luxuries we offer are unnecessary, but we at Schnell & Sons believe that a loved one's home going should be as comfortable and stress-free as possible. Now, if you'll follow me."

He leads her down a dimly lit corridor that features several framed pictures of men and women stiffly posed, staring coldly at passersby.

They enter a much larger room that is empty, except for a collection of folded chairs on one side of the room. The floor is linoleum, gray and lifeless, contrasting starkly with garish, illuminated stained glass windows that flank an elaborate podium.

"This is our banquet room where all of our services are held. This room is equipped with advanced lighting technology to provide subtle-colored lighting to illuminate the final appearance of your mother. Music services are provided via our large database of pre-recorded music or we can provide live musicians. Music has been proven to bring comfort to our guests during services and we can provide whatever style of music you desire."

Felona nods, forcing a smile.

Jacob leads her back into the corridor and they pass several other empty rooms similar to the previous one, before coming to a brightly lit showroom full of open caskets.

"This is our showcase room featuring our casket and vault collection. We offer many different sizes, colors and customizations that might fit your mother's personality."

"Beautiful," she says aloud, not realizing it, as she runs her fingers along the satin that's inside one of the caskets.

Jacob turns to her proudly with his hands clasped together, smiling. "They are a work of art. It's almost a shame to bury them, but what a lovely memorial to create of our loved one as we see them for the last time."

"I've never considered how death could be made to be… beautiful," Felona says in astonishment.

"Death is inevitable for all of us. While you will miss your mother when she's gone from here, the memories retained of her should be made beautiful."

Felona looks away thoughtfully while Jacob continues, "Our caskets can be customized to help create that memory that you would like to capture."

He points to a closed, brushed metal casket with 'United States Marine Corps' spelled out and its logo engraved in the center. He then gestures to a less dignified and baby blue, pearlescent casket that is open. The interior is crush velvet pink with quilted padding and shiny, gold buttons throughout.

"Wow. Pink and blue," Felona responds. "Somewhere right now a pimp is on his deathbed comforted with the fact that his most desired resting place awaits him."

Jacob chuckles nervously.

"What things does your mother like to do?"

"What?" she asks, puzzled.

"Does your mother have any… hobbies or belong to any organizations?"

Felona looks down and scowls.

I've never thought about my mother from the perspective that she might have likes and passions. All I've known is that I wasn't one of them.

"She was very active with her church," she finally looks up and says.

"That's wonderful. Did she sing in a choir or teach children? How was she active?"

Her scowl returns.

"Umm... my mother and I haven't been that close in the last few years. I don't live here now and we...."

"Oh, I see. That's no problem. Not a problem at all. We'll figure that out later."

Felona nods and turns her attention to the long aisle of caskets. As she walks, she carefully studies each one, running her fingers along the sundry of textures and finishes.

Which of these containers would best suit my burying my mother's ugly past in? she mulls.

A hint of delight accompanies her as she takes in the smells and appearance of lacquered oak and new linen.

"What are these for?" she turns to ask, pointing at a display of assorted vases.

"Those are vaults," Jacob, who has been following behind, answers. "Or as most people know them, urns. If you decide to have your mother cremated, these vaults would contain her ashes. As you can see, they come in a variety of elegant styles and finishes."

"Oh, wow," she says, unaware that her fascination is aloud

or that she's smiling. "How long does it take? The cremation process?"

"Well, state law requires that we wait two days before cremation. Would you want a viewing before the cremation?"

"A viewing?" she frowns.

"Yes. Some families need a visible sense of closure so we also provide that type of service previous to cremation."

"I'm not sure that my mother wishes to be reduced to a few pounds of ash and put in a vase, but the idea is enticing to me," she says as she places one of the urns back on the shelf.

Again, Jacob chuckles uncomfortably at what he surmises as Felona's dry sense of humor.

"What are these for?" she asks, holding up a deck of what appears to be business cards.

"Those are prayer cards. On one side is typically the twenty-third Psalm, but we can accommodate whatever inscription you'd like. Prayer cards are given to guests during the memorial service as a keepsake. On the other side, there is usually a picture of the one being memorialized."

"Prayer cards, urns, pimped out caskets, and waiting rooms. Who knew that there was so much to planning a funeral? You really do offer a litany of services."

"Thank you for saying that," he smiles and bows.

"No. Thank you for taking the time to educate me. Planning a funeral is almost like planning a surprise party."

Jacob stammers, "Well... that's... one way to look at it. I–I guess, it is like that in a way. You're planning her going away party."

Felona smiles and nods, "Yes. Exactly."

"We would love to help you." He bows again and hands her a card and pen. "Why don't you fill this out with all of your information and we can send you a packet with more details and pricing so that when you're ready, we can make your loved one's transition much easier on you and your family."

The faint ringtone of her cell phone interrupts her attention.

"Excuse me. I'll be right back," she says as she fumbles through an oversized handbag while walking away.

"Hey, bella," Vin greets on the other end. "Are you okay? How are things going there?"

"Vin! Hey. Things are going okay. I was just about to leave the funeral home and head back to the hospital."

Felona makes her way back to the lobby to walk outside.

"What?! Funeral home? Why are you –? Oh no. Felona, I'm sorry."

"No, Vin. It's not like that. I'm just being proactive so that I know what follows. Did you get the message I left earlier?"

"Uh, yeah. I saw that I missed your call, but I was in a meeting. That's been my whole day so far. I didn't take the time to listen to your voicemail. I just called you back instead."

"Well, you know how I like to stay busy. I can't just sit around in a hospital room waiting for something to happen."

"Are you sure you're okay? You sound strange."

"Strange? I'm fine. What do you mean?"

"You sound... happy."

"Should I sound depressed to hear from you, mister?

I'm just trying to be like Ny and see the positive side of this. In all honesty though, I'm numb. The doctors will be removing her from the respirator today and then it's just a matter of waiting for her to die. How are things going there? How did your meeting go?"

"The meeting went better than expected. We're officially acquiring Brisbane Properties, but since they were already in Chapter 11 negotiations, we will be inheriting fewer of their liabilities than we thought. The court will ultimately decide what we're responsible for, but in short, we had a huge win and guess who the new VP is going to –"

The call drops.

Felona looks at her phone to redial Vin, but it rings before she can do so.

"Vin? I'm sorry about that."

"Felona?"

"Tobias?"

She looks at her phone and immediately realizes that she must have accidentally answered an incoming call from Tobias instead of redialing Vin.

She sighs, "Tobias, what's going on?"

"Hey. You sound better than you did last night. A good night's rest must've helped."

"Tobias, what's going on?" she repeats.

"You know how last night when we were talking about your mom and you got angry about my trying to tell you what to do? I thought about that afterward and I'm sorry. I'm really sorry. I had no right to try to tell you how to manage your mother's business. I mean, it doesn't matter what we do, God's gonna intervene and do what he wants to do, right? Whether we're right or wrong, God's gonna do what he wants."

Felona opens her mouth to respond, but Tobias keeps talking.

"Hasty decision or not, miracles happen all the time. I may have had my string of bad luck, but I've still been witness to miracles in my life. I mean, I saw more than my share of bad situations when I was stationed in Iraq, but –"

"Tobias, stop! Jesus, man! Can you save the dissertation please? What's going on? Was there a purpose to your call or are you just calling to chitchat? Because if you're just calling to chit chat, maybe you should let me in on the conversation too."

"I'm sorry. What I'm trying to get to, Felona, is that you were right. Your mom was very weak, hooked up to those machines for all that time. But she didn't even wait for the doctor to remove her from the machine. She took control of her own fate by the hand of God. She did it, Felona. I'm at the hospital right now and I wanted to tell you personally before the doctor called you. Your mom passed –"

And the line goes dead.

10

One Summer

2000

Summer has always been known as a time to explore and get lost in adolescence, but for Felona, the summer of her seventeenth year yielded the consequence of her youth's greatest indiscretion.

And with it, she felt alone. But that was nothing new. She seldom got any degree of emotional support from her mother, yet she would still seek it.

The outcome was always the same, though – mangled pangs of abandonment and betrayal.

"I'll be back in an hour," her mother informed her as she dropped her off in the parking lot of the abortion clinic.

There weren't many cars in the parking lot and a lone, middle-aged man in a security uniform stood guard at the entrance. He took a long drag on a cigarette and nodded hello at Felona as she rushed past him to go inside.

A loud melody, akin to a doorbell, chimed as she stepped into the waiting room. Everyone who was seated looked up in unison and studied her in silence as she made her way to the reception area.

After listening to Felona's answers to the same routine questions that they, themselves, had to endure under scrutiny, her audience resumed their previous activities and conversation, satisfied with this unspoken initiation of shame.

Felona wanted her mother to hold her hand in the waiting room and tell her that everything was going to be okay. She was afraid of what they would do to her. And even more so, of going through it alone when she didn't want to have an abortion at all.

She looked down at her feet to avoid trading glances with any of the other girls there. She was afraid they would see through her and judge her like she secretly judged them.

When she would steal occasional glimpses of the room, she saw girls of varying ages. Some were older women. The girls with younger faces appeared normal and unaffected. They were carrying on conversations with others, while a few were just staring into silent space, holding their stomachs as if to hide their shame or somehow connect with what was inside before saying goodbye.

There were two guys, both older men, who were there. They were seated alone, probably waiting for their counterparts to return from the back... emptied out.

Felona found out that she was pregnant at the end of her senior year in high school. Even though she understood the basic principles of sex, she was perplexed because she'd only had sex one awkward time and it didn't seem like something that would culminate in a life changing event.

After much guilty deliberation, she finally told her mother, knowing that she would be disappointed in her, but she thought at some point, motherly love and compassion would kick in. It never did.

She just flatly responded with, "If you have that baby, you'll mess up your life like I did. You're going to get rid of it. That's the end of that."

So there Felona sat, afraid and alone in the waiting room of the abortion clinic, waiting to "get rid of it" because she was, otherwise, too immature to protest.

Felona and Tobias grew up together and were in most of the same classes during their senior year of high school. They shared everything.

But two weeks after Felona's abortion and sudden absence, Tobias finally saw her and asked, "Where you been hiding, Curlytop? You get a job you didn't tell me about? I haven't seen you in a while. What's going on with you?"

"I've been... busy," was all she said in response.

"Are you angry with me? You've been acting strange ever since we —"

It was all over her face that things would never be the same again. But Tobias had no idea when things changed or why.

She wanted to tell him, but was too ashamed.

They were best friends and shared everything... including their virginity.

Felona wanted to tell Tobias that her mother had forced her to have an abortion after she found out that she was pregnant with their child, but she couldn't. She was afraid of how he might respond – of how he might reject her. So she left him before he would leave her.

And she felt more alone than ever.

11

Closure

I can't believe she's dead," Felona mutters to herself over and over, blankly staring at the sprawl of traffic that is between her and the hospital.

"I was just there and now she's not."

In most cities, rush hour traffic typically starts around 4:00PM, but in Nathaniel, today at least, it has started early.

Felona finds herself moving forward just enough to gain a slight momentum, only to feel defeated when she has to come to a complete stop again.

She growls, frustrated, before picking up the phone and hitting redial.

"Hey, bella. You must be in a bad area."

"This whole town is a bad area, Vin," she sighs. "I just got the call that my mother just died."

"What? Oh no. I'm sorry, bella."

"I'm on my way to the hospital now"

"Bel – ck – ut – ry –."

"Vin? Hello?"

Their connection drops again.

"Damnit!" Felona exclaims and slings the phone onto the

passenger seat.

She grips the steering wheel and violently rocks back and forth.

"Fuck fuck fuck! I hate this town!"

She falls back into her seat as traffic crawls forward again.

"I'm not ready for this. I'm not ready for total strangers to feign sorrow for me and offer up the same tired line... 'I'm sorry for your loss.' Can someone come up with a new cliché? I mean seriously. What does it even mean? And when did this become the standard response to someone's loss?"

"My cat just died. I'm sorry for your loss."

"My baby died during childbirth. I'm sorry for your loss."

"My entire family was massacred with a machete during a random burglary gone wrong by a lone meth head. I'm sorry for your loss."

"The dog ate my homework. I'm sorry for your loss."

I can't believe she's dead. What's more is that I can't believe that this is starting to affect me. I feel something, but I'm not sure if it's frustration, anger, resentment, or... sadness.

She exhales.

I don't want to be in my head right now. I need to talk to Ny.

She reaches for her phone, but realizes that it bounced to the floor as a result of her earlier tantrum.

She pushes the call button on the steering wheel and articulates slowly, "Kinaya Odoyo."

A series of beeps over the speaker are followed by a voicemail message, "You've reached the voicemail of Dr. Kinaya Odoyo. If this is a medical emergency, please dial 911, otherwise leave a brief message and I'll return your call as soon as possible."

Felona abruptly ends the call and resigns that the next fifteen minutes, or however long it takes for her to get to the hospital, will be spent alone with her wandering thoughts.

She pushes a button on the door panel and the window slides down. Hot, humid air rushes in.

She immediately pushes the button for the window to return to its closed position.

"My curls aren't ready for that kind of confrontation today," she mumbles.

Her cell rings. It's Ny calling her back.

"Thank goodness. Hey, girl."

"Hey, Felo. You okay, sweetie? What's wrong?"

"Ny, she's gone."

"What?!"

"My mother. She's dead."

"What happened? When did this happen? Where are you?"

"I just got a call that... that she passed. I don't know the details yet. I'm on my way to the hospital now."

Ny gushes, "Oh , Felo, I'm so sorry."

A wave of emotion shivers through Felona at Ny's response, culminating in a stream of tears.

She's startled at the reaction and quickly swipes her hand across her face, clearing any evidence that she bears sentiment or feelings in this matter.

I hate that I was already on the verge of tears for the woman who condemned my existence. I hate that I'm the one she chose to suffer alone through this process... no doubt, her last sadistic intention toward me.

"Felona? Are you still there?"

"Yeah. I–I was just thinking. You know, you wake up, you eat breakfast, you go to work, you do all of the normal things you do every day and, in the nebula of a second, everything can change. Just like that. You're gone. She's gone, Ny. She's dead."

"I'm so sorry, love," Ny's voice trembles.

"I don't know what or how to feel."

Ny's voice quivers, "It's okay to feel whatever you feel, love, even if you don't feel anything right now. It's okay. Let it come naturally. Allow yourself the freedom to just... be."

Felona sharply inhales and then quietly exhales.

"Felo?"

"Yeah?"

"I'm on my way there now, sweetie. You're not going through this alone."

"Ny, I don't know how long... let me call you back and we can..."

"Felo," she firmly interrupts. "There's nothing to talk about. I'm on my way. I'll call you when I'm close. We're family. This is what we do for each other. I am going to be there for you."

Felona relents with, "O–okay. I'll see you soon, then."

"Alright, hun. Love you."

I thought I was prepared for this.

Felona pulls into the hospital parking garage.

When I was at the funeral home, the reality of my mother's impending death was starting to feel real. I was coming to terms with the finality of it all and how any hope of ever reconciling with her would be gone. I didn't expect her to be gone so suddenly, though.

The car comes to rest in a familiar parking space.

But she is dead now.

Felona pivots the rearview mirror toward her, and dabs her red eyes with a tissue.

In two weeks, I will be Mrs. Felona Ricci and this day... this experience... will soon be in the past. I can't reconcile with my mother now. She can't apologize for the horrible things she said to me, did to me or made me do.

She retrieves her phone from the floor and tosses it in her handbag.

I guess there's some degree of closure in that I can stop looking for it to fall out of the sky someday. It won't. Ever. I can move forward to become the woman that everyone already thinks that I am.

Felona takes one last look at herself in the reflection of her car window. With a selection of her mother's dresses draped over her arm, she walks toward the hospital entrance with a confident resolve.

Life goes on. Except for my mother.

12
Except for My Mother

The door to Room 433 is gaping open and the room is empty. All of the machines that were sustaining Dianne Mabel are gone. And so is she.

Felona walks fully into the brightly lit room. The bed is gone, too.

"I'm not sure what I was expecting, but I suppose they wouldn't just leave her lying here dead. But where is she?" she mumbles.

She steps back into the hallway toward the information desk.

A young woman, who is seated at the desk, immediately greets her with a cheerful and toothy smile.

"Hello. How may I help you?"

"Hi. My mother, Dianne Mabel, was in Room 433 and I'm trying to find where they took her."

"Oh, okay. Let me just look and see what I can find here," the woman, who looks to be barely beyond her teenage years, cheerily says.

She starts typing rapidly and looking at a monitor in front of her. She glances up at Felona midway through her task, makes a gesture at her own neck and says, "Like, I love your tattoo!"

"Thank you," Felona replies, touching the soft of her neck where her tattoo is. "I sometimes forget that it's there until someone makes a remark about it."

"It's pretty. Like, what does it mean?"

"It's called ouroboros. It's representative of a serpent eating its own tail which represents wholeness and recreation."

"That's deep. I like that. It's, like, very bold. I like that," she enthusiastically nods and resumes looking at the monitor.

"Thank you."

"Did you say her name is Dianne Mabel?"

"Yes, that's her."

"Okay, it says here that she was transferred down to three, but there's no room number. Let me try something else here."

She pecks on the keyboard and leans back, looking impatiently at the monitor, smiling nervously at Felona at intervals.

"I'm sorry. Sometimes these computers take, like, a long time. I'm just waiting for it to do whatever it's doing."

"No problem."

"Like, do you mind if I ask you a question?"

The young woman leans forward as if her forthcoming query is a secret between them.

"Sure. What?"

"Like... what are you?"

"Umm? Excuse me?"

"What are you? Like... you're so pretty, but I can't tell what you. Are you... like... black or Spanish or mixed up or something?"

"Spanish? Are you seriously asking me if I'm a language?"

The young woman returns silence and a quizzical stare.

"I'm Black," Felona relents and sighs.

"Seriously? You're too pretty to be black. You don't look it," she naively smirks.

"Wait... what? Too pretty to be black?"

"I mean, you got like hazel eyes, freckles and hair like a white girl... but you don't look like most white girls. You just don't look black, either. You look kind of... like... you're not from here. Like... exotic."

Felona scoffs under her breath before saying, "How old are you?"

She sits up proudly in her chair and smiles, "I'm twenty-three."

Felona's tone flattens.

"You sound like you're twelve. You don't ask a person what she is. That's insulting. What kind of question is that? What if I asked you what you are?"

"I would say that I'm Latina."

"No no no. I wasn't really asking you. I don't care. It shouldn't matter. But if you ever want to know, there are better ways to ask someone. Like maybe if you'd asked me what was my nationality... or what was my ethnicity... or what was my background."

The young woman rolls her eyes and quietly returns her attention to the monitor. She picks up the phone receiver and coldly says, "I don't see a room number for your mother so let me call the desk and see exactly where −"

"Nevermind," Felona snaps. "I'll just go down there myself. Thank you."

She turns and abruptly walks away.

As soon as she steps off of the elevator onto the third floor, Felona walks straight to the information desk, but no one is there. She waits a few moments for someone to return, but no one does.

With no hint of patience remaining, she resigns her wait and slowly walks through the hallway in search of a nurse, doctor, or anyone who appears to be in charge that might be able to help her find her mother.

Countless eyes fall on her as she roams about looking for some clue. She wanders through the conglomerate maze of hallways, imagining what she will encounter when she finally sees her mother's dead body.

Perhaps, she'll walk into a cold, sterile room where the hospital keeps the recently deceased and see her nude body covered with a white sheet, lying on a stainless steel table. The attendant will fold the sheet back to reveal her face to her.

Perhaps, Dianne Mabel's eyes will be closed, but unlike earlier this morning, her chest won't be moving up and down nor will any other part of her body be moving. Her face will be drawn in and colorless. Felona may tilt her head ever so slightly to try to recognize her beneath her withdrawn appearance.

Perhaps, her hands will nervously hover above her mother's face, wanting to make contact, but afraid of what a touch might reveal of her cold, lifeless corpse.

Perhaps, Felona will finally confess, "I'm sorry that I wasn't Iris. I'm sorry that I wasn't good enough to fill the void that your favorite daughter left behind. I tried my best to please you."

And perhaps, with that said, tears will fall from her eyes. She'll wipe her face and dab tear-moistened fingertips to her mother's lips while whispering, "Goodbye, mom. You didn't want me, but I loved you anyway."

Suddenly, past the commotion of her imagination, thoughts and the hospital's white noise and hallway activity, Felona hears the end of a familiar laugh.

"Tobias?"

She immediately stops walking and listens for more evidence of where the voice is coming from.

A woman accidentally runs into Felona, not expecting her to suddenly stop in the middle of the hallway.

"Excuse me," the woman, who appears to be in some sort of daze, mumbles as she recovers and walks past.

"I'm sorry," Felona politely mouths, pressed against the wall.

She strains to listen for the source of the laughter, but she no longer hears it.

"Okay. Am I losing it or what? I could have sworn I just heard Tobias. But now I don't."

She slowly walks, looking up and down the near empty hallway, listening.

She looks up at the domed mirror in the ceiling that gives her a perspective view around the corners into the adjacent hallway.

Finally, she hears the voice again and hastily walks toward the source where the sound might be coming from.

"I'm not crazy after all."

She pushes open the nearest door and peeks inside to see a nurse assisting a patient with his hospital gown. His back is turned to the door, but the nurse seems alarmed at her entry. The patient seems feeble and is barely keeping his balance as he holds onto a support railing beside his bed.

"May I help you?" the nurse asks.

"I'm sorry. Wrong room."

Felona says as she backs into the hallway.

"Felona?" a voice from behind her asks.

She turns to see, "Tobias!"

Mistaking her expression as warm, he pulls her into a hug. "Come here, girl."

Instead of returning the enthusiastic greeting, she turns rigid and pats his back with her free hand before pulling away.

"What happened?"

"I tried to call you back to tell you, but the call kept dropping or I couldn't get a call out. This hospital must have some kind of a firewall or signal blocker because even my text messages wouldn't send. I was just coming out to walk across the street to try you again. I figured you would be here soon though."

"Coming out? Where were you? Where did they take my mother?"

Tobias takes her hand and leads her to a room two doors down from where they were standing.

"Your mom awaits you."

As he pushes open the door for her to enter first, she scowls at him, confused.

"Wait... what? I heard you laughing earlier. Who were you talking to?"

"Who do you think?"

She peers at him, waiting for more.

He smirks.

"Didn't I tell you? I knew if you just placed your trust in him, God would come through. I knew that your mom would pass God's test."

"Pass God's... what are you talking about, man?" frustrated, she shoves him back toward the door and turns from him, looking across the room.

Felona's eyes widen at the sight of her mother who is very much alive, conscious and propped up against several pillows in bed weakly looking back at her.

An icy shiver scampers down Felona's back as she stares in disbelief.

"Ain't it awesome?" Tobias excitedly says from behind her. "God did intervene. On his terms."

Felona opens her mouth to say something, but only hushed air escapes.

Tobias nudges her to step closer, but she remains immovable. And silent.

Then, Felona's handbag slides down her arm and thuds to the floor.

The dresses in her arms follow as they crumple to the floor. And then, so does she.

13

Hurt People

2007

Shortly after Felona finished college, an inexplicable thing arose within her that provoked her to want to see the face of the man who sired her.

For most of her life, she had struggled with what ethnicity and culture she was supposed to identify with and give allegiance to. More often than not, she was ill–received by women of color who thought she wasn't "black enough" while white women judged that she was "too black" and "too pretty to be trusted."

Felona wanted to know more about her father's side. Whether it was a moment of morbid curiosity or a genuine need born of a chronic identity crisis, she sought him out.

It was no easy task either. He'd been transferred to a handful of different facilities over time due to a number of reasons including overcrowding, bad behavior and an increased sentence.

She eventually located where he was incarcerated, but he wasn't allowed visitors at the time because of continued violent behavior.

Since Felona was the last known contact to attempt communication with Ignazi Bernardi, she was on record as the next of kin.

As a result, early one morning, an official representing the state called her instead of her mother.

She said, "I'm sorry to be the bearer of bad news, but your father passed away last night."

Silence was Felona's only response.

"Ma'am? Are you there?"

"Yes?"

"I'm sorry, but your father passed away last night."

Still unsure of what exactly to say or how to respond, Felona stammered and says, "O–okay. Thank you."

She then abruptly hung up the phone, embarrassed of her pursuit of a stranger, undeserving of her time and effort, who'd caused her mother such harm.

There were no other details of what led to his death. And if there were, Felona never learned of them. Nor did she care.

Felona's relationship with her mother grew more detached while she was in college. While there was phone contact, the sole focus of those aloof conversations was to keep her mother apprised of her progress with school. The proverbial elephant in the room – Felona's abortion – was never visited.

As she progressed through college and started an internship following graduation, the stunted conversations between them declined in frequency until they were no more than missed calls and unreturned voicemails.

Although, once she received news of her father's death, Felona felt compelled to inform her mother in person, thinking that it might free her of what held her in hatred's grasp for years.

Felona felt a kinship, in that they could grieve and celebrate for the same reason and do so together. She felt that death might be a bridge to the resurrection of a mother and daughter relationship.

"He's dead, mom," Felona started, as she sat down on the couch beside her mother, clasping her hand.

She knew that saying his name wasn't allowed so she didn't.

"The bastard who's tormented your memories and thoughts for years... he's gone."

But Felona's mother didn't throw her arms around her and rejoice that the man who'd raped her was now dead and damned to hell. She didn't burst into tears accompanied by silence, while grasping her daughter's hand in some new, unspoken unity. She didn't recant her abuse and curses with a heartfelt confession and apology.

Instead, she was fixated on something much less significant at the time.

"How do you know?" she asked with her head cocked to the side and a tinge of bitterness in her voice.

She slid her hand away from Felona's.

"They called and told me."

"Who?"

"The prison. They called and told me that he died."

Dianne Mabel looked down thoughtfully at the floor. Felona's eyes were locked on her, waiting for her glance to return to her.

Then she looked up at her pitifully and asked, "Why... why would they call you? How did they get your number? How would they even know to contact you?"

Felona felt she had no reason to be ashamed of seeking the identity and face of her father, but her mother's tone caused her to feel that she'd done something reprehensible.

"I–I gave it to them when I tried to visit him."

"Visit him? Why would you do that?"

"It was awhile ago, mom. I wanted to know who he was. I wanted to know the face of the other person I came from."

Dianne sat back on the couch, creating a discernible physical distance between them.

"I already told you who he was... what he was!" she shouted.

Felona lowered her head and swallowed loudly before speaking.

"Mom, I know of all of the things that you told me. But I still wanted to see for myself the other half of where I came from."

"Why, Felona?" her mother whined. "For what? I told you where you came from. I told you about that monster and what he did to me."

"Yes, you told me what I came from. I heard it all the time. Too much, frankly. But as much as you reminded me that I was conceived of a horrible thing done to you, it never answered the question of where I came from – my heritage on my father's side."

"Your father? Don't call him that. Going to see that monster... that sorry excuse for a human being... was not going to answer any questions that you had about yourself. If you wanted to know anything about anything, you could have asked me."

"Asked you? I recall asking you once and you nearly took my head off with a slap across the face. What mom slaps her twelve-year old daughter for simply asking about visiting her paternal grandmother for Thanksgiving?"

"Stop lyin'. That never happened," she denied, crossing her arms and looking away.

"You did a lot of things that you conveniently forget, mom."

A weighted pause lingered before her mother turned to her.

Her voice trembled, "I sacrificed everything for you. And you treat me like I'm less than a stray dog with sores."

In disbelief and confusion, Felona yelled, "How am I treating you like a dog? By seeking out the people, who on my father's side, I'm connected to by blood?"

"By turning your back on me? I've given the last twenty-four years of my life for you. The least that you can do is show a little faithfulness to me. Blood is thicker than water."

Felona softened for a moment and searched her mother's eyes for something other than the hatred that was glaring back at her. She found nothing and hardened as well.

"This isn't about faithfulness," she said tersely through a tightened jaw. "I look in the mirror and I don't see your features. I see a woman who looks like she's from somewhere... someone else. When I was in high school, I didn't fit in because of how I looked. People would ask me what I was as if I was some mongoloid or creature from outside of humanity. And then I would come home to you."

Her lips quivered as she continued, "You would make me feel even worse, criticizing everything about me from my freckles to my skin color to the way that I dressed. Not only did I feel like I didn't fit in, I've had to suffer for the sin of some wretched man, who I've never even met, for twenty-four years. I had every right to know who he was and what he looked like."

Felona threw her arms up in surrender and her mother made the trembling gasp that she often made right before she would start to cry.

Felona got up to leave, but turned to face her mother who was seated on the couch with her head down, whimpering softly.

"And as far as faithfulness is concerned, I come to tell you that Ignazio is dead and all you hear is how I didn't come across that information in the right way? What difference does it make?" she shrieks. "He's dead, mom. He's dead!"

Felona's mother looked up, her face wet with tears.

"He may be dead, but it won't cure me of any of the pain, heartbreak and loss that I've suffered. I worked hard to have the life that I had and he took it all away from me. I lost everything!"

"You lost everything? What about me? You had me."

She looked down, shaking her head.

"I had you, but you came with the price of a lot of heartbreak."

"Heartbreak? You had a daughter who... all she wanted was..."

Felona looked away, closing her eyes tightly, commanding tears back.

"Child, you just don't understand."

Felona turned and glared at her defiantly.

"I know, I know. I'm just a stupid, clumsy, ugly, pale, dirty-faced, tangle-headed mistake! Did I get all of the words right, mom? Oh, wait, I did forget that I am also a dirty, red-headed whore!"

In one swift movement, her mother leapt from her seemingly helpless, whimpering posture and was upon Felona before she could do anything more than knock over a few figurines and a lamp, attempting to avoid her lunge.

Her attempt was in vain.

Dianne had gathered the collar of her blouse in her fist and was holding her against the wall, choking her as a result. Felona squeezed her mother's arm tightly with both hands, trying to wrestle away her mother's strangling grip.

"You watch your tone with me in my house, you ungrateful, little heifer! I'm your mother."

"Y–you're hurting me," Felona managed to gasp,

struggling to breathe.

"And all you've done is hurt me!" she exclaimed before relaxing her hold. "All you've ever done is walk around here like some fake white girl, like you're better than everyone else... thinking the world owes you something."

Felona jerked away from her to create distance between them.

"What is wrong with you? Are you crazy?" she shrieked. "I came to share something with you so that we could move forward and you attack me? Fake white girl? Better than everybody else? You have constantly made me feel like I was less than everybody else. Whatever hint of a healthy esteem that you think you saw was fake and born of insecurity! All I've ever wanted was for you to tell me I was good enough. I should have never come here! I was right to stay away all this time!"

"You lower your voice!"

"All I ever wanted was for you to love me! All I ever wanted was for you to forget what I came from... and acknowledge that I was a gift from God!"

"My gift from God left me a long time ago... because of you."

Felona returned a puzzled and betrayed look.

"W–what? Your gift? Iris was in an accident."

"I'm talking about Brent."

A scathing heat of realization melted the puzzled frown from Felona's face. All the while she was growing up, she thought her mother didn't accept her because she was a reminder of the bad. But the fact is, she never accepted her because her ex-husband never accepted her. Iris's death only made it more difficult for him to stay and, eventually, he left.

"You know what? This is fucked up. You rejected me because of some man?"

"He wasn't just some man. He was my husband! And he was a good man until –"

"And I'm your daughter!" she shrieked, flailing her arms in sheer frustration.

Despite the physical distance between them, Felona's mother managed to make a wide step forward with such speed and coverage that she may as well have teleported across the room. Her momentum was only stopped once her knuckles found their target – Felona's face.

She didn't have the opportunity to dodge her mother's boxing styled haymaker nor put up any semblance of a defensive posture. She barely saw her spring toward her before she was struck.

The force made her stagger backward, but she recovered her composure just before her legs buckled underneath her.

"W–why did you hit me?" she wailed, as blood sputtered from her mouth.

Though she'd received many slaps and punches from her mother in a similar manner before, that time was different. She couldn't understand why her mother was violent or why she was the recipient of such rage under the condition.

Just as sudden as the violent lunge, her mother's face transformed to a surprised expression of regret.

"Lona, I'm sorry."

Felona stumbled to the door.

"You're crazy! Fuck your sorry! Fuck you! I hate you. I'm never coming back here!"

She flung the front door open with such force that it slammed against the wall and shattered glass tinkled from one of the windows.

"Lona, wait!"

The tears that Felona had fought to reserve, spilled down her face. She briefly paused on the porch to spit a stream of blood at her mother's flowerbed before she staggered to her car, fumbling for keys from her handbag.

She mumbled to herself, "This will be the last time she ever puts her hands on me! I'm no one's punching bag!"

Nothing but hurt was born on 1865 Barbaro Way. She vowed to never return as she peeled out of the driveway, leaving black skid marks on her mother's, otherwise perfect, driveway.

Meanwhile, her mother stood on the porch and watched her skid away. Tears spilled down her face as well as she leaned against the door.

Felona was hurt. Dianne was hurt. Their wounds were too deep to be soothed by news of a dead man.

There was no way to avoid the fact that hurt people hurt people.

14
She Was...

Felona? Felona, can you hear me?"

Felona opens her eyes and bristles at the close proximity of Tobias's warm breath and wide grin.

"You okay, Felona?"

"Where am I?" she moans as she tries to lift herself from the chair.

"Take it easy," Tobias says, gently coaxing her to return to her reclined position.

"You're in the hospital. You fainted."

"W–what?"

"You walked into the room about ten minutes ago and then you just fainted. It's a good thing I was standing behind you to catch you or you would've busted your curly head on the door."

"How is she doing, sir? Is she conscious yet?" asks a voice from behind Tobias.

He turns and stands up, nodding. A woman wearing nurse scrubs comes from behind him and stoops to Felona's level, placing her palm across her forehead.

"What happened, ma'am?"

"I don't know. I blacked out?"

While taking Felona's pulse, the nurse asks, "Is anything hurting you?"

"No. I just got warm and dizzy all of a sudden."

Felona sits up, wiping her hands across her face.

Tobias looks over the nurse's shoulder and says, "Maybe she got too hot. It is kind of warm in here. Her mom complained about being hot as soon as they brought her in here."

At the mention of her mother, Felona remembers. She anxiously looks around the room and attempts to stand up, but the nurse protests by grasping her by the arm.

"Ma'am, you might need to be still and rest for a few minutes."

Felona ignores her instruction and snatches her arm away, looking to her left as she steps past to see her mother lying in the bed across the room with her eyes closed.

She staggers closer.

Her chest is moving and there are tubes running from her nose, but there is no machine like before.

"She's asleep. She's been in and out since I called you," Tobias says from behind Felona.

She swings around to look at him.

"What the hell happened? Why did you say she was dead?"

Tobias scowls, "What? I didn't say that? I called you to tell you that she was alive. While the nurses were prepping her to be removed from the ventilator, her brain waves and pulse rate fluctuated from where she'd been steady. By the time the doctor got to her, she was conscious and trying to talk."

"But you said... you said she was dead."

"No. Why would I say that she was dead? I said she had passed God's test. That's what I said."

"Ugh! I heard you say that she had passed."

"I'm sorry, Felona. I really am. I tried to call you back too. I couldn't get a signal."

She looks away from Tobias to her sleeping mother. The nurse has turned her attention to her as well and is checking her bandage dressing, her IV tube and the monitor.

After a few seconds of staring at her mother in silence, Felona turns back to Tobias.

"Why can't you talk like normal people talk? Huh? Why? Most people would've started the conversation with, 'Your mother is alive, Felona,' and went on from there. But you... do you even realize that you take three hundred words simply to say three?"

His smile relaxes and his eyes widen as a puppy that has just been scolded for peeing on the living room floor. He looks past Felona at her mother and the nurse who is pretending not to hear them.

"She needs her rest and we need to finish this in the hallway," he says sternly with one finger to his lips.

He firmly grasps Felona by the wrist and leads her into the hallway. She follows without contest.

Once in the hallway, Tobias looks around before saying in

a whisper, "You need to drop the attitude, Felona. If it weren't for me, your mom wouldn't even be here."

"I thought my mother was dead, Tobias. I'm a little on edge right now. You might want to cut me a little slack."

"I get that. I get that you're frustrated being thrown into all of this, but that gives you no excuse to be selfish, Felona. You act as if everyone owes you something. Like you're better than everyone else. Like you're the only one who's been through something. But you know... you're not."

"Look, you don't know."

"I'm not done. See? You think it's all about you. You may be pretty and used to how everyone does everything for you because of your looks, but that don't give you the right to treat me like your tool. I have no idea what happened to you, Felona, but all of a sudden, one day you just changed and started treating me like shit... ignoring me like I don't even exist."

"Look. I don't mean to be rude. I appreciate you being here for my mother and for calling me about her. I really do. But you've got to understand."

"No! I don't have to understand a thing. I'm not your whipping boy, Felona. I'm not stupid either. Your mom talks about you all the time. She tells me that ever since you moved to the city, you won't even talk to her. It's like some part of you died."

Felona looks down at the floor.

Some part of me did die, she thinks.

I killed it. I killed our baby and I can't even look at him without thinking about what I've done. What my mother made me do. And now she's alive. I'm right back where I was before. I thought I'd finally found peace, but apparently I was wrong.

She looks up from the floor at Tobias.

"I need some time with my mother. Alone. We can finish this some other time. Not now. Not here."

Tobias doesn't say anything as his jaws tighten. He just nods and walks away with his head lowered.

15
Maybe

Dianne Mabel's eyes finally flutter open.
Felona's breath quickens and she subconsciously steps back.

Her eyes look in Felona's direction, but she isn't able to fully focus.

"L–lona," her weak voice finally exhales. "Issat – y–you?"

Nostalgia and regret rushes through Felona.

Lona? She only called me that when things were good between us… when I was little. It's been so long since then that I'd almost forgotten about that name.

"Yes?" Felona answers timidly as her expression softens in the moment.

"Oh mmm – havenn seeeen – you. Kum kose – ssssso I kin geh uh goo – geh uh goo –"

Dianne's speech is slow and slurred. She nudges her frail arm slightly, trying to raise it, gesturing for her daughter to come closer.

She continues, "W–whuh yooo – sssstannin way o – dere?"

Felona stiffens in place.

Dianne Mabel was never a large woman, but, before her

coma, she was five foot four and weighed one hundred and seventy pounds. Her figure, busty with wide hips, was considered shapely by many standards.

Now, she barely weighs one hundred pounds as she stretches her thin, ashen arm toward her daughter, who says, "How're you feeling?" interrupting the lump in her throat.

Dianne doesn't answer, but just blankly gazes at her, still reaching her fingers outward.

She timidly steps forward, narrowing the distance between her mother and herself.

She then sits on the edge of the bed, careful not to touch her hips or any part of her body to her mother's.

Dianne lays her hand on Felona's thigh and she stiffens at the contact, clasping her hands together in her lap, staying vigilant not to return the touch.

Felona nervously clears her throat and says again, louder, "How're you feeling?"

Her mother reaches with her other hand toward the tubes coming from her nose, but the IV tube that's feeding into her arm, limits her range of movement.

"M—my dote – my dote huts. Annnn," she swallows loudly, "my head – f–feelsss duffy."

Felona strains to understand her mother's thick, nasally words.

"Do you know what happened to you?" she leans in, articulating loudly.

Her mother drops her hand back to her side and tries to shift her body to face Felona, who instinctively reaches to help her, but quickly withdraws just before doing so.

"I don memma mush – buh Bias tole me dat – dat I pass out ann I was – inna coma. He tole me dat it was uh m –"

She pauses, as tears twinkle in her eyes, before continuing.

"He tole me dat duh docduh had loss hope – dat I would survive and dat it wuh uh miracuh dat I woke up."

Dianne closes her eyes tightly and inhales sharply. Felona leans away in apprehension and tenses up.

"He said duh docduh cuh–nn splane how I woke up – annn stodded breeding on hum own. They wuh jusss boud tuh moov me fum duh mmsheen – den ah woke up."

Tears flow down the side of her face into the pillow.

Felona stares back in silence at Dianne.

"Id wonn mah time yed. G–god give me m–mo time tuh make id right – wid muh people – wid you."

She directs her gaze away from Felona and lifts her weakened hand to wipe her tears.

Make it right with me? Whatever, Dianne. Your crocodile tears don't move me.

Dianne smears wetness across her face with her trembling hands.

I've had enough of this soap opera.

Felona stands abruptly, crossing her arms.

But if I leave now, I look like the asshole.

She sighs loudly and her arms drop to her side.

"Fuck," she says under her breath.

She aggressively plucks a handful of tissues from the box on the table beside the bed.

Why the hell am I feeling an ounce of compassion for this woman?

She moves closer and leans over Dianne, who looks up at her daughter with pleading eyes.

Felona softens.

She dabs her mother's face of wetness.

Dianne smiles, saying nothing else. Her eyes flutter weakly before closing.

Felona returns to her perch on the bedside, placing her hand on top of her mother's. She tilts her head and studies her face.

She doesn't look like the hardened and hateful woman I've known for so long. She looks benign. Has a near-death experience changed her? It changed me.

She sighs again.

Sort of.

She looks different now. She looks at peace. She looks like someone's mom. Like mine.

Felona takes hold of her mother's hand.

Maybe everything does happen for a reason, she considers. *Maybe I can get the opportunity to experience a mom who loves and accepts me. Maybe I, too, can accept her for who she is. Maybe I get a second chance in this as well. Maybe there is hope for this mom and daughter after all.*

16
Breaking News

The din of conversation, laughter and dishes clinking animates the patio that's brimming with diners adorned in suits, evening gowns and flashy accoutrements. The sun has begun to set and paint the sky with smudges of orange, purple and blue while strategically placed streetlights ensure that dusk is barely noticeable.

Danielle Dashley sips from a glass filled with red wine as she sits alone at a table. Her blond hair hangs in front of her face, disgusing her, as she steals glances at people walking past the restaurant. She picks up her cell phone from the table, studies it for a few seconds and puts it back down.

"Excuse me," a middle-aged woman, who is seated at the table next to her, whispers. "Aren't you the woman from the news?"

Danielle tosses her hair back and smiles, "Why? Are you saying I look like her?"

The woman, who is wearing a large, white pearl necklace with matching earrings, abruptly stands and extends her hand to her.

"Oh my! You are her!" she exclaims, smiling widely.

"I would know that blue-eyed glint from anywhere. I watch you every night before I go to bed. I'm so honored to meet you. I feel like I already know you."

"The pleasure is all mine," Danielle nods as she shakes the woman's hand. "And thank you for watching me every night."

The woman turns back to her table.

"Frank? Frank," she whines. "I told you this was her!"

"I hear you! I ain't deaf," her husband gruffly says as he approaches the table.

"Doesn't she look so pretty and tiny in person? Just like a little Barbie doll."

"Thank you! You're so sweet."

"It's nice to meet you, Mrs. Dashley," he says, shaking Danielle's hand.

"It's Miss."

"Huh?" he answers back loudly, leaning in closer.

"It's not Mrs. It's Miss. I'm not married."

"Well, all of the men of Admah City are dang fools if they don't snatch you up soon."

Danielle blushes while glancing past the couple.

Just outside of the dining area on the street, a few people have begun to congregate, looking in Danielle's direction.

Not shy of attention now that's she's been exposed, she waves as one of the men in the small group holds up his phone to take a picture.

Two women approach Danielle holding up a camera and one of them asks, "Ms. Dashley, do you mind if we –"

"Of course not," Danielle returns.

"We think you're gorgeous," the women say in unison as they lean in to have their picture taken with Danielle by the woman wearing the white pearl necklace.

"Thank you so much," she beams.

"Excuse me," says a deep voice from behind the older couple.

They turn to see a statuesque, blue-eyed man with brunette hair and defined cheekbones towering over them. He's wearing a tailored, dark suit that hints at his muscular build beneath.

The man, Vin, hesitantly smiles.

"This is Danielle Dashley – the lady from TV," Anne says to him.

"I know," he returns. "May I?" he asks, gesturing to sit down as the two women nod their thanks, walking away.

"Oh, please excuse us. I didn't know. We'll get out of your way and let you fine people have your dinner," Anne says.

She leans in and mouths to Danielle, "He's handsome. Good job," nodding toward Vin.

Danielle smiles politely as Vin sits.

"Hey, you," she brightly greets.

"So what's so important that you have to call and text me incessantly?"

"Nice to see you again, too," Danielle coldly returns. "Geez, why're you so rude?"

"I'm not being rude. But I didn't agree to meet you for small talk. You said that you had to see me. What's going on?"

"I had to see you because it's been so long since we –", she blushes, nodding her head, "you know."

Vin frowns.

"I don't have time for this," he announces as he gets up to leave.

Danielle reaches out for him.

"Wait! Okay, fine. I need to talk to you about something. It's about Felona."

He pauses his departure and glares at her, waiting for her to say more.

"You're too serious right now," she pouts. "Please. Sit down for a few. Have a drink."

Vin sighs before reluctantly sitting down.

"So why did you start ignoring me? Why did you stop returning my calls?"

"We've been through this, Danielle. I'm engaged to Felona. Us meeting like this... this can't be anymore. We can't carry on like before. I want to start right with her."

"Start right? You haven't been right with her before. Or do you forget?"

"That was different."

"Different? So it's okay to cheat on your girlfriend for three months, but not your fiancé?"

"Yes. It's different. As a single man, it's okay to have several different women. That's not cheating. But with my wife –"

"Oh. So I was just one of your whores?" she exclaims.

"Would you lower your voice?" he sternly whispers. "No, you were not one of my whores."

He pauses and exhales, looking around nervously.

"You were my only. And at the time, you were the best

I ever had," he smirks.

Danielle glares at him and grips her near-empty wine glass.

A thick silence falls between them, but her glare melts into a smile and then a chuckle.

She leans in close to him, sliding her hand under the table up his leg toward his crotch.

"You're damn right I was."

She raises her glass just enough for the waiter to see and takes the remaining swig before handing it to him as he approaches.

"Would you like anything right now, sir?" he asks Vin.

"No, thank you. I'm fine," Vin says. "But, could you provide a little more privacy for us? We don't want pictures or interruptions from any more of your patrons."

The waiter nervously smiles and says, "Sir, I don't think I can –"

"It would be a great help if you did."

Vin cups a $100 bill in the hand of the waiter who looks down and then replies with a smile, "I'll see that no one else bothers you, sir and ma'am."

"Thank you," Vin nods.

"So what's this all about, Danielle?" he asks as he leans in.

"I wanted to see you. Geeez. Is that so wrong?"

"Yes. I have a lot of work to do. You just said you had something important to tell me that concerned Felona."

She smiles slyly.

"Well, I figured since the freckle-faced cat is away,

we could have a few drinks and go fucking play."

Vin scowls.

"You're wasting my time with this. I told you... we're done. I'm marrying Felona."

"Yeah. Felona. You act like you're so in love with her. You even made a public production of proposing to her for the entire world to see. Nice publicity stunt to boost her ratings. But you don't really love her."

"What? What're you talking about?"

"Come on, Vincenzo. Don't play stupid. You and I both know that you proposed to Felona only after you got caught fucking around with me. That ring was an expensive yet lame attempt at trying to smooth over the fact that you got busted fucking her co-worker and former friend."

"Would you have rather that I proposed to you instead? Is that what this is about?"

"No. That's not me. I don't need that. I was only in it with you to have fun. I don't need the headache of a husband. You all fuck around anyway."

"Alright. I'm glad we had this little talk. Have a happy life," Vin snaps as he abruptly stands.

"I'm not done. Sit down!" Danielle tersely says, turning serious.

Vin cocks his head and frowns.

"Who do you think you are talking to me like that?"

"I said sit down! You've ignored me long enough. You will hear me, even if I have to shout at you as you walk away."

He returns and leans in close to Danielle's ear and says in a low voice, "I don't owe you shit. We had our fling and I'm done with that. Don't fuck with what I'm trying to build here just because you're not a part of it. Leave me and Felona alone."

Danielle calmly smiles and moves to kiss Vin, who jumps back.

"Well, you can't blame a girl for trying to break the news to you gently."

He scoffs as Danielle sits up in her chair and stares straight ahead.

"This is Danielle Dashley reporting live on the scene with Vincenzo Ricci, reported playboy and fiancé of reporter Felona Mabel. The allegedly happy couple is planning to exchange nuptials within two weeks while, I, Danielle Dashely, am pregnant with Vincenzo's love child. Details are still developing, but we'll keep you informed right here. Reporting live in Admah City, this is Danielle Dashley. Now back to you, Vin."

She relaxes and takes a long gulp of wine.

Vin falls back into the chair.

"W–what?" he says with a puzzled look.

"I'm pregnant, Vin. With your child."

"Oh, I see," he nods his head. "You said this was about Felona. So what? You tell her or –? Is this some kind of extortion?"

"I don't need your fucking money, asshole. I'm just letting you know. I'd have to be a cold-hearted bitch to not at least tell you. But don't worry. I'm getting rid of it. I don't want your seed in me. You don't even love me. For that matter, you don't love your fiancé either. And while I don't like her, I feel sorry for her to be trapped with a man like you because you're not interested in her happiness. It's all about you, isn't it, Mr. Tall, Dark and Italian?"

Vin returns to silence as his glare falls to the ground.

"Yeah. You have no words now, do you? Well, you and Felona can have your fake little happily ever after."

17
Uppity Bitch

Felona loiters in the vicinity of hope for long moments, watching her mother sleep, until her hunger lets her linger no more.

Earlier on her way in, she noticed a café across the street within walking distance.

As soon as she leaves the hospital to get some food, her cell phone chimes that she has missed messages from Vin and Ny.

She calls Vin back, but his voicemail is all that greets her. She then calls Ny back.

"Where are you?" Felona immediately asks when Ny answers.

"I'm less than thirty minutes before my exit, according to GPS."

"Dang, girl. You're flying. You have heard of felony speeding, right?"

"Ha! For your information, I'm moving with traffic. Don't worry your curly little head about me, sweetie. I tried to call you earlier. How're you holding up?"

"Actually, that's what I called to tell you. But first, I want you to pull over into the right lane and slow down."

"Pull over into the slow lane? Felo, what's up?"

"My mom."

"Your mom what?"

"She's... she's not dead."

"What?" Ny shrieks. "Maybe I do need to pull over. Hold on. She's not dead?"

"No, Ny. She's not dead. I misunderstood the call that I got earlier because it cut off in the middle. Based on what I heard, I was under every impression that she'd died. But she didn't. I got to the hospital and to my shock, she was both alive and awake."

"She is conscious? Felo, you're blowing my mind over here. She's alive and awake? From the coma? That's – wow!"

"Yeah. I'm still reeling from the shock. Basically, she woke up just as they were about to remove her from the ventilator."

"Oh my god. That's amazing, Felo. Are you okay? I can't begin to imagine how you must feel right now."

"It's like it never happened, but then at the same time, something happened. I just spoke to her and she seemed... different."

"Different? Different how?"

"I don't know. There was a kindness about her that I haven't seen. At least, I've never seen it directed at me."

"This is amazing, Felo. I can't wait to finally meet her and give you the biggest hug ever. You poor thing. You've had quite a time. What an emotional roller-coaster, huh?"

Felona smiles brightly to herself at the thought of Ny joining her in a place that she would rather not be. Before today she would've been skeptical for anyone to meet the disaster that is her mother, but in the moment, things do feel different.

"I can't wait to see you too. I appreciate you so much."

"Appreciate me? What do I always say to you, Felo?"

"That I'm right?"

"No. I mean when you're not dreaming, what do I tell you?"

"That we're family?"

"That's right. And this is what we do."

Felona smiles and exhales.

"Okay. Swan Providence Medical Center, Room 315."

"Got it. Love you. See you soon."

"Love you."

While waiting for her order, Felona listens to her voicemail.

3:17 PM from Vin. "Bella, I tried to call you back. I'm so sorry about your mother. Call me."

4:16 PM from Ny. "Hey, Felo. I just wanted to give you a status on where I am. Rush hour traffic out of Admah City slowed me down, but I'm finally out of the city and it's wide open. Oh, maybe I shouldn't say that too soon. I'll call you back when I get closer."

5:35 PM from Vin. "You must be in a bad area. You keep going straight to voicemail. Call me back to let me know where you are so that I can make arrangements on when you need me there."

Felona looks at her phone, puzzled for a moment.

Her bewilderment is interrupted with, "I gotta turkey melt, a side Casear, and a Diet Coke."

"Oh, that's me," she says, forcing a smile while holding her receipt up. "Thank you."

The wiry man behind the sandwich counter nods and smiles back and a glint of light catches his front, gold-capped teeth and Felona's attention. She tries to contain her surprise.

"You need anything else with that, Ms. Lady?"

She glances down at her tray and then back at his sulfurous smile.

"No, thanks. This is good."

As she takes her food, he continues, "I mean, if you want some soup or chips or a man or something, I can hook you up."

"Oh, so you're pimping soup and men, huh?"

He laughs, "You got jokes. And you fine. I like that. I can work with that."

As he leans across the counter, he sucks his teeth, nodding his head, scanning her up and down.

He then lowers his voice and says, "How 'bout you give one of the dark brothers a chance? I bet I could make you scream."

"I bet you could too,"

She backs away.

Failing to grasp Felona's tone and sarcasm, he leans back surprised and responds, "Word?"

"No, not word. I have a man."

She holds up her ring finger and smirks, "Have a good day."

He mumbles, "Beige ass, uppity bitch," as she's

walking away.

Felona pauses and muses for a moment.

Now I'm no prude and I've been the recipient of many rude and lustful things said to me by men. In my lifetime, I've been ignorantly labeled a number of things – half breed, mulatto, mutt, stuck up, fake white girl, wannabe, uppity – but the word, bitch, just rubs me raw. I've always been bothered by the fact that any woman would be defiled and disrespected with such a word so I can't just walk to my table and eat my food, pretending that this fool didn't just call me one.

She whips around and walks back toward the counter, saying, "Does it take me being an uppity bitch to know that you're ignorant? I'm not going to criticize your sad means of getting the attention of a woman when clearly you're immature in that area."

He looks around nervous at the attention Felona's raised voice has garnered from other patrons in the restaurant.

"But I will criticize your lack of professionalism. Your job is to take my order and, when it is prepared, pass that order to me. Nothing more. I'm sure this is not your first failure with women, but you should take this one as a sign that perhaps, in a place of business, you should focus on your work and save play for another time, before you lose your job."

He grimaces and steps back, mumbling something to himself incoherently and wiping his hands on his shirt.

She concludes, "Oh, and for the record, I have no issue with, as you put it, the dark brothers. For those women who do, it's probably because of fools like you."

She winks a fake smile and walks away, leaving him no audience for a response.

18
Weak Smile

An inordinate expanse of time lapses between biting and chewing and dwelling on the last few hours of events, but Felona eventually returns to her mother's room.

She finds that the nurse, who was there earlier when she fainted, is helping her mother back into the bed.

"How's she doing?" Felona asks as she enters.

"You just missed Dr. Amos. He said that she's doing remarkably well. If she continues to improve at this rate, he sees no reason why she can't be discharged by the weekend."

"Oh, that's good to know."

"The man that was here earlier – your husband or brother? He talked to the doctor."

Felona ponders for a second before she realizes that the nurse is talking about, "Tobias Coles. He's a friend of the family."

"Okay. Well, the doctor talked to Mr. Coles right before I changed your mom's bed dressing and gave her a sponge bath. He asked a lot of questions on your behalf."

"That sounds like him," Felona nods. "Hopefully, he let you get a word in edgewise."

"Dr. Amos will be back in a couple of hours to check on your mom, should you have further questions about her condition."

"Okay. Thank you."

The nurse turns to open the door, which is already swinging open toward her.

She steps back just in time to avoid getting hit as Tobias barges in.

Upon noticing the near-collision, he says, smiling, "Oh, I'm sorry. You okay?"

"Yeah. That was a close call," she nervously laughs as she finally exits.

"Hey," Tobias says as his smile fades and he walks past Felona to return to the chair where he was previously.

"Hey yourself," she mumbles back before turning her attention to her mother who is awake again.

"How're you feeling, mom?" Felona says brightly as she runs her hand along the side of the bed.

Her words are still slow and deliberate as she answers, "I'm – okay. Mmmah head is – throbbin', but – the nurse gave me somethin' for it."

Felona's eyes widen at the clarity of her mother's speech as she sits on the edge of the bed.

Mom? I don't think I've called her mom in years, she thinks. *It sounds weird to hear it leave my mouth when I don't even refer to her as mom to other people. But it just came out naturally, as if I've been waiting for any given emotional opportunity to release it into the wild and test the feeling.*

Felona puts her hand on her mother's arm and says, "So the doctor told you that you might be able to go home soon?"

"Yessss. Yes, lord," she sighs. "I can't – wait – to get outta – thisss bed."

"I bet you can't. It's amazing. Your being here, that is. You beat it. You kicked that coma's ass."

Felona catches her mother's matronly glare and stutters, "S–sorry. Butt. You kicked that coma's butt."

She weakly smiles and Felona smiles back.

"I feel ssso weak. I wanna – move, but – mah body don't – don't wanna do – what I want it to."

"Well, mom, you have been in a coma for five weeks. It's going to take some time to get back to where you were. You have to be patient and give your body time to heal."

"Your muscles have atrophied from lack of circulation," Tobias chimes in from behind her. "You're scheduled to go to physical therapy in the morning and a couple more times through the day. They'll get you back on your feet. You'll be back at home and in that garden in no time."

Felona turns to look at him.

"Aren't you just full of facts, Dr. Cole," she teases.

"Well, we're all full of something," he responds.

"Bias has been – sush – sush a sweetheart, Lona. Since his momma passed – bless huh heart, he been – like uh son – checkin' on me – and treatin' me like his own."

She smiles sweetly and Tobias blows a kiss at her from across the room, as he cycles through various television channels with the remote.

"Do you wanna watch this?" he asks as he ends his cycle on a badly scripted, clichéd one-liner of a sitcom about three women who are best friends and share a commonality in that they are all successful professionals who are miserably single. The show is neither funny nor flattering to women, but it's extremely popular.

"Mmm hmm," she mumbles and tries to reposition herself into a more comfortable position.

Felona stares at her mother who is gazing in the direction of the TV.

The color is returning to her face. I was always envious of the deep, velvet soot that is her skin color. When I was a child, I wanted nothing more than to be dark-skinned so people wouldn't constantly tease me as that fake white girl. I hated that. And whenever I was out with my mom, people would stare and whisper.

Her haircut is the same as I remember, too. She always wore it dyed red; short on the sides while curled on top. I don't understand why she kept her haircut low, but gave me such a hard time when I decided to start wearing mine cut low as well. So much, of who I am, came from her.

Her mother glances from the direction of the television and asks, "Why you – lookin' at – me like that, Lona?"

Felona faintly smiles, "I haven't seen you in a while. Can't I look at my own mom?"

"Yes, you can. I haven't seen you – in so long. Look at you. You done gained a little weight – like you –"

Felona tenses up and holds her breath.

"You filled out – in all the right places. I wish – I wish

I had your figure. You grown into – such a beautiful woman, Lona. We got a lot of catching up to do. I'm glad you here."

Felona quietly exhales.

"Dinner time!" a voice announces.

Felona turns to see a portly nurse entering the room, pushing a silver cart stocked with trays of food. She pushes the cart toward her, as if she's not in her path.

Felona stands to move out of the nurse's way, just in time to avoid becoming a casualty of the rolling dinner cart.

The nurse briskly works, rolling the bedside table from its previous position and raising its top.

"I want you to eat something now," she instructs Dianne, as she places one of the trays on the table.

"You make sure she eats something," she advises Felona and Tobias before making an exit that was as abrupt as her entry.

"Baked chicken, green beans, beets, applesauce and orange juice," Tobias says as he stands across the room.

Felona exchanges a glance with him and sits back down on the bed beside Dianne.

"Why don't we start with something easy," she says.

She offers a spoonful of applesauce, but Dianne protests with, "I'm not really hungry right now," frowning at the smell of the food, that has filled the room.

"Mom, you need to eat if you want to get out of this bed and out of this hospital any time soon."

"Momma Mabel, eat a little something," Tobias pleads from across the room.

Felona nudges closer to her mom, but hesitates for a moment before sliding one hand between her head and the pillow. She forms a cradle with her hand and slightly lifts her head, holding the spoon closer to her mouth.

Her mother opens her mouth.

Loudly smacking her lips from the taste, she says, "This is sweeter than I remember applesauce being."

"More?" Felona asks with another spoonful.

She nods and Felona leans her forward again, musing at the role reversal of mother and child.

"This is sweeter than I remember, too," Felona says through a smile.

19

Engagement Ring

Knock knock," announces a bright voice from behind Felona, who turns to see her best friend, Ny, peeking from behind a bouquet of flowers.

Though she only stands at five foot, two inches, Ny's presence immediately floods the room.

"Look who's here," she says, standing up, grinning from ear to ear.

"Hey, sweetie," Ny says, kissing Felona on the cheek as she leans in, holding an empty bowl in one hand and a spoon in the other.

"I'm so happy to see you! Let me introduce you to someone," Felona nods toward her mom. "Ny, this is my mom. Mom this is my best friend, Kinaya Odoyo. Doctor Kinaya Odoyo."

Her mom smiles and nods her head. "Hello. Nice – to meet you. My name is Dianne."

Ny reaches over the bed and gently pulls Dianne into a full embrace while kissing her on the forehead as her long, dreaded locks fall from around her shoulders as if to join in the embrace.

She whispers in her ear, "You're so strong. It wasn't your

time to leave us. I'm so glad that you're still here and I finally get a chance to meet you."

Ny straightens up and says, "These flowers are for you, Mrs. Mabel. I'll put them right here."

She places the bountiful arrangement of Stargazer lilies and blue iris blooms in front of the tray of food.

"Hopefully, they'll make you feel better so we can get you out of here soon."

"They smell so good!" Felona enthusiastically says.

Her mother cocks her head sideways, looking at them admirably as her face brightens with delight. "Ohh – thank you so much. They – lovely."

"Mmm hmm! You're welcome," Ny responds.

Felona directs Ny to Tobias who stands from his previously seated position.

"Ny, this is my friend from back in the day, Tobias. Tobias, this is Kinaya."

Tobias reaches out to shake Ny's hand. "Pleased to meet you," he widely grins. "So you're a doctor?"

"It's an honor to meet you and yes, I'm an obstetrician."

"That's awesome... I think. What's an obstetrician?"

They both laugh.

"Women's plumbing. And babies."

Tobias chuckles knowingly, "Oh, okay."

"What do you do, Tobias?"

"A little of this and a little of that," Tobias proudly answers. "I'm in the Army Reserve. I, not too long ago, finished my second tour in Afghanistan. I, also, just finished school and next week, I'll be taking the aptitude test to become a fire-fighter. I've already passed the psych, first aid and driving tests, as well as the physical."

"Nice, Mister Everything. My dad is retired Army. Thank you for serving our country. And pre-congratulations on passing that firefighters exam."

Tobias nods humbly.

"You're very handsome, by the way. You'll make a fine addition to the firefighter's calendar."

"Ny! I can't believe you just said that aloud," Felona whines.

"Well, it's true. And I'm not flirting with the man; I'm happily married, thank you. I'm just telling the truth. We need to lift our black men up when they're doing well. And looking good."

"Thank you," Tobias smiles and bows. "On behalf of all black men, I thank you."

"See, if I said the same thing to a man I just met, he would think I was thrusting my vagina in his face," Felona says.

Dianne and Ny chuckle.

Ny can say pretty much anything to anyone and they receive it in the purest and most positive way. She just exudes good vibes and makes people feel good around her. She makes me feel good about my freckles, short hair and all.

"How you say your name?" Dianne asks of Ny. "Kee ni ni?"

"Kee–Ny–Uh," Ny slowly enunciates.

"Oh, okay. Kee–Ny–Uh."

"Yes. That's it. You got it!"

"Kinaya – you say that you married?"

"Yes ma'am."

"That's – that's nice."

Dianne smiles.

She turns her attention to Felona, who is moving the uneaten tray of food to the side table and out of the way.

"Lona, when you gone fine – when you gone fine you a man – tuh settle down wit?"

Felona is sobered by the question and her expression widens, suddenly made aware of the reality that she hasn't spoken to her mother in eight years. Her mother doesn't know of her two-year courtship and engagement to Vincenzo Ricci. Her mother doesn't know that her daughter's wedding is inside of two weeks away. Her mother doesn't know that her daughter had no intention of ever talking to her again and, therefore, she wasn't invited to the wedding.

"Ummmm."

"Felona's never had a problem with finding a man," Ny volunteers jokingly. "Her problem was finding which one she was going to marry."

"Ny!" Felona interrupts.

Ny looks at Felona and then at her mother.

"Oh," Ny resolves as her tone drops.

"What just happened?" Tobias asks, laughing nervously.

Felona looks at her mother apologetically and wrings her hands. Her mother returns a look of concern.

"What is it, Lona?"

"I–I already found a man to settle down with, mom."

Felona lifts her ring finger to show her engagement ring.

Her mother says feebly, "You engaged, Lona?"

"Y–yes, mom, I am."

She strains forward and squints at Felona's hand.

"It's – nice. When?"

"I was going to tell you. When you got out of the hospital, I was going to catch you up on everything. Remember what you said earlier? We have to catch up. On a lot."

Dianne stares back at Felona suspiciously.

"When?"

"Soon. But mom, let's... let's not make this about me right now. We're here for you."

"Why can't you tell me? What's the big secret? When?"

Felona nervously fidgets, almost like a child who is negotiating her way out of trouble.

"Mom, let's talk about this when you get your strength back, okay?"

Dianne frowns thoughtfully and relaxes back onto her pillow.

"So – 'fore today – you had no 'tention uh tellin' me?"

Felona looks down as a scorned child and says nothing in response.

Dianne continues, her voice now quivering, "Before I got sick – you was jus gone get 'gaged, married and have my granchil'ren and I – I obviously wasn't invited."

"Mom, come on. You know what happened between us before –"

"You really had no 'tention uh ever –"

"Momma Mabel, I don't think it was like that," Ny defends.

"No? How you know?"

Ny returns silence, unsure of what to say as Dianne continues, "I can't say – too much. I only have muhself tuh blame. It's been eight years. What can I 'spect? Even though I tried – calling for uh while – Lona wouldn't – wouldn't take my calls."

Dianne looks down, sulking.

"I made sacrifices fo huh alla huh life – and dis – dis is how she repays me – treats me like uh dog? I may not ha' been the puhfect mother – but I did the best I could. I did the best that I –"

She inhales and gasps at once, raising her hand to her face.

"Mom? I'm sorry I didn't mean to hurt your feelings."

Dianne turns on her side, away from her captive audience, and begins to cry.

Felona sighs loudly.

20

Fleeting

Blessed is the woman who has never had anything to love. She can never know the heartbreak that comes with losing it.

Some have said that Felona is fortunate to have many things – stunning beauty, intelligence, a job that offers adventure, a celebrity-like lifestyle and a rich, handsome fiancé.

But, in reality, all that she knows is loss.

All of her life, lovely things unattainable have dangled just beyond Felona's reach. She thought for a scant moment that she might experience what it's like to truly know a mother's love and acceptance, yet now, in this moment, she's discouraged. And her hope is fleeting.

She stands beside the bed waiting for her mother to stop crying. Ny and Tobias are the supporting cast of silence.

"Mom?" Felona calls to her in a desperate whisper, but her mother only answers with whimpering.

After several unyielding tries, she finally turns to Ny and asks, "Can we talk in the hall for a moment?"

"Sure, sweetie," she says as she gently leads her by the arm. "We'll be right back," she says to Tobias.

He nods as they disappear into the hallway.

Ny clasps Felona's hands in hers and exclaims in a hushed tone, "I'm sorry, Felo. I didn't know."

"You have no reason to apologize, Ny. You didn't do anything wrong. My mom can be... dramatic."

"I know this is very stressful for you, love. One moment you're losing your mom and the next, she's back in the land of the living."

She's back alright, Felona frowns thoughtfully. *When I looked into her eyes earlier, she seemed different; like she wanted to repair everything wrong between us. And beyond all of the bad things she's done to me, I felt it too.*

Her frown deepens as she peers at Ny, shaking her head.

"But... I'm not sure people can really change, Ny. I'm just not sure about any of this. I shouldn't be here. I shouldn't have come."

"She's your mom, Felo. I get why you would much rather run in the opposite direction, but she needs you right now. I get why you had no intention of her coming to your wedding."

"Do you?" Felona interrupts.

"Well, kind of. Okay, no, not really. But I trust that you had a good reason. And things have been whatever they've been between you and her in the past, but that's not to say that they have to continue that way at this point. Maybe this is the beginning of change. Her nearly dying to bring you back here seems like the perfect catalyst for such. But you have to play a role in that change. It won't just happen in an instant or overnight. And it takes time."

"I don't know," she sighs.

"She's been in a persistent state of unconsciousness for five weeks and as a result, her muscle acuity is deficient, she's likely experiencing temporary dementia, and her irritability is a direct side effect from all of the medicine and toxins built up in her body right now."

"I hate when you use medical terminology and rationale to makes sense."

Ny chuckles.

"I honestly don't know whether to be angry with her undercurrent of manipulation or saddened by the fact that she knows how to get to me. I wanted to hug her... and smother her at the same time, Ny."

Ny raises her eyebrows.

"Uh oh. Was I too honest?" Felona smirks.

"Felo, I know this is difficult, but –"

"No," she whines. "You don't know. She would cry as a way to... to break me down. She's dramatic for no reason. I mean, you saw it. What was that about?"

"She's just dealing with a lot right now. Just try to be patient with her, love."

Felona breathes in deeply and follows it with a long sigh. "I can't promise much, but I'll try."

"I love you, Felo. I do. But you need to do more than try. You almost lost your chance to fix whatever was broken with you two. That resistance? That's your pride getting in the way. One of you has to be the more resilient one. I believe that one is you."

Felona shakes her head, staring at the floor.

"Look, I know I just got here, but I'm going to give you two some time to talk in private."

"She won't talk to me. The next words that come from her mouth will be insults and name calling."

"Well, I'm going to hope for the best while I'm gone. I need to see what I can find to eat at this late hour in your quaint little town."

"Quaint? I'm certain you'll have more colorful words to describe this place when you return from your expedition. Quaint will not be one of them."

"Maybe. But while you're changing the subject, know that you have the means to overcome this. The Felona I know may be sarcastic, but she's also intelligent, loving and compassionate. I've seen it. You're my best friend and you've been there for me. I know that you can come out on the other side of this in a brilliant way. It's not going to be easy when all you've known of your mother has been bad experiences, but you can do this. It comes down to patience. There was this quote about patience that I remember from college. How did it go?"

Ny taps her lip with her finger and studies the ground before concluding, "Our patience will achieve more than our force. Edmund Burke."

Felona snaps her fingers.

"I also remember a quote. I can be as patient as the next woman, assuming that at the end of the day, I get my way. Felona Mabel."

"Felo. I'm serious. I know it's going to be tough under the circumstances, but try to be a little patient with your mom. You're more resilient than she. You'll be surprised at how she'll respond to your persistent kindness. Eventually, she'll follow your lead."

"You don't know my mom."

"But I know you."

"I'll try."

Ny pulls Felona into an embrace.

"I love you, curly girlie."

"Love you too, Ny. Thank you."

Ny disappears down the hall onto the elevator.

Felona stares into the distance.

Patience. What will patience lead to? Distrust is whispering in my ear that this is a fool's errand and I'm inclined to think there is no greater wisdom right now.

21

Disturbance

Felona quietly walks back into the room. Despite the exchange a few moments earlier, Tobias is already nodding off in his chair, but he jerks awake at her entry.

"Is she asleep?" Felona whispers.

Dianne is still lying on her side with her back facing them.

"Yeah, I think so," he drowsily says as the television hums at a low volume.

She collapses in the chair near Tobias and exhales loudly, "This has been some day."

He looks at her and smirks, "Some day indeed."

Felona suddenly sits up and leans forward, staring straight ahead for a moment.

She turns to face Tobias and her expression softens. "I had no excuse to treat you the way that I have. You've been nothing short of nice and I've been an ass."

"Yeah, you have," he quickly agrees.

"I'm sorry, Tobias. So much has changed. Coming back here reminds me of all that I left and tried to forget."

"Including me, Curlytop? Your former best friend of all time?"

Best friends of all time? That was a lifetime and a tragedy ago, she thinks before saying, "Come on, Tobias."

"No, really. What happened with us? If you're offering apologies and confessing your sins, you might as well bring it all into the light. Once upon a time, we were inseparable and now you can barely look me in the eyes for more than two seconds."

Felona looks away, as if on cue, at Dianne who is lying still under the covers.

"It's not you. It's me."

Tobias laughs heartily. "Really, Felona? Clichés now?"

"No, really," she says with a grimace, relaxing back into the chair. "It's all on me. You didn't do anything wrong. I changed. Everything changed. Our friendship was just collateral damage of all of that change."

"But why?"

Felona bites her lip and hovers, for a moment, over the idea of telling him everything.

"It just did, Tobias," she finally exhales. "It just did."

"Well, what about now? Is there any way to fix us now? Can't we repair what we once had?"

"Tobias, we were kids. What we once had was a consequence of who we were then. Things are different now. We live in different places... literally and figuratively. I'm engaged to be married in a couple of weeks."

"So I heard. I saw your ring earlier, but I didn't assume it was an engagement ring. These days, some women wear rings on that finger to discourage men from approaching them so much."

Felona nods.

"So who's the lucky man?" he continues.

"His name is Vin. Vincenzo Ricci."

"Vincenzo? Italian?"

"It is."

"Is he?"

Dianne stirs.

"Felona?" Tobias asks.

"Y–yeah?" she answers, briefly distracted by Dianne's movement.

"Is he Italian?"

"Yes. He's Italian. So?"

"I just can't imagine you being into the Jersey-boy type."

She looks down at the floor, thoughtfully.

"I'm not and he's far from the Jersey-boy type. He's a good guy. A great guy, actually."

"I would hope so. What does he do for a living?"

She raises her eyebrows and looks at Tobias, searching for the intent of his question.

"Come on," he smiles "Don't I have the right to know? I have to make sure that he's right for my little sister."

Felona cocks her head sideways and frowns, coldly repeating, "Your little sister?"

"Yeah. Well, you know what I mean."

"No, Tobias. I don't. What do you mean?"

Before he can answer, her cell phone in her handbag beside her chair rings, startling her.

She quickly recovers it.

"Vin. Hey. I tried calling you earlier, but went straight to voicemail."

"Oh. Really? I'm not sure why."

"Reception here sucks. It's even worse in the hospital."

She glances at Tobias who appears distracted at something across the room.

"Let me call you back when I step outside."

She looks over to her mother who is laboring to sit up in the bed.

"Love you," she says in a lowered voice before hanging up.

"Momma Mabel, do you need help? What do you want me to do?" Tobias asks as he stands.

"Can you – put these pillows under me?" she says, as she looks at Felona strangely. "I can't – get comfortable. I need tuh sit up."

Felona stands, as if in reverence of her mother's glare.

"I know I tried – tuh be a good mother tuh you," her mother starts. "I sacrificed all that I had for you tuh be here. What's wrong with you, girl? Have you lost your mind?"

Felona looks puzzled at Tobias who looks back at her with same stunned expression.

"W–what? Mom, what are you talking about?"

"Are you always looking for new ways tuh break my heart?"

Felona steps closer to her mother.

"I–I don't understand."

"You runnin 'round wit Italian men?"

"What? What difference does –"

"That man – who raped me – he was Italian too!"

"So every Italian is evil because of one? Mom, you're being irrational."

"How could you get involved with someone like him?"

"Wh–what? You don't even know him."

"Are you pregnant? Is that it?"

"Mom, no. What difference would it make if I was?"

"I dun want no Guinea gran'baby."

"Guinea? Like me? That's a new one. I don't think you called me that one before. That man – the one who raped you – is not who I'm engaged to, mom!"

"He may as well be. They all the same – greasy hair and greedy hands. They all the same! I don't understand why you wouldn't find a man like – like –"

"Like who? Like Brent?"

"No. Like Bias."

Felona looks at Tobias who appears embarrassed at the inclusion. He averts his eyes to the floor.

"Oh, so all the while I was a teenager, you didn't think Tobias was good enough, but now he is?"

"I never – I never said that." Dianne looks at Tobias, who is standing quietly over her. "Bias, I never said that you weren't good enough, honey."

Felona scoffs.

"Are you serious? You specifically didn't want Tobias and

I to end up together. Do you forget the lengths you went through to assure that we didn't?"

Felona glances at a confused Tobias while her mom's voice starts to quiver.

"Do you realize what I went through to have you?"

Oh, here we go! I really thought we were past this.

"Yes, mom. I do realize what you had to go through to have me because you told me about it every chance you got!"

Tobias puts his hand on Felona's shoulder and tries to lead her away from the bedside.

"Felona, why are you so angry? Maybe we should all just calm down before things are said that can't be taken back."

She jerks away from his grasp.

"I only told you about it so you would know to not make the same mistakes that I made," Dianne says as she begins to manifest tears.

"The same mistakes? What mistakes did you make? Me? Oh yeah. I remember now. And you made goddamn sure that I wouldn't make that same mistake, right?"

Dianne lowers her quivering voice and looks away.

"That's not what I meant and you know it."

Felona leans in so close to her mother, who is wiping tears from her eyes, that her breath warms the side of her face.

"I don't care what you meant. What I do know is every chance you got, you reminded me that you could have... you should have... aborted me. I made your life difficult. I wasn't as pure or worthy as Iris. I made Brent leave you. Whenever you looked at me, you saw Ignazio. Yeah, I said his name. Ignazio

Bernardi, Well, I'm not him! And neither is my fiancé!"

The door swings open and a nurse rushes in urgently.

"What is going on in here, people?" she sings with a thick Jamaican accent. "Do you all realize that it's late and some of the patients are sleeping?"

"I'm sorry. We'll lower it down," Tobias volunteers. "We were just having a... uh... a spirited family discussion.

"Family, my freckled ass," Felona mumbles under her breath as she turns to retrieve her handbag from the floor. She yanks it up and starts walking to the door to leave.

"Felona, don't do your mom like this," Tobias calls behind her.

She passes the nurse and whips around.

"Do my mom like what? Like she's been doing me for years? You don't even know the half of it, Tobias. This time I'm leaving before she gets her strength back to do more of the same."

"You always had a bad temper," her mother says through tears and a shaking head.

"And you always had a bad backhand, mother!"

"Ma'am," the nurse interrupts Felona, who ignores her and starts making her toward her mother again.

"Well, you don't have to worry about me. You don't have to worry about whom I'm engaged to. I'll save you the trouble of having to look in his white, greasy, Guinea face. Or see him kiss me – his bride – at the wedding!"

"Ma'am, you're being a disturbance now. It's in the late hour. If you can't be quiet, I going to have to call security."

Felona continues, "And no, I'm not pregnant, but if I were, that's all the more reason to keep away from you! You're hateful and toxic! Clearly nothing can change that. Not even a near-death experience."

"You're going to have to leave, ma'am," the nurse says, now standing between Felona and the bed. "You're being a disturbance to this room and you're upsetting the patients on the floor."

"Don't worry. I'll leave. For good!"

Felona turns and violently swings the door open, but the tensioner prevents it from hitting the wall and it quietly yawns back closed as the sound of angry heels clicking against the floor fade down the hallway.

22

Crash

Violently flashing blue lights appear from out of nowhere behind Felona. She looks down at the speedometer and even though her foot is now relaxing from the gas, she's suddenly conscious that she'd been driving well over 85mph since she sped away from the hospital.

"Shit!"

Widened, hazel eyes glance in the rear view mirror. The vein on the side of her temple is throbbing, indicative of how rapid her heartbeat is pounding. Her hands become tacky with sweat as she grips the steering wheel tightly. She pulls into the right lane, slowing further, but the flashing blue lights don't pull into the right lane with her.

The police car speeds past, while the siren begins to wail. A second police car follows behind it in the same manner.

She exhales loudly.

That was too close. As heartless as it may sound, I'm thankful for someone else's tragedy that needs police attention. I can't be stuck in this God-forsaken town any longer than I need to be.

A little over twenty-four hours ago, Felona was headed in the opposite direction to Nathaniel to see to the final arrangements of a dying mother. Now, her temper is fueling her irrational decision to cancel all plans of reconciliation with her mother and head back to Admah City without much regard for anything else.

"I need to get gas and I need to find Ny. There is no reason to stay here another night."

She slows into the turn lane to make a left into the gas station.

The clicking of her blinker is interrupted with a forceful thud and the sound of metal and glass.

She screams.

The shove from the impact behind jerks her back into her seat from her previously leaning forward posture.

The seat belt tightens around her as the vehicle spasms into the lane of oncoming traffic, but she regains control before any opposing cars come.

She let's her car coast into the parking lot. Once the moment of shock passes, she realizes that she's been hit from behind by another vehicle that was going at a high rate of speed.

The car that crashed into her pulls in behind her.

She closes her eyes and rests her head against the headrest.

"This can't be happening. Fuck! Shit! Fuuuuuck! Damnit!"

She repeatedly slams her palms against the steering wheel, blowing the horn angrily as a result.

After her tantrum, she takes a deep breath before she gets out of the car.

She immediately walks to the back to see what damage has

been done. She gasps at the sight of her once-flawless, white Range Rover in its now-mangled appearance. The bumper on the right side is flayed and the back end is smashed. The back window has been pulverized and glass is sprayed throughout the interior. She walks back around toward the front of her car.

The driver of the other vehicle meets her halfway.

She's a small, brunette woman with short gel-spiked hair. Her pale, haggard face, nose ring and arm tattoos aren't enough to mask the brightness of her eyes, which have an innocence about them. Coupled with her stature, she barely looks old enough to be driving.

"I'm so sorry," she whines with a cartoonish, high-pitched voice.

"What the hell?" Felona fires back. "There were two whole lanes that you could drive in. And you pick mine? Didn't you see me?"

"I tried to stop."

Felona glances at the woman's car, an early model Buick that is barely scathed, minus a broken headlight and scuffed paint.

"You successfully did that. With my car! You could have killed me!"

"You don't have to yell, lady. I said I was sorry. It was an accident."

"You barreled right into me. You've didn't even put on brakes. Did you call the police?"

She crosses her arms and frowns, "No. Why? You don't look hurt."

"Why? To report this accident. Your piece of shit car may be fine, but do you see what you did to mine?"

She doesn't say anything, but just looks around nervously.

Felona scoffs, "Forget it. I'll call them."

She walks back to her car to retrieve her phone from the middle console. While standing on the driver's side rifling through her handbag for her license, the passenger door opens and the woman gets in.

"What the hell are you doing?"

"Leaving the scene of the crime."

"What? What are you –?"

Steel fingers bite into the back of Felona's neck and shoves her head forward, holding her in place, keeping her from turning around. Every muscle in her body tightens. Something blunt is thrust into her side with so much force that it feels like a dull knife, a pipe… or a gun.

"Don't scream and I won't hurt you," a gravely voice behind her threatens.

His breath smells of marijuana laced with bad hygiene.

"Step back… slowly."

His fingers tighten around her neck and he pulls her back from the driver's side of her car. She reaches for her handbag, which is still sitting on the seat, but he yanks her back too abruptly for her to grasp it in time.

"W–what do you want?" she asks, unable to see her perpetrator and attempting to remain calm.

"I want whatever I decide I want. Don't talk to me and don't look at me."

He squeezes her neck tighter still.

"Let's go. We ain't got time for playing," the woman says, as she leans across the driver's side.

"Hol' on! Don't rush me."

"You gone fuck up again! Let's go. This ain't the plan!"

"The plan wasn't to fuck up the car with all that backend damage either. We're s'posed to chop this into parts and make three times the amount that this is worth whole. But we can't sell fucked up parts. You takin' money outta my cut with that shit. 'Sides, this lady fine as hell. I wanna keep her for a while to make up for your fuck up."

He slides the gun down from her waist to her hip to her inner thigh. Felona clenches her jaw and closes her eyes tightly. A tear escapes them anyway as he applies greater pressure to her crotch and leans in where his lips are touching her ear.

"Nah, fool! We don't need no repeat of last time. Get in here, nigga. Let's go!"

Despite her small, wiry stature, clearly the woman is the one calling the shots because he relaxes his ill-stained intent.

"That wasn't my fault. That lady bucked. What was I s'posed to do?"

"Nothing ain't ever your fault. We don't need the trouble this time. Let's go!"

"Fine!"

He shoves Felona forward so hard that she stumbles to the ground. Her cell phone falls from her hand as she tries to break her fall and not land on her face. By the time she turns around to see her assailant, the car door has already been shut. She steals a glimpse of him past her tear-blurred vision and the gun, which he is pointing out the window at her, as they pull away.

"Help! Help me! I've been robbed!" Felona starts to scream desperately, looking around to see if any witnesses will come to her aid, but there is no one in proximity.

She's alone in the gas station parking lot as she watches her car speed away without her driving it.

"I hate this fucking town!" she sneers.

23
Police Report

Nine minutes later, Felona is still shaking when the police arrive with their blue lights flashing. They pull alongside the car that the thieves left behind.

"Ny, I'm fine. I'm – I'm fine. Ny, calm down," Felona raises her voice on the phone as she paces beside the car. "Ny, the police are here. I'll call you right back after I talk to them."

Felona instinctively reaches to slip the phone into her handbag, before remembering that it was stolen – along with the car that she'd only had for four months.

Her hands and forearm are scratched and bloodied from her fall and her right knee is throbbing with pain. She looks down and slightly lifts the hem of her skirt to inspect the extent of her injury. Her otherwise pale, freckled skin is reddened, puffy and bleeding.

She limps toward the police as they get out of their car.

I wonder if these are the same police that sped past me earlier. Is them being here a form of poetic justice since I was thankful for someone else's misfortune earlier that caused them to overlook my speeding?

"Good evening, ma'am," greets one of the officers

approaching her. He's short and chunky and from underneath his hat, wisps of thinning hair peek out. Despite his squat shape, he has broad shoulders and a wide smile that commands a sense of safety and presence. "Are you the one who called 911?"

"I am," her voice trembles despite struggling to sound composed.

The second officer trailing behind him is a woman who has a grimace, contrary to her friendlier partner. She doesn't say anything or make eye contact as she peers in the windows of the abandoned car.

"Can you tell me what happened?"

"I was preparing to make a left turn when I got hit from behind," she points at the thieves' abandoned car. "I pulled in to this parking lot and when I got out to look at the damage, I was held at gunpoint and they stole my car. They took off that way."

She points as the policeman scribbles in a notepad.

He absently says, "Mmm hmm" as he continues to write.

He finally looks up and asks, "Do you have any identification on you, ma'am?"

"No, my handbag was in the car when they took off. Fortunately, I was holding my phone."

"Let me get your name and address, ma'am."

"It's Felona Mabel."

He looks up from his notepad with a controlled smirk.

"I thought you looked familiar. You're that lady from the news."

"Yep, that's me."

He chuckles to himself, shaking his head, and continues writing.

"What's that address?"

"I live in Admah City. 1039 Crescent Trail."

"If you had any credit or bank cards, you're going to want to cancel them as soon as possible. You don't want to also become a victim of identity theft," the female officer says as she completes her walk-around inspection of the other car. With her hands resting on her belt in an official stance, she informs her partner, "McDermott, I'm going to run the registration on this one, but I'm pretty sure it was stolen too."

Officer McDermott nods yes and turns his attention to her. "You're bleeding. Do you need an ambulance?"

"No."

"Are you in any pain? Neck stiffness? Back aches?"

She rubs her right forearm, slightly brushing gravel and dirt from the dried blood.

"My knee hurts, but I'm fine."

"How fast do you think the perpetrators were driving when they ran into you?"

She shrugs, "Very fast? I don't know."

He chuckles to himself and resumes writing in his notepad as he walks around to the front of the thieves' car.

"What is the make and model of your vehicle?"

"It's... wait... huh?"

"What kind of car is it?"

"It's a white Range Rover. 2011."

He scribbles intently.

"What kind of damage did your vehicle sustain?"

"The backend was smashed pretty badly so the bumper was kind of hanging down on the right side and the back glass was gone."

He peers at the front of the vehicle where the headlight is broken and scuffs of white paint from her car are apparent on the hood.

"Okay. Good."

He turns his head and speaks into the speaker contraption on his left shoulder, "Twenty-two traffic."

"Twenty-two," a female voice squawks back.

"All points on a 2011 white Range Rover with passenger-side, extensive backend damage, last seen northbound on Washington."

"Ten four, twenty two."

He returns his attention to Felona.

"Did you get a good look at either of them?"

"I did see the woman. She was a few inches shorter than me; about five foot, two; Caucasian; brunette, shoulder-length hair; hoop nose ring; a lot of tattoos on both arms; light blue T-shirt; black jeans."

"You said they held you at gunpoint? How many people were there?"

"Two. The other one was a man and he's the one that had the gun on me. I never saw his face."

"Ms. Mabel, will you need us to give you a ride anywhere?"

"I don't think so. I have a friend who's near that can pick

me up."

"That's fine. If you could wait here, we're going to continue our investigation. We may have a few more questions for you."

He hands a card to Felona as his partner returns from her inquiry.

"What about my car?"

"We will do our best to recover your car. My report will be available in two to three days for your insurance company." He points his chubby index finger at the printed information on the card. "This is your case number and this is my number, should you have any questions."

"It's stolen," announces the female officer from behind him. "It was reported stolen two weeks ago."

"Great," Felona throws her hands up in frustrated surrender. "So you accidentally recovered someone else's vehicle two weeks later. Is that how you plan on recovering mine? The next victim they rob will be smashed by my car that's left at the scene?"

The female officer speaks up, "Ma'am, I can assure you that we will do our best to recover your property, but your vehicle is not the only one that was stolen this week or even this night."

Felona crosses her arms with an abrupt motion, momentarily forgetting that they're hurting.

"Owww," she mumbles.

"So if Nathaniel's crime rate is getting out of control like that then I would think that you would have a greater sense of urgency to solve some of these crimes before your town is overrun with car thieves or worse."

The female officer places both of her hands on her utility belt and squares her shoulders as she moves closer to Felona.

"Ma'am, we're well aware of the crime rate and what we need to do. That's why we're out here. We're trying to help –"

Her partner intervenes by reaching between them, handing Felona his notepad.

"Ms. Mabel, if you could jot down a contact number, we will get in touch with you as soon as we find anything."

Felona rolls her eyes at the female officer, before writing her number in the notepad.

***

The officers walk around the stolen car a couple more times, writing things in their notepads, before relocating their investigation inside the car, searching the glove box, the trunk and under the seats.

Felona paces back and forth on the curb next to the gas station. The attendant inside suddenly appears from the back of the store, peering through the glass, curious at the commotion that he missed since his absence. He walks over to the door and pulls on it, making sure that it's still locked before he takes residence behind the counter on a stool.

Felona sees him from the corner of her eye.

Now he shows up. Where was this dude when a crime was happening in his own parking lot?

She turns her attention to the police.

I'm not sure what they're looking for, but if dusting for fingerprints was ever a consideration, it's too late now. They've pretty much contaminated any forensic evidence left behind in their search for something else.

A tow truck pulls into the parking lot just as Felona is finishing a call with Tobias, who she asked to come pick her up. As she is about to call Ny back, she notices that she has four missed calls from her because her phone was on silent while she talked to the police.

"Oh my god, Felo! Are you okay? We must've lost our signal. And I've been calling and calling," she greets her on the other end.

"I said that the police were here and I would call you right back."

"What happened? I was so worried and had no clue how to find you."

"I'm so sorry. I had to talk to the police. I didn't mean to worry you. We don't need to have the both of us stressed out."

"So what happened?"

After Felona has told Ny about how the conversation with her mother went downhill fast shortly after she left, how she'd reached her tolerance threshold and how there was no practical application of patience that could be applied under the circumstances, Ny interrupts impatiently.

"You already told me all of that! What happened to you

after you left the hospital and why are you talking to the cops? Are you okay? Where are you?"

"I got hit by someone – my car, that is – got hit by another car. It was intentional. I was carjacked."

"Oh my god!"

"These assholes smashed me from behind and when I got out to check the damage, they pulled a gun on me and stole my car and my handbag."

"Are you okay? Did they hurt you?"

"I'm scuffed up a bit, but I guess it could've been worse."

"Oh my god. I'm so glad you're okay, Felo! Where are you? I can come get you."

"No need for you to get lost in an unfamiliar town in the middle of the night. Tobias is on his way to come pick me up. I was going to have him drop me off wherever you are so I can stay with you for the night. Where are you?"

"I'm at this hotel about fifteen minutes away from the hospital. Thelma's Bed and Breakfast. It's off of Riverside."

Felona sighs, watching the tow truck pull the stolen car onto its flatbed while the police look on.

"Every time I come here, something bad happens. There's a reason I haven't been here in a while."

A noisy, blue 1971 Toyota Corolla pulls into the parking lot and slowly passes the tow truck and police car, obviously to steal a glance of what's going on.

The female officer scowls and moves toward the car with one hand tucked in her belt and the other one hovering over her gun holster.

The driver, Tobias, doesn't linger after satisfying his curiosity and he whips the car around the gas pumps and pulls up to the curb where Felona is waiting.

The engine is obnoxious enough that Felona has to raise her voice in order for Ny to hear her.

"Tobias is here! I'll see you in a few minutes!"

"Give me a moment," Felona shouts to Tobias over the noisy engine, before she walks over to talk with the police.

Felona returns a few minutes later to find Tobias looking like he isn't too pleased to see her. He leans over to the passenger side and unlocks the door.

Felona pulls the handle to open the door, to no avail.

"Pull hard," Tobias yells over the idling engine.

Felona yanks the handle with all of her weight and the door opens with a loud squeak. The car sits a lot lower than what she's accustomed to with her Range Rover, so she accidentally collapses into the seat.

"Thank you for coming to get me," she turns to him, nervously smiling.

He doesn't smile back nor does he ask her why she needed him to pick her up in the middle of the night at a gas station when she has a car.

Instead, with a grim expression, he turns to her and calmly says, "After you left, your mom and I had a conversation. She was very upset, but I learned a few things that make more sense now."

Felona frowns, confused.

Tobias continues, "She told me what you did, Felona. Your mom told me why you turned cold toward me and left Nathaniel years ago."

24
Post Partum

2000 - 2001

Immediately following her abortion, Felona felt nothing. And that nothing was a dull and odorless void that tasted of copper and Valium.

She wanted to tell Tobias that she had been emptied of the child that they inadvertently conceived together, but she was afraid.

She was afraid that he would hate her or that she would hate him for whatever his response might be. So she didn't tell him. And he never knew anything other than the fact that, for seemingly no reason, she distanced herself and changed toward him.

But Felona wasn't the only one who was altered as a result of her abortion.

Her mother changed too.

Where she was once the cold, calloused mother who dared abandon her pregnant daughter in the parking lot of an abortion clinic, guilt overtook her.

One day, or more specifically, four days after Felona's abortion, her mother asked, "Lona, do you want me to make you anything special for dinner?"

"No. I'm not hungry," Felona flatly answered, lying on her stomach across her bed.

"Are you feeling okay? You haven't been eating. You need to get your strength back up."

Felona didn't answer further. She instead returned to her silence accompanied by red, swollen eyes.

If by okay, she means an acute fixation with wanting to stop breathing then I guess I'm doing fucking well, she thought to herself.

Eventually, the dull and odorless void that tasted of copper and Valium turned into a vacuum, much like that which was used to withdraw life from her womb.

Felona continued to bleed for almost a month afterward and, at times, the bleeding carried with it dollops of flesh and streaks of intense pain with cramping. She felt dirty, guilty and alone, all at once.

She had neither appetite nor much motivation to do anything but lie in bed, yet not at the consequence of sleep. It evaded her.

But during those rare times when she slept, her dreams would hear the indistinct cooing of babies to the point that she thought she was losing what little two-fingered grasp that she had with reality.

Felona wanted the noise and the bad feelings to stop at any cost. She began fantasizing more and more about dying. Soon, death became an elusive suitor that she longed to court.

Rather than being distracted by preparation for her first

semester of college, her mind dwelled in a place of death, tombs and catacombs.

She went from feeling nothing to savoring the peace that accompanied her resolve to kill herself.

The consideration of the best method of suicide isn't exactly the type of discussion that could be had with just anyone.

Felona had distanced herself from Tobias. Under any other circumstances, he would have been the first person that she would consult with.

Despite the fact that she essentially blamed her mother for everything that had happened to her, there was still a nagging compulsion within her to reach out. But she didn't.

She couldn't.

One doesn't go to the hardware store looking to buy bread. She'd made that mistake several dozen times before, thinking that, one random day, her mother would surprise her with a love, compassion and acceptance that she desperately needed. So she was left to her own resources and imagination.

Painless and peaceful – that's how most people wish to die, whether self-inflicted or of natural causes. That precluded jumping, cutting or shooting and left the only logical solution in its wake – pills.

Felona resolved to kill herself by eating a handful of muscle relaxers that she stole from her mother's medicine cabinet.

She gained knowledge of their existence when she was given a couple on the night of her abortion for the purpose of easing her cramping and to help her sleep. Felona had never felt as high as she felt that night. She floated above pain and loneliness that night.

What seemed poetic and like a good idea at the time was her undoing. Not entirely sure why, she wanted to die in a public place instead of at home. She didn't want her mother to stop her or commit her to some psychiatric ward afterward. She simply wanted to stop existing. No questions. No interruptions. She decided that she would go to the mall.

A crowded place, slow emergency response time, and endless shopping. What more could a self-destructive girl ask for? she darkly joked.

Her mother was asleep and Felona had just gotten her driver's license. Her final defiant act would be to steal her life and her mother's car.

She swallowed a handful of pills before leaving home. She didn't count them. It didn't matter.

Her rationale was that if two made her float above her bed, a handful would float her all the way to heaven.

What she didn't take into account was that a handful would also numb her nervous system and act a lot more aggressive, retarding her motor skills; motor skills that she needed to drive.

She never made it to the mall, which was only eight miles away. Her eyes closed at around mile five before her mother's car smashed into a retaining wall to a bridge underpass.

Felona awakened to the sight of fire dancing between the front of the crumpled car and the damaged wall. She could feel the heat of flames and the warmth of the engine on her face as it lay on the hood of the car.

She hadn't been wearing her seatbelt and was catapulted through the windshield on impact. She wasn't thrown clear of the car though. She was sprawled between the dashboard and the hood.

When she attempted to move and escape the volatile danger that fire and leaking gasoline presented, she felt glass dislodge from her neck and shoulders. She struggled to move and steal a glance at the damage that her body had endured. Her blouse was soaked with her own blood.

Panic suddenly flickered through her mind, but the pills that she'd taken dulled her heart rate and reflexes. She tried to scream for help, but all that her effort produced was a muffled gurgle followed by streaks of intense pain. Her throat had been crushed.

Taking a handful of pills and driving to the mall to die seemed poetic and like a good idea at the time, but there Felona was – mangled and unable to successfully carry out a seemingly simple thing such as ending her life.

She'd only succeeded at making things incredibly worse.

The streaks of pain yielded to the drugs in her system as she heard sirens getting closer. She lost consciousness again.

Felona's suicide attempt and near-fatal car accident didn't avail her of her emotional pain though. And she was still seeking some form of liberation three months later as her freshman year of college had begun.

Unfortunately, every time she looked in the mirror, she saw the scar – the scar from the emergency tracheotomy that the paramedics had to perform on her when her larynx was crushed in the car accident. This scar she wore was a reminder of her stupidity, but also the mark of her miraculous survival.

The human brain can only go without oxygen for about four to six minutes. Felona's airway was blocked and she'd started to aspirate on her own blood and saliva. If the paramedics hadn't made an incision to her trachea to allow an airway, she would have suffocated and died.

Felona wanted to hide that ugly reminder on the soft spot just below her throat so she came up with the idea of covering it with a tattoo, yet she didn't have any idea what she would cover it with.

She discovered a tattoo shop a couple of miles from Edison State University in Admah City, where she was attending on an academic scholarship. Felona was relieved to be away from the guilt and memories of Nathaniel and the abuse from her mother. She was ready to experience independence and the things associated with college life like meeting new people, experiencing new things and, perhaps, finally being accepted.

"Yer stunnin'. Who's gonna be lookin' at ya neck?" Clint, the proprietor and tattoo artist of Viper's Skullduggery and Body Art, asked her after she told him that she didn't want people staring at her tracheotomy scar and wanted to mask it with something.

"Well, I have to look at it and I don't like it. I want to artfully cover it with something significant and subtle. What would you suggest?"

All of the walls were wallpapered with tribal scribblings, subcultural motifs and a splurge of color. Clint had his heavily tattooed arms crossed with a discerning finger on his chin as he toggled between looking at Felona and the wall of options before them.

"No matta what I put there, it's gonna stand out 'cause it's on yer neck. And yer skin tone is very light. People are gonna probably stare at you more. And since they gonna ask you what the ink means or whateva, you want somethin' that at least got an interestin' story."

"Hmm. So would that exclude a smiley face?"

He looked at her blankly, unaware that she was joking.

"Just kidding."

"How 'bout this?"

He pointed to an illustration of a bandage.

"No. I think that draws more attention than I want. I want something a little more —"

"Conservative?"

Felona frowned, unsure if his assertion was a compliment or criticism.

"Uhh, yeah. Not in your face or a cliché."

He nodded and continued to survey the illustrated walls and after a few moments of him pacing back and forth, he abruptly turned to Felona and snapped his fingers.

"I got it!"

"O–okay. What?" she nervously smiled.

"Well, the moment you walked in, I was distracted by how beautiful you are." He waved his hands above his head in an exaggerated motion, "I was entranced by yer beauty."

"Thank you."

"Now a lotta pretty girls come in here, but yer look is different. Exotic. It's yer freckles. I love yer freckles. They're like a sky fulla stars. And yer big, hazel eyes are like planets mankind can never know."

Felona blushed as he continued, "We should go with a galaxy theme. And I would suggest this."

He turned from her and reached up so high that he was nearly tiptoeing. His boney finger pointed to a star.

"A Texas star?" Felona winced.

"No, it's not a Texas star. Well, it is, but that's not the meanin' here It's a nautical star, which represents new direction."

"Pass!"

"But –"

"No! I'm not going to walk around with a Texas star on my neck. What else you got?"

Clint frowned and rubbed his chin as he stared at the floor.

Felona continued, "I want it to represent starting over, being made whole, being reborn or something like that."

After some quiet consideration, he brightened and said, "I got a perfect idea fer you, but I'm gonna need to sketch it out. Give me twenty minutes?"

Felona shrugged.

"Umm... sure."

———

"Ouroboros!" Clint exclaimed fifteen minutes later as he came from behind the counter holding a sheet of paper.

"Bless you," Felona joked.

"No. Bless you."

He presented the paper to Felona by holding it up and a few inches away from her face.

"Ouroboros is an ancient, circular symbol of a serpent eatin' its own tail which symbolizes re-creatin' oneself or wholeness. But I figured yer not the type o' hottie that wants a reptile on her neck so I simplified it ta look like a brush stroke of the same thing."

Felona smiled widely, beaming, "I like it!"

Clint gently took her by the arm and led her to the counter before he reclaimed the sketch from her.

"But wait! There's more."

He colored an irregular dot in the center of the drawing and stepped away from the counter so she could see what he'd done.

"A circle with a dot in the middle was a common Egyptian and Greek symbol for the sun or for fire. Now I hope ya don't think I'm reachin', but fire can represent rebirth to a lotta people."

"Oh my god! I love it! And the dot looks like a little heart lying on its side."

Clint leaned in and squinted at his handiwork.

"Hold on. That's supposed ta be a circle. Let me fix it."

Felona snatched the drawing and held it closely to her.

"No! I love it just like this. A heart on its side. This is what I want... colored the same as my freckles."

Prep didn't take long and before she knew it, she was in the back of Viper's Skullduggery and Body Art, sitting in what was akin to a barber's chair with a towel draped over her shoulders.

She winced at the first sting, baring her teeth and clinching her eyes tightly.

Clint pulled the buzzing instrument away from her throat and chuckled.

"You might wanna think happy thoughts fer the next thirty minutes or so. If you use that much energy every time the needle touches you, you'll wear yerself out 'fore I'm halfway done drawin' the lines on you."

With her eyes closed and as the instrument hummed in her ear, Felona began thinking of her post-partum rebirth – college, womanhood and freedom from her mother's castigation.

25
Fear

The only constant in life is change.

And heartbreak. And fear. And sometimes, loneliness.

I'm ready for something a little less than obstinate at this point, Felona thinks as Tobias drives in sullen quiet.

I feel like I've been falling from heaven with the same momentum for most of my life. My fear isn't in the falling, as much as not knowing what hitting the bottom will feel like. Am I already there? Can I start to get up yet?

I have no idea what my mother could have possibly said to Tobias once I left that has him this quiet. There's no way she could have told him about the abortion. But what? she ponders.

Finally she breaks the pregnant silence with, "Aren't you going to ask me what happened to me? To my car?"

Tobias scowls at her and loudly exhales.

"What happened to you? And your car?"

Felona rubs her elbows and looks away from him, out the window. "I got carjacked."

He abandons his grim, quiet stance. "What?"

"Carjacked. It's when someone steals your car by weapon or force."

Tobias sighs. "I know what the word means. Why're you like that?"

She turns to him. "Like what?"

"So sarcastic?"

"I'm not sarcastic. I just have a healthy sense of humor about life."

"That's not a sense of humor. That's being a smart ass and covering up how you really feel. It also pushes people who care about you away."

"Okay, Dr. Coles. I didn't know that I had you on retainer. And you make gas station calls in the middle of the night too? Nice."

"Dr. Coles? See? You prove my point. So what happened exactly?"

"While I was driving, I was hit from behind, but it was just a ruse to get me to get out of my car. At that point, I was held at gunpoint and my car was stolen."

"Jesus, Felona! You could have been killed! You should have called the cops instead of getting out of your car in the middle of the night."

"Well, I got out of my car in a well-lit parking lot. How was I to know that well-lit gas stations are no longer safe places? How was I to know that no one would come to my aid, even after the thugs drove off with my car? I bet if I'd tried to steal some gas and drive away, there would've been witnesses. They would've had it on HD quality video."

"I'm sorry that happened. Are you okay?"

She scoffs and rolls her eyes before looking down at her

scuffed hands and arms. "I guess... physically, anyway. I am now carless and trapped in the very place I couldn't leave fast enough. I feel like I'm about to lose my mind any second, so whatever bomb you're about to drop, you've been warned."

"It's not even like that, Felona. Calm down. Your mom said that you –"

She interrupts, leaning forward, "Wait! Where're you driving to?"

"Back to the hospital. I thought –"

"No no no! I can't go back there. I will not go back there. Would you drop me off at the bed and breakfast off of Riverside Parkway? Thelma's? Kinaya is staying there, so I'm going to stay with her for the night."

"Are you sure?"

"I've never been more certain."

"Okay. I can drop you off where your friend is, but we need to talk first."

"Tobias, it's late. I'm exhausted in every way imaginable and I'm sore. I just want to take a hot shower and collapse into unconsciousness. I don't have the energy to talk about anything. Can't this wait?"

He nods his head, saying nothing else.

But then Felona realizes that he's not driving in the direction of the hospital nor Thelma's Bed and Breakfast. He's heading toward her mother's house.

Last night around this time Felona was sitting in her car
in the rain in front of a house that looked almost identical
to the one that Tobias is parked in front of now.

He turns the idling, yet noisy, engine off and turns his
attention to her.

Felona averts her eyes from him and toward the house.

"Why did you bring me here, Tobias? I told you, I'm
emotionally and physically exhausted. Are you so selfish that
this has to happen now?"

"Felona, I fear that if I drop you off, I won't get this chance
again because you'll leave for good. So I'm taking the one
shot that I might have."

She scoffs.

He continues, "Your mom said that you left Nathaniel
because of me."

"W–what?"

Her breathing becomes shallow and panicked.

"She said that, shortly after we had sex, you told her what
happened to you."

"I–I did? Told her? Why would I tell her?"

"She said you told her that what we did exposed feelings
that you weren't ready to face."

"Tobias, I don't think –"

"Wait. Let me finish," he says calmly, raising his hands
to pause her objection. "It makes perfect sense. We were
kids and we crossed a line, but we never talked about it. We
tried to carry on like everything was normal, but it wasn't.
Everything had changed. The first time we were together, you

were in immense pain and I was awkward and scared. The second attempt, it felt more like sex was supposed to feel, I guess. But we didn't really say much about it and opportunity didn't allow for further attempts. Suddenly, school activities were more important to you and by the time we graduated and had the opportunity to talk, you seemed cold toward me. I didn't understand what was happening at the time, but it makes perfect sense now."

Tobias reaches out and places his hand on Felona's shoulder. Instead of turning to look at him, she stiffens and continues looking out the window, trying not to tear up.

She says nothing out loud, but her head is full of commotion and regret.

I want to tell him the truth. I want to tell him about all that we once had in common. And how I messed up. But this isn't the time.

"Felona?"

I've been afraid of rejection ever since. The selfish thing that I did – that I was forced to do – has left me feeling more alone than my mother could ever singly do. Not even Ny knows because I feel like she would judge me and think me a horrible woman. She's trying to become a vessel to bring life into the world and I just poured out mine.

"Felona?"

But maybe if I told Tobias the truth, there is some forgiveness to be had. Maybe my being here, the chapter that I have to close, is this very thing. All of my past wasn't entirely horrible. Was it?

Compartmentalizing the bad stuff away has also buried the

good memories. He was once my best friend and now I can't bear to look at him. I can't bear to be reminded of what I lost... of what I experienced. I want to forget forever. But it's not his fault. He doesn't deserve –

"I need air!" she blurts out loud, as she briefly struggles with the latch to open the door before shoving her way out of the car.

"Felona!" Tobias calls after her, as she steps from the street-lit sidewalk into the shadows created by the trees in her mother's yard.

She's spent the last ten plus years trying to escape where so many of her bitter memories were born and now she finds herself seeking temporary refuge at this very place.

She collapses into a seated position on the damp grass.

"Felona, are you alright?" Tobias asks as he walks around his car.

She looks away, hiding her expression in the shadows as he approaches.

He kneels down in front of her and whispers, "I'm sorry. I never meant to hurt you or mess us up. I'm so sorry that I didn't tell you then how important you were to me. I'm so sorry, Felona."

As liberated tears trickle from her eyes, he smooths his hand across her face. She jerks away; surprised by his touch, but not before he feels the wetness of her tears and knows that she's crying.

"Hey," he whines. "What's wrong? Why're you crying?"

Not saying anything, Felona just shakes her head back

and forth, although in the darkness, Tobias can't see her mute response. As far as he can tell, Felona is non-responsive so he continues to fill the silence.

"I'm sorry, I didn't mean to bring up the past, but now that I know where we messed up, I'm not going anywhere. I'll always be your friend. No matter where you go or what you do, I'll always be here for you. What I was too immature to say then, I can say now. I love you. I've always loved you. That will never change."

At some point in their lives, most women want to hear some assemblage of the words "I love you" from a man who expresses and intends them with all sincerity. Every fairy tale ending consists of them.

But Felona simply shuts her eyes tightly, to prevent more tears from coming forth.

The background noise of crickets and distant trucks on the highway becomes Felona's soundtrack of evasion while Tobias continues to say things she can no longer hear.

All she hears is the continued ramblings in her own head.

Tobias deserves more than my mute offerings. He's trying to make peace and I'm the one who should be pleading for his forgiveness right now. I'm a coward. Just like my mother said, I don't deserve anything good.

Nothing good has come of this town. Does that include me? Running away didn't stop me from being who I am; who I've become. Everywhere I go, there I am.

Finally an audible sigh escapes her mouth and Tobias stops mid-sentence of whatever it is that he was saying.

Her voice quivers, "Tobias, I... I'm sorry."

Felona opens her mouth to say more, but nothing further comes out.

She looks down and pauses for a moment before she unexpectedly leans forward to kiss him.

26

Faint Water Stains

Y ou did what?" shrieks Ny, jumping up and down on the bed. "Felo, what the hell? Did you forget that you were engaged to a certain man named Vincenzo Ricci? Remember him?"

"I didn't say that we passionately kissed. As a matter of fact, I surprised him more than I was surprised at my own impulse."

"Care to explain those impulses?"

"Honestly, I wish I could. But like I said, those impulses surprised me. Tobias told me that he loved me. Something malfunctioned somewhere in a glimmer and a brain fart of a moment and I leaned in to kiss him. I'm not really sure why or what I expected to come of it."

She falls back on the pillow and stares up at the popcorn ceiling with faint water stains bleeding from the side of the air vents and continues, "I kissed Tobias and for a moment, I think he kissed me back. But he pulled away. He pulled away like he was repulsed by me."

"Under the circumstances, are you surprised, love?"

"I guess not. He told me that he didn't want to taint what

we have like he once did. He said that I needed to settle whatever chaos was going on within me before we –"

"What you have? What do you have, Felo?"

Felona says nothing and continues to stare up at the ceiling. Ny continues, "And chaos? You mean with your mom?"

"Chaos with everything. Coming back here to experience all that I'd thought I'd escaped, only confirms that I haven't escaped anything. I can't run away from who I really am."

"Who you really are? What do you mean?"

Felona searches in silence for a moment before answering, "I'm a grown, educated woman who has gathered many successes for herself in a short time. People judge me by what they see. They assume because of my looks, that I have it made. They comment on how they want to be me or be like me or be with me, but they don't know how hard it is… being me… in my skin… not belonging to a race, a group, a family or anything."

She shakes her head, and her lip begins to quiver and Ny looks at her.

"I've wanted to be happy for a long time, but I don't know how. For a long time I've wanted to feel like I belong to something. I've wanted to feel more like an intent than an accident."

Tears follow her words. Ny falls beside her, hugging her tightly.

27
Haiku

"Rise and shine, curly girlie!" Ny sings as Felona slowly emerges from the fog of sleep.

I abhor morning people, is her first thought. *Especially when I've barely gotten two hours of sleep. How is it that she closed her eyes the same time as I, but now she's bouncing around full of energy and life, opening curtains, flinging on clothes and singing? I love her, but I hate her right now.*

Metal rings squealing along curtain rods coincide with daylight suddenly washing the room with brilliance.

"Are you serious? Close the damn curtains! Why are you up so early? I need sleep!"

"You need to get up, sweetie. A better world today summons you. Your phone has been buzzing like a beehive all morning."

"All morning?"

She exhumes her face from the muted comfort of her pillow, struggling to open one eye past a squint. "What time is it?"

"It's Felo'clock. Get up!"

"You're not my favorite person right now. Where's my phone?"

"I don't know. It's probably buried under the covers with you."

As she continues her horizontal protest, Felona fans her arms under the pillows next to her and underneath the covers, in search of her phone. Her wrist finds it just as it's accidentally knocked to the floor.

"Can you get that for me, Ny?" she mumbles from her pillow before raising her head to clarify in a less muffled tone. "Ny? Can you pick up my phone for me?"

After a few silent moments, Felona sits up in the bed to see that Ny has left the room. The sound of running water is coming from behind the closed door of the bathroom.

She sighs loudly and falls back onto her pillow.

Sitting on the edge of the bed after several moments of sleepy procrastination, Felona studies her retrieved phone as she drags her fingers through her hair.

She's accumulated several unread text messages from the past two days, but most of them are work-related. She skims past them to discover that Vin has left her a text message.

12:45 – "You never called me back, bella. Are you upset with me for any reason? Call me in the morning. I'm going to come be with you. Love you."

A few text messages from Tobias follow.

3:01 – "I hope you get plenty of rest. I'll probably spend the night at the hospital with your mom. I'll keep you posted."

4:36 – "Your mom is having a restless night. I didn't tell her about the accident, but I slipped up and told her I saw you. She's asking me a lot of questions right now, but she's also kind of drugged up."

8:20 – "Good morning. I'm sorry that I reacted the way I did last night. I wasn't rejecting you. You just surprised me. I hope we can talk about it later. Give me a call when you get up."

"You want to go by the hospital before we get some breakfast?" Ny asks, exiting the bathroom.

Felona looks up from her phone with a raised eyebrow.

"Hell no."

"And you're sure that you want to head back home so soon?"

"Yes. Very sure."

"Okay. Just double-checking. How're your arms feeling?"

Felona stretches her arms out and rotates them to look at Ny's bandaged handiwork from last night.

"Still a little sore."

"What about your knees?"

She looks at her legs dangling over the side of the bed. They, too, are wrapped in gauze.

"The same. I won't be wearing short skirts for a while."

"Well, it's a blessing that you didn't suffer any broken bones or fractures."

"Yeah. Crutches aren't cute with a wedding dress."

"I'll rewrap them and put some more anesthetic on you after you shower. That'll help with the swelling and pain."

"Thanks. A shower is exactly what I need to wake up at this point. That and a lot of caffeine."

———————————————————

Felona takes a deep breath, looking at the stretch of highway before her as Ny stares straight ahead driving and tapping her finger on the steering wheel to a familiar pop R&B tune playing on the radio.

"This expanse of asphalt meant something totally different a couple of days ago," she sighs as she ends yet another call attending to the monotonous business of canceling various credit cards and filing an insurance claim on her stolen car.

She smiles, "Thank you for coming, Ny. For being present."

Ny glances a smile back at her.

"Of course, curly girlie."

"I'm sorry I've been on the phone most of this time while you're just driving, but I needed to go ahead and –"

"Stop being silly, girl. I'm fine over here. Handle your business."

"I just have one more call to make and then I can keep you company for the rest of the trip."

"You saved the best for last, huh?"

"You know it."

Felona dials Vin.

"Vin, hey. I'm on my way back home now."

"Bella? You're on your way back? Already?" he says, above clamor on his end. "I was about to head out there.

Did you get my message?"

"I'm sorry, Vin. I got your message. I didn't mean to worry you. It's just that a lot has happened since we got cut off last night. Long story, short... I'm headed back with Ny. My assistance here is no longer needed."

"Pardon me?" he says as the background noise on his end crescendos.

"I said, I'm riding back with Ny. My mother is fine."

"Your mom is fine? Kinaya is there?"

"Yes," she answers loudly.

"Wait. Why're you riding with her? Where's your car?"

"My car got stolen last night. I was carjacked," she says matter-of-factly.

"Hold on. What did you say? Your car is where? I'm having a hard time hearing you."

"Where are you? What is all of that commotion in the background?"

"I was having a celebratory lunch with Ed, Karl and Riley before I got on the road."

Felona turns to Ny in disbelief.

Ny, seeing Felona's expression, glances away from the road long enough to whisper, "What is it?"

"Wait. Let me get this straight. You're having lunch with your buddies while your wife-to-be is in another town waiting for you to come be by her side?"

"What?" shrieks Ny.

"What?" he nearly shouts. "I didn't hear you. What did you say?"

"Ugh! Nevermind. I'll see you in an hour or so. I'll tell you then. Enjoy your lunch! Ugh!"

Felona hangs up the phone.

"Are you okay, Felo?" Ny asks as she mutes the radio.

"Can you believe this? Vin should have beaten you here to be by my side and he's still in Admah City having lunch with his buddies. I swear that man's insensitivity frustrates me. He can be such a knucklehead sometimes."

"But we're headed back now. Why would you want him to be on the way here?"

"I know it may seem petty, but it's the principle, Ny."

"No, it's not petty. I understand, but you're already under a lot of stress. Why put this on your plate too? Just have a heart to heart with him when you get back so that you and he can be on the same page."

"Yeah, you're right. As always. These past couple of days could be summarized as three lines that don't make sense. I'm not sure whether that's akin to haiku or heroin, but at this point it doesn't really matter. I need to stop looking behind me at the past so that I can stop stumbling over everything in the present."

28

Engagement Party

2013

Every woman is the star of her own romance, but romance was never quite what Felona was seeking.

Vin happened by accident, in that she wasn't expecting to meet him, like him, go out on a date with him and ultimately, get engaged to him.

Yet there she was at their engagement party, announcing to the world that they, as a couple, were engaged to be married.

It was Vin's idea to host a little get-together with his family and their friends. Always the charismatic one in the mix, he loved hosting, whether it was a casual business meeting with contemporaries or a Super Bowl party with his peers.

"Felona," he shouted from downstairs. "Come on! The guests'll be here any minute. What are you doing up there?"

Felona had changed clothes for the third time because her first two attempts didn't meet Vin's standard of engagement party attire.

"You're the hostess and will be the center of attention," he'd proclaimed. "Your dress should look the part."

Rather than make a big fuss about it, she complied,

but was running out of options. They didn't live together so Felona had a limited selection of outfits at Vin's house.

"Yes. I'm coming down now," she sang, as she walked downstairs wearing a black, lacy cocktail dress that she'd only worn one other time, when Vin and she had gone out for dancing and dinner.

A cacophony of garlic, basil and oregano greeted her as she neared the kitchen.

When he had time, Vin loved to cook. Growing up in Napoli where his family owned several restaurants, he was practically raised in the kitchen.

"It smells good in here," she purred in his ear from behind as she wrapped her arms around him. "And you smell good too. Am I going to get this treatment all the time when I become Mrs. Ricci?"

"Grazie," he said as he turned to face her. "But only if you play nice. Here, let me take a look at you."

She stepped back and spun around like a ballerina on a turnstile display. After her fouetté turn was complete, she looked to his expression for endorsement, but it wasn't the expression she was hoping for.

"Cristo, bella! Your boobs are spilling out of that dress!"

"My boobs? Are you serious? I don't have much of anything to spill out. It's the dress! You said to put on something sexier."

"My ma is going to be here though," he whined.

"I know. I've met your mom before. She loves me. So what?"

"So, I don't want her thinking."

"Thinking what? That she is about to inherit a gorgeous and sexy daughter-in-law?"

"No, it's not that. I just... I don't want to deal with her saying stuff."

"Saying stuff?"

"Yeah. Plus, I don't want all the men staring at your tits the whole time."

Felona looked down at her dress and then back at him.

"I wore this dress when we went dancing and you didn't seem to have a problem with it then."

"That was different. It was just you and I. We were on a date. You're supposed to look sexy when you're with me."

She frowned, "What? I'm supposed to? Ugh! That makes no sense. I'm not changing again, Vin. Get over it."

The doorbell rang just as Vin leaned in closer to protest further.

It didn't take long before nearly fifty guests filled Vin's foyer, kitchen and dining area. His two thousand square foot home suddenly seemed small and cozy as people talked, ate, drank and, seemingly, had a good time.

Most of the guests there were Vin's people – his friends and family.

Felona, on the other hand, had a small circle of friends that included Ny and her husband, Mosi, Ny's mom and Guy, Felona's producer and friend from work.

Felona hadn't spent much time around Vin's mother, Alda, but she liked her from the very first time they met. Her demeanor was gentle and humble, until she was well into her second glass of Pinot grigio. From that point, Alda spoke with a frankness and sense of humor that would draw even the most conservative into a lively conversation.

She was pale, small and stout in appearance, but larger than life in every other way. Knowing her, it was clear where Vin's charm, passion and charisma came from.

Alda loudly tapped a spoon on the stem of her empty wine glass.

"Ciao! May I have your attention please, yes?" she announced, her Italian accent so laden that she enunciated every vowel and dragged out every consonant as if she were singing them.

A few people quieted and looked in her direction, while her small stature hid her from the view of some.

"Ere, hold this," she handed Felona her wine glass and spoon and disappeared into the standing crowd of people.

A few moments later, she reappeared, standing on the couch where everyone could not only hear her, but they could also see her.

"Felona," she said to her over the crowd. "Bring another glass to me."

Felona nodded and smiled as Alda turned her attention to everyone else.

"Ciao, ciao! May I 'ave your attention, yes?" she announced in a loud voice. "I want to tank all of you for coming to congratulate my son and 'is beautiful fiancé. Vincenzo, come up 'ere."

She energetically waved him forward as the crowd of people cleared a pathway for him to approach.

"Tell the people your love story of you and Felona. It was colpo di fulmine, no?"

Vin chuckled and turned to face the audience of people, who by now, had crowded into the family room space.

"Sì, ma. It was love at first sight. Where are you, bella?"

Vin scanned the heads in the crowd as Felona made her way to him.

"There my bella is," Vin crooned as the sea of people parted to reveal her, holding two full, wine glasses above her head.

She offered a glass to Alda and then stood beside her.

"Like my ma just said, thank you all for coming tonight. It means a lot to Felona and me that you came to celebrate with us."

A lone clap from the audience initiated eventual applause from others.

As soon as the clapping and chatter died down, someone from the crowd challenged, "Tell us how you got engaged."

Vin laughed, "Ah, yes. The elaborate scheme that I came up with to make my bella say yes?"

Felona looked away from her audience, blushing.

"Well, I think it sounds better from Felona's point of view so she should tell it."

He gestured for her to speak, but she playfully declined the offer until a few jeers from the crowd caused her to relent.

"Okay okay. It's actually an awesome story and I'm not

just saying that because I got a ring at the end of it."

Everyone laughed.

"So, I'm an art geek and I love going to museums. I was excited about this Egyptian artifacts and jewelry exhibit that was being held in the Arts District at AC Hall. How often do you get to see the intricate work of Egyptian artisans up close, right? I convinced my girls – Ny, Mandy and Tierra – to go with me. While we were walking around marveling at these amazing crowns, bracelets and necklaces, Ny noticed that there was this woman taking pictures of us. Now I'm immediately thinking to myself that the museum doesn't allow people to take pictures so what's this chick's deal, right? Well, Ny, being Ny –"

Some people in the audience laughed.

"Ny walks up to this woman and is about to confront her in the nice way that only Ny would, but the woman proactively informs her that she works for the curator of the museum and was taking pictures for the quarterly magazine. She flashed her ACH badge, so we were satisfied with her explanation and resumed enjoying the exhibit. Of course, now that we were aware that we were in the interest of the paparazzi, some of us... I won't name any names... couldn't help but to be more conscious of artful posing while facing the camera."

Felona tiptoed, looking into the audience.

"Weren't we, Tierra?

Tierra giggled from the audience and shouted, "You can't prove nothing, man!"

"Anyway, we'd gone through the entire exhibit and were on the final piece, which was this ring in an elaborate case. But this ring doesn't look like all of the rest of the pieces that were more intricately designed. This ring was simple and gorgeous, but it seemed far too modern to be a part of this collection. My curiosity was piqued as to what royal figure this piece originally belonged to and so I read the information card, which was very intriguing. The card had three lines. The first had the initials, V.R. The second line had the date of that particular day, which was September 23, 2012. And the final line read, "Ricci Engagement Ring."

"In that moment, it dawned on me what I was looking at and I began to scream and the girls screamed with me, jumping up and down with me. And then Vin appeared from out of nowhere, dressed in a perfectly tailored, Italian suit, looking as handsome as ever."

Felona looks over to Vin, who is smugly looking out over the audience, before he returns her glance.

"He lifted the case and removed the ring before getting on one knee before me and professing his love for me. He asked me to marry him. I said yes and kissed him while everyone around us clapped."

As if on cue, the captive audience erupted into applause. Vin smiled from ear to ear and kissed Felona.

"A toast to my 'andsome son and 'is gorgeous fiancé," Alda proclaimed, raising her near-empty glass. The sound of glasses clinking filled the room.

Vin's mother dramatically tossed her head back to receive

the remnants of wine, before she held the empty glass in front
of me, shaking it.

"Tesoro, bring another glass to me, yes?"

As women approached her, Felona absently arched her
wrist and pivoted her hand to catch just the right amount of
light and would await their judgment.

"It's beautiful."

"I'm so happy for you."

"Oh my god, he must really love you."

"Wow, that must've set Vin back a few mortgage payments."

"Congratulations again."

"Nice ring. That's almost as big as the one that my
boyfriend is going to give me."

"We love you guys so much, Felona. I'm happy for you,"

"Your ring is a'ight," Ny teased, with her mocking street
dialect. "I guess he love you and stuff."

But then she broke character and hugged Felona tightly.

"I love you, curly girlie."

Ny stood barefoot at five foot, two while Felona had on
four-inch heels, in addition to her own height of five foot,
seven. She had to nearly get on her knees to hug her back.

Ny's long locks, pulled back into a bun smelled of
lemongrass and patchouli.

"I love you too, shorty McNy."

Felona took Ny by the arm and lead her into the kitchen,

away from the crowd of people.

"Thank you for being here to remind me that there is sanity and integrity still in the world," she whispered.

"What're you talking about, Felo?"

"Ny, I don't know most of these people. And they seem to be so concerned with superficial things like my ring or my dress or how much more makeup than usual I'm wearing. Does it not matter anymore what's inside a person? Beyond a three-carat ring, does it matter whether the engaged couple is in love with one another or not? Not once did anyone ask me what our plans were for the start of a fulfilling marriage or whether we were doing premarital counseling. Instead people were more concerned with, 'Where are you planning your honeymoon?' or 'How big will your wedding be and where?'"

Ny chuckled.

"Well, some people don't know what to talk about other than the surface things when they don't know you. Plus, this seems to be a conservative bunch here. Everyone can't be as awesome as you and I."

"True. True."

Ny glanced in the direction of her husband.

"You see Mosi? He's walking around taking all of the credit for introducing you and Vin together. You would think that he's the one that just got engaged, the way his chest is all proudly puffed out at the hint of his matchmaking prowess."

"Wait. Wasn't Mosi against playing matchmaker in the first place?" Felona asks.

"Yeah. Remember? He and I had a little argument over

the whole ordeal. Technically, I'm the one you have to thank for all of this."

Felona smiled at Ny and sarcastically responded, "Or blame."

As the food and alcohol diminished, so did the guests. The last one to leave with her long, lingering goodbye was Vin's mom, Alda.

"Everything turned out pretty well, wouldn't you say?" Felona asked Vin as she collected used glassware from various places that the guests saw convenient to abandon them.

He mumbled something incoherently from the couch.

"Your mom is funny. It's a good thing that her friend, Rosa, gave her a ride home because she was in no condition to walk, let alone drive. I'm surprised you didn't just ask her to stay overnight. Did you see the gift that the Odoyo's gave us? Wasn't that awes–"

Felona paused when she looked up and noticed that Vin didn't seem to be actively listening to what she was saying. He just stared ahead with a grim look on his face.

"Vin? Are you okay? Are you listening to me?"

"I hear you. Of course I see you... in that dress. Who wouldn't?"

Felona frowned, confused at his tone.

"W–what? What're you talking about?"

He stood up from the couch and staggered toward the kitchen where she was clearing the counter of empty bottles.

"Did you have a good time, Felona?"

"Vin, what's–?"

She raised her hand to place on his chest, but he backed away.

"I know my guests had a good time gawking at you in that dress the whole time."

She looked down at her dress.

"You remember Larry?" he asked.

"Larry? He was the one who went to Edison State, right?

"Yeah. You and he seemed like old buddies."

"Vin, when I found out that we went to the same college, of course, we would have some things in common. What's wrong with that? I, nor he, was out of line or disrespectful."

"I'm saying you were extra friendly with him! And he was close enough to you that you might as well have given him a lap dance."

"Lap dance? What the hell are you talking about? You're drunk."

Felona reached out a second time to touch Vin, but he abruptly pushed her hand away.

"I'm not drunk! Not enough anyway. I had to stay sober to make sure that none of my guests tried anything with you."

"Tried anything? I'm a grown woman and your fiancé. It doesn't matter what anyone tries, they're not getting anywhere. You don't need to watch over me like I'm some child. And you don't need to talk to me with that tone."

"Clearly, you're a grown and developed woman. And clearly, you were flirting with Larry."

"I was being friendly as I was being to everyone, Vin! Men and women. When have I ever disrespected you? I wasn't flirting!"

"Look at that dress. That's disrespectful. I told you that dress was too revealing with your boobs falling out. I'm talking to the guys and instead of looking at me, I catch them constantly checking you out the whole time!"

"Well, you could have worn the dress and gotten the attention then," she joked.

"That's not fucking funny, Felona!"

"I can't control what anyone else looks at, Vin! I can't change how I look. What do you want me to do? Wear a burkha?"

"I want you to not flirt with my friends or wear suggestive stuff in front of them."

"Suggestive? What's suggestive about what I have on, Vin?"

She spread her arms out.

"I told you. Your boobs are out, the dress is hiked up to your waist, and you have on those stilettos!"

She looked down at herself again.

"I barely have boobs! My dress isn't hiked up to my waist. My legs are long! And my shoes? Really, Vin? When I had on pants and a blouse, you told me that I looked too plain. When I had on a fancy dress, you said I looked like I was going to work. So I find something in-between and you accuse me of dressing like a whore? Need I remind you, this is the same dress I wore when you and I went to dinner and dancing a while ago? Ugh!"

She turned away from Vin and leaned against the counter.

"I didn't call you a whore. I just don't want men looking at you like you're their sex object," he said in a lowered voice.

She flung around with a deep scowl on her face.

"Everyone doesn't think like you, Vincenzo! Just because you think with your dick doesn't mean that everyone does."

"I thought you forgave me for that and now you're going to throw it in my face?"

"Throw it in your face? Vin, you cheated on me with my co-worker – a conniving, cutthroat heifer I can't stand. Don't you dare try to play victim because I'm bringing that up. I forgave you, but don't think that makes me a fool just because you followed up your apology with an engagement ring. I'm not that skank you charmed into fucking so don't assume that any man can come along and do the same with me. And as far as being a sex object, I don't care how other people look at me. I can't control that. I've had to deal with that my whole life... people judging me based on my looks. Even my own mother treated me differently because of how I look. I can't remove my freckles or darken my skin or change my shape. But how do you look at me, Vin?"

His face hardened in defense.

"You're my fiancé. I don't care about other people either. But I do care about how you present yourself. That represents me."

Felona scoffed.

"You didn't answer my question."

"I asked you to marry me. You already have your answer."

She loudly sighed.

"I'm sorry if I was too friendly with your friends. I meant you no disrespect and you know it. I don't understand why you're so upset."

Vin said nothing as he clinched his jaw, looking away.

"Don't you want me to get along with your friends? Your family? Anyone that is a part of your world?" Felona continued.

"My friends? No! They're my friends. You don't have to be friends with them."

"I was just trying to be nice, Vin!"

"Nice? The girls at the strip club are nice, Felona. You're my fiancé. You don't have to hustle for attention anymore. You have mine."

"Hustle for attention?" her voice quivered. "You make me sound like some attention-starved whore. Is that what you think of me?"

A tear ran down her cheek just before Vin pulled her into an embrace, but Felona stiffened at returning any degree of affection.

"Attention-starved? No. And if you're anyone's whore, you're mine, Felona. No one else has the right to that fantasy. I'm the man that will be your husband. I'm the man who loves you."

Felona looked up at him and softened. More tears were all that she had to offer at that point as Vin wiped her face and continued in silence.

29
Stranger In The Mirror

Neither super strength, nor telepathy, nor flight, nor telekinesis, nor any aberrant ability will ever be as great as the innate ability that a woman has when she is able to control her own mind.

It's 4:34 AM and Felona lies in her own bed, once again in Admah City, unable to fall asleep because she is unable to control her own mind that is rattling noisily with a recollection of the events of the last two days.

The cedar scent of hardwood floors and silence within the walls of her North Wells loft accompany her as she stares at apparitions swinging above her like weighted shadows threatening to fall and crush her if she blinks.

She reaches for her cell phone that bears the scars of her carjacking to check the time, before slinging the covers off of her, abandoning all hope of slumber.

There's something enchanting about the dawn. The world is still sleeping while time seems to tiptoe, so as not to wake anyone too soon. Those who are awake during those hours find themselves mentally energized by the illusion of control gleaned from the quiet.

Felona pads barefooted across the floor to tap a light switch and light fills the open space room with life.

Three large paintings run along one of the beige walls and converge where her wedding dress hangs in the corner of her bedroom, next to her closet. The opposite, brick-exposed wall features two large windows that allow natural light in, giving the wedding dress the illusion that it's glowing and floating above the floor.

In a few days, I'll be wearing this and gazing into the eyes of the man who will gaze back at me. And he will vow, 'I do.'

She runs her fingers across the intricate lace, pearls, sequins and loops.

How many hands took part in creating this dress? How many fingers ran across these same seams before it was considered beautiful enough and complete? And after I wear this on my wedding day, what will become of it? Do I wrap it up and tuck it away in the back of my closet for keeping so that one day I can pass it on to the daughter that I never had; the one that I –

She closes her eyes tightly and lets out a loud sigh.

She opens her eyes again and drops her head, looking at the floor. And her toes.

I like my toes, she smiles to herself. *They're not too long or too chubby, they smell nice and they're the one part of me that doesn't yet have freckles. They're perfect.*

She continues to look down at her feet as she walks to

the other side of the room until she is in front of a full-length mirror that sits at an angle against the brick-exposed wall.

She looks up and leans in close, pulling matted curls away from her head, but they spring back to their position when she releases them.

I was letting my hair grow out for the wedding, but I'm so tempted to get it cut. I hate this in-between stage when my hair is neither here nor there.

Of course, as soon as I get it cut, I'll long for it to grow back to the same length that it was right before I cut it and when it does, I'll repeat the bipolar cycle all over again.

People often say, "I love your hair. I wish mine was like that. Your hair looks so healthy."

Such a contrast to my mother telling me that it was too short kinky and unmanageable.

"You have hair like a Jew. I don't know why you wear it like this," she was notorious for saying. "You need to perm it. You look so pretty when it's straight."

She steps back to look at herself in full view.

Usually when I'm standing before the judgment of the mirror that never lies, I'm fully clothed. But now, all I see is me... naked, raw and vulnerable me.

She stares into sunken, sad, hazel eyes that sometimes appear green in certain light.

Men most often comment on my eyes. They say that they're dreamy, entrancing or, expressive. I wish that I saw them the way others see them. But I don't.

From my vantage point, I see eyes that are, as my mother

would describe, sleepy or like a person with cataracts. Ghost eyes.

She traces the line of her eyebrows with her fingers.

Eyebrows – the archway and curvy compliment to one's soul. I've met women who are amazed that I don't get my eyebrows done. They're naturally the way that they are; not too thick; not too thin; naturally arched.

But my mother would say that they were too bushy and if I didn't get them trimmed, I would have a unibrow.

She places fingers on both sides of her nose and contorts the shape of it.

When I was a little girl, she would tell me to develop the habit of pushing the tip of my nose in for two minutes when I woke up in the morning so that it wouldn't grow pointy and make me look like a fake white girl.

This very nose, according to others, is what adds to my exotic appeal.

I don't feel very exotic at all though; especially when most of my skin is covered in freckles. My mother would tell me to play outside in the sun, thinking that my skin would darken and my freckles would blend better, but I came away with darker freckles and sunburn.

She places her pinky finger in the cleft of her chin.

I've yet to meet another woman who has one, yet Ny insists that it gives me a beauty that sets me apart from everyone else. Personally, I could do without it. Every time I look at it, I'm reminded of how my mother constantly said that it made me look masculine.

She brushes the tattoo on her throat with her fingertips

and smiles.

Coupled with the reflection of the wedding dress behind me, this scene feels symbolic to the fact that I'm finally moving away from who I once was. I can't help but chuckle at the clumsy rebellion that ultimately led to this brand on my neck. My little ouroboros. I still love it.

Felona glances at her brief smile.

I need to smile more. I like my face when I... I want to smile more.

She runs her fingers down to her breasts.

Vin tells me not to bare too much cleavage. What cleavage? There isn't a whole lot to behold of my A cups, she scoffs.

I would get a boob job if I weren't such a punk. But no one is cutting me or sticking a needle in me unless I'm dying and am in need of emergency assistance. That's another reason why I'm proud of my tattoo. I bore so much pain to get it... before and during.

Her hands slide down to her belly and she turns to look at herself sideways.

"I have a flat stomach," Felona says aloud proudly.

And then she twists and looks behind her.

"Ooh. I also have a flat ass."

She pivots back around, caressing her stomach.

What would I look like if I were pregnant? Every time Vin brings up the topic of children, I can't. He really wants kids.

What kind of mother would I be? I'm so screwed up by the example of my own mother, I might turn out to be the same as her. I'd rather never have children if that were the case.

And it's an inevitable poetic justice that I would get pregnant and something bad will turn up; just like it did with my mother. If I'm not suddenly diagnosed with inheriting lupus from her, I might find that I can't carry a baby full term and then I'll miscarry like Ny did. Or maybe I can't even get pregnant. What if something got messed up with the abortion and I blew my only chance at ever being a mom? Would Vin even want me anymore?

She looks down at her legs that are wrapped in gauze at the knees.

My mother would give me such a hard time about my legs and how I was always falling and scraping them up. I guess some things are simply as they are.

She chuckles.

But before I was car jacked, I had flawless legs with nary a blemish in sight. If I can't bare children, at least my long, curvy legs that go on for days might make Vin want to keep me. Maybe.

And I would finally have someone who accepts me. As small of a number two is, it's more of a family than one.

She steps back further from the mirror, taking in the sight of all of herself at once.

If I were sleeping right now, as I should be, I might be floating in this same space, looking in this same mirror at every curve and imperfection. Instead of finding fault with the stranger in the mirror, I might love her... accept her and her external and innate beauty.

But dreams are for the sleeping while I'm wide-awake.

30
Pitfalls of the Suburban Lifestyle

"Vin, do you love me?" Felona bluntly asks him as he shovels food into his mouth, sitting across the dining table from her.

"Look at your finger and ask me that again," he smacks through a mouthful, pointing with his fork.

She glances down at her engagement ring, but returns to his face, awaiting a response from him as he slouches over his bowl of pasta, continuing to stuff his mouth with food.

Despite a long day replete with errands and a lingering exhaustion, Felona's desire to return to some sense of normalcy fueled enough energy to prepare dinner for her fiancé in honor of his promotion.

"Say it then."

"Say what?"

"Say that you love me."

"I say it all the time," Vin laughs nervously. "What in the hell?"

"Say it now."

"Love you," he sarcastically returns.

"No. You don't say it right," she whines.

"What?"

His eyes widen, as he chews.

"I'm your beloved fiancé and you don't say it like I am. You say it in such a routine way like you don't even think about the meaning of it. You just say it."

"What? So there's a specific way that I'm supposed to express myself to you now? What's going on with you, Felona? Can't we talk about what happened in Nathaniel instead of this silliness?"

"We're getting married in a few days, Vin. Sometimes it feels like I'm the apple of your eye and other times I feel like I'm just an accessory. I'm just seeking a little affirmation right now. Is that so wrong?"

"Affirmation? I'm not trying to be an asshole here, but I'm the one that asked you to marry me and gave you that ring, remember? Of course you're not an accessory."

"Anyone can ask, Vin. That's the easy part. So many people jump into marriage without realizing that it takes hard work to make it a healthy and lasting relationship."

He frowns.

"I just don't want to end up like everyone else – divorced. I want to know in the beginning that you love me enough to do whatever it takes to make our marriage a great one."

"Are you sore with me because I couldn't go with you to your mother's? I told you I feel horrible about what happened to your car. I don't know what I would have done if something had happened to you."

"No. This has nothing to do with that. Well, it kind of

does, but... not really."

Vin frowns thoughtfully.

"Well, are you having second thoughts about marrying me?"

Felona shakes her head.

"I just think we both need to be sure that we're sure that we want this."

"We talked to that preacher and if he surmised that we weren't so sure, he wouldn't be marrying us."

"The pre-marital counseling with the priest is something that we had to go through in order to use the church that was so important to you for us to get married in. Besides, you fed the priest exactly what you thought he wanted to hear."

He smirks.

"That's not true. I'm not having second thoughts. I'm just as certain now as I was when I proposed."

Felona searches his eyes, but he resumes eating.

"I had to drop by the station to clean up some loose ends before my vacation and guess who I ran into?"

Vin shrugs nonchalantly.

"Danielle," she continues. "Since we're now on separate shifts, I rarely see her these days, but there she was."

Vin steals a furtive glance and nods.

"It was strange though. She seemed... different. Her eyes were kind of sad. I guess conning her way into that anchor position hasn't made her as happy as she thought it would. I felt sorry for her for a second, but then I remembered she made herself my sworn enemy when she tried to seduce you.

Does she ever try to contact you at all anymore?"

"No," he shakes. "Why? Why would she? Why is that even a question? Why are we even talking about her? Is this why you're acting strange? Because you ran into her? You're the one I want, bella. I made a mistake last year. But even if she did try to contact me, it wouldn't matter."

He gets up from the table, taking his empty bowl with him.

"Do you want anything else?" he asks from the kitchen.

"This baked ziti is awesome. You outdid yourself this time."

"No, Vin. Thank you," she answers as she looks down at her lukewarm salad, asparagus and ziti that is untouched.

"Soooo... are you excited about honeymooning in Venice with your husband-to-be, bella? The man who loves you? I, personally, can't wait to see the architecture in person there. And the food there... the food there is amazing."

He returns to the table with a full bowl, stirring the contents while studying Felona's expression.

"Did you hear me?" he asks. "Are you excited about our honeymoon?"

"Vin, say that you love me," she commands, relentlessly.

His shoulders drop and he sighs heavily as he looks up from his bowl.

"Really? Again with this? I'm asking you about our upcoming honeymoon. A honeymoon. Something that happens after two people get married. Two people who love each other."

"Say it."

"Bella, saying I love you in some exaggerated and breathy way isn't what men naturally do. It's something that they do if they're trying to emotionally control you. I'm not interested in that."

"You're not interested in controlling me?"

Vin scoffs, before slurping loudly from his glass.

"No."

"So when we're married, I can wear what I want, talk to who I want, go out with my friends when I want and you're not trying to control me?"

He leans back in his chair and studies her face, as if she's just made a clever chess move that's forced him to wisely contemplate his next strategy.

He sighs.

"Felona, I love you."

Routine, while it has its charm and security, can be one of the biggest pitfalls of suburban life. For children, it is a necessary element to a healthy environment for them to flourish and grow, but for an adult, it can feel like a looming death sentence after a while.

So many of those adults talk about their lives with little to no vigor or excitement whatsoever. The most adventure that they know is to look forward to vacations to the same lake house, cruise ship, ski resort or beach year after year, never deviating from rigid and controlled comfort to the abandon of adventure and living in a true sense of discovery.

The comfort and disaster that befalls them is that they

know and can predict with a certainty what their lives will be like every day that they wake up.

For the past year, Vin has consistently been romantic and creatively so, but what if that's reached its lifespan, Felona wonders to herself as she's placing dishes in the dishwasher. *Despite the spontaneity we've been privy to, suddenly I'm aware... or paranoid... that we've already begun to creep into normal.*

"Dinner was exquisite, bella," Vin says behind her as he joins her in the kitchen. "Thank you."

She turns to him, smiling sleepily.

"I can't cook like your mama, but I try. I want you to know that I love you and I'm proud of you."

"You look tired. You should get some sleep."

Felona turns away, sarcastically saying, "I look tired? Gee, thanks."

He wraps his arms around her from behind and pulls her to him.

"You know what I mean. I'm going to go and let you get some rest, but before I go... it's been a long time since I've shown you that I love you."

"Vin, you talk like it's been weeks. It's been a couple of days."

He softly kisses the side of her neck.

"Come on. Let me show you."

He tongues her ear lobe, gripping the sides of her waist, holding her firmly to him.

Her voice trembles, "O–okay."

She turns to face him and they begin kissing, fumbling

their way to her bed, tangled in an embrace of skin, tongues and teeth, shedding clothes, as breadcrumbs that will lead them back once the fires of passion have been satisfied.

Vin's massive frame dwarfs Felona's otherwise tall, svelte stature as he lifts her weightlessly and flings her onto the bed.

He slowly lowers his body to meet hers as she bites his lip. He gropes her breast and kisses her back with an unloosed intensity. In return, she grasps his buttocks, biting her fingernails into his fleshy muscle, pulling his weight between her thighs.

His tongue dances on her neck and she shivers before she thrusts her boney waist into his and they connect as one.

"You feel my love for you now?" he breathes into her ear.

Felona quivers from the tickling vibration that his deep voice causes.

"Oh, I feel you. I feel you good," she playfully responds in a whispering sultry tone.

"You feel how deep it is?"

"Yes," she whines.

"How deep is it? Tell me how deep my love is!" he barks, arching his back sharply before falling into her again and again.

She moans and flails her arms, gripping for the sheets.

"It's... you... so deep. I can't... I can't hold you in.... Harder!"

His thrusts become more feverish and uncontrolled.

"You feel this? You were a bad girl to doubt my love. Don't you... ever doubt... my love for you!"

"I was... a bad girl. Fuck... forgive me."

"Who's your man?"

"Y–you."

"Who's your Superman?"

"You! You're... S–superman. You saved... s–stop... stop talking!"

"Say my name."

"Vinnn –"

"Say my whole name!"

"Vincenz – Vinc –. Shit! Vincenzo Alon – Alonzo Ricci."

"Whose pussy is this?"

"Yours!"

"Will you marry me, bella?"

His thrusts become wilder.

"Y–yes!"

"So you're mine?"

"Yes! Shut up. Harder. Don't sto–"

Vin's whole body hardens as he thrusts even faster.

"Yeah! You're mine!"

"Yes!"

"You're my everything!"

"Yes!"

"You're my whore!"

"Yes, baby."

"You're my bitch!"

"Yes... wait. B–bitch? Wait. What?"

He wails a loud groan, shudders and falls to the side of her, moaning.

An obscure amount of time passes and Felona is unable to sleep as Vin is, sleeping face down on the pillow next to her. One of his arms is across her chest and it's so heavy that all she can do is lie still on her back, staring up at the ceiling thinking, *Bitch? Was that just in the heat of the moment, dirty talk or did he mean something by it? I hate that word. He's never used it with me before? Why would he say it? Where did that come from?*

Her cell phone, on the nightstand beside her bed, vibrates, interrupting her thought.

She picks it up to see that it's her mother who's been relentlessly calling her for the past couple of days.

She tosses the phone back where it was previously and the clanging sound that it makes on impact does little to stir Vin. He continues to lie still while intermittently snoring.

Felona sighs.

Is this what married life will be like? Routine and monotonous with minute bursts of passion? Vin says that he loves me and I love him so why do I feel incomplete in this? I should be looking forward to marrying this man, but I feel like I'm wildly searching for reasons to do otherwise. Maybe this is simply the wedding jitters that Ny said that she had a few days before she married Mosi.

She sighs again.

Or maybe, because I deserve no better, this is the chasm that I'm destined to resign to.

31
Voicemail

"Vin?" Felona softly calls out as she's awakened by the click of her front door closing.

She gets up and walks to the large bay window. It's still dark outside.

She slightly parts the curtains, peering through to see his car roll from the curb across the street onto the street and away.

Just as the curtains fall back into place, headlights from another vehicle that was parked a few spaces behind Vin's car, turn on. The vehicle rolls down the street as well.

Felona dismisses it, shaking her head as she returns to her bed. On the way, she glances to her left to see a glint and sparkle of light caught by her wedding dress hanging in the corner of the room.

She stares at it for long minutes and a smile dawns on her face before she falls back onto her bed and slides under the cover.

I really need to get some sleep. I have brunch with the girls in the morning.

Felona buries her face in the pillow that still smells of

Vin's cologne of sandalwood, coriander and jasmine.

Restless, she rolls onto her back, staring at the ceiling before sharply sighing.

"But I'm wide awake now. What time is it?"

She retrieves her cell phone from the nightstand.

"4:42? It's already morning."

Thumbing through the apps on her phone, she notices that Tobias has left several text messages since she left Nathaniel.

The messages are innocuous enough as they read like, "Just checking on you," "Your mom is home now," "I hope you're doing okay," and "Give me a call. I would love to catch up under better circumstances."

I would love to catch up too, she says to herself. *But catch up to what? Or why? At this juncture in life, what's the point?*

As Felona continues to browse through her phone, she sees several missed calls from her mother – seven, to be exact. She doesn't bother with listening to the voicemails associated with them, but simply deletes them as she discovers them amongst the sundry of unchecked messages.

Instead of deleting her mother's final voicemail, she accidentally plays it.

It starts off in an agitated tone, "Felona, you need to pick up your phone. I'm trying to help you, you ungrateful heif –!"

The voice pauses and resumes in a calmer tone.

"Felona, you need to... you need to think about what you doing. You're not happy! I could see it in your face. If you were happy, you getting married wouldn't be a secret. You woulda told me that you got engaged. Even if it was to hurt me, you woulda told me. But you didn't. I think you ashamed or settling or whatever. But you don't need to settle, Felona."

Dianne's breathing becomes labored.

"You said you ain't pregnant, but I don't know. And Tobias told me about you two."

Felona sits up.

"You know, my momma always told me that a woman who's kissing two men is either confused or a whore. I think you're confused, Felona. You still love Tobias. And he sure does love you. He needs to know the truth. About everything. He deserves to know. And he deserves to hear it from you. But if you don't or won't tell him, I will. You stirred up a lot of feelings in him and it's not right. He deserves to be happy just like you claim to be. You need to tell him or God's not going to bless your life or anything."

The voicemail ends and Felona groans.

I really wish I could unhear that. I've been struggling with regret that she didn't die in a coma. And then I feel horrible that I'm even having such thoughts.

Dianne never fails to validate my contempt for her existence. She may not have died, but she's dead to me now.

32
Felony

1983

Worldwide it's accepted that the day of your birth is the one holiday that you inherit by default. Regardless of culture or nationality, most people celebrate their birthday and some of them can even recount the details of the day of their birth that was told to them by their parents.

However, very few people can or would want to recount the tale of how, when and where they were conceived.

Felona wishes that her mother had never shared such information with her. She wishes she didn't know the level of detail that she does of her conception day.

But she does. All too well and clear.

Her mother, Dianne Mabel, was 26 when it happened.

Nathaniel was a very segregated city. Dianne, her husband, Brent, and two-year old Iris lived on the south side of town – "the black-hand side."

Dianne was a teacher who took an acute interest in her students. One student in particular whose name was Anthony. He was one of a handful of white students that were bussed in from the east side of town.

Apparently, the local government was attempting to expand their voter base through school integration, deferred taxes, mortgages for first-time house buyers and financial incentives for the owners of decayed rental housing – otherwise known as gentrification.

Anthony was an Italian immigrant who lived in the part of town known as The Woods. The streets had names like Oak Avenue, Kudzu Lane, Birch Street, and Pine Drive. The people who lived in The Woods were typically employed as day laborers, housekeepers, lawn maintenance workers and handymen. Most of them were first generation immigrants and broken English was their second language.

Regardless of being an educator, Dianne was narrow-minded of anyone who didn't speak English. She didn't care for whites either. Or fair-skinned black men. She pretty much didn't like anyone who didn't look or talk like her.

But she loved her students. As long as they were in her classroom, they had no skin color or language barrier.

Despite Anthony's struggle with speaking English, he demonstrated to be a very bright and promising student otherwise. Dianne was determined to help him get caught up since he started the school year late.

One Saturday, she promised to deliver work sheets and extra credit assignments to his home. He'd scribbled down his address for her, but she wasn't aware that he had his sixes and nines mixed up when she showed up at the wrong house. He and his mom were at home, two houses down and across the street.

No one was at the home where Dianne knocked.

"Who you looking for?" said a voice from behind her as she stood at the door waiting for someone to answer. She jumped, startled and unaware that anyone was standing behind her at the base of the stairs.

She turned to see a man who looked to be in his thirties. He had a receding hairline that left behind a snatch of curly, black hair on top of his head. His eyes were large and green like traffic lights while scraggly remnants of a failed shave created the contrast that made him appear both destitute and kind.

"Oh! I didn't see you standing there. You scared me. I'm looking for the Rossis. I'm Anthony's teacher, Mrs. Mabel. Do you know them?"

He took a thoughtful drag from the cigarette that carelessly dangled from the corner his lips.

"I might. Did he give you this address?"

"Yes," she answered as she fumbled in her handbag for a sliver of paper. She held it out in front of her. He walked halfway up the steps, took the paper and squinted to read past the smoke.

"129 Kudzu Lane. Yep. You got the right house."

While the paper read 129 Kudzu Lane and that is indeed where they stood, Anthony Rossi actually lived in house 126.

He continued, "You can't be too careful these days with kids and all, you know? But he's not home. He went off with his momma. He should be home in a few minutes though."

He walked up the remaining steps past her to the door,

removing keys from his pocket. After fidgeting with the lock for a second, he pushed the door open.

"You welcome to wait inside if you want, though."

He inhaled deeply from his cigarette one final time before he flicked it into the bushes by the steps.

"Wait. You live here? Who are you?"

"I am his uncle. I live here, yes."

"Oh," she says thoughtfully. "Well, can I just leave these with you?"

She handed him a folder that was thick with sheets of paper.

"No. I imagine he would be very happy to see you and it would break his little heart to know that he just missed you. He'll be here any minute. You welcome to wait inside for him if you want."

Dianne became fidgety and smiled, "No. I'll just wait in the car."

"Suit yourself," he shrugged, looking her up and down.

She turned to walk down the stairs and he called out, "You don't look too much older than the students themselves. You go to school around there?"

She turned and smiled.

"Thank you. I graduated from Nathaniel State College."

"Oh, yeah? I have a co-worker who went there and now he talking about how his kid will be going there next year."

"Co-worker? What do you do?"

"Me? Back home, I'm what you call a carpenter. I make things with wood... mostly furniture."

"Oh, wow. That's impressive."

He steps aside from the door that's ajar.

"Would you like to see some of my work? I have a few pieces right here in the living room."

"No, thank you. I wouldn't want to bother you."

"It no bother. Come. Anthony will be here in a moment anyway."

Caution signs and yellow flags should have fallen in front of Dianne Mabel. This man, whom she'd just met, was inviting her into his home. He spoke fairly good English with a hint of an accent, yet he claimed to be the live-in uncle of her student whose struggle with speaking English was the reason she was there in the first place.

But caution signs and yellow flags didn't fall in front of her. And her prejudice and suspicious nature didn't stop her from following him in.

It was only after she entered that she knew that she'd made the wrong decision. She stood at the entryway looking around the living room and there was no custom-made furniture. There was no furniture of any kind. The room was practically bare, short of a TV tray in the far corner that had some tools lying on top and a bare, carpeted floor littered with trash from former tenants.

Panic flashed through her and she swung around to leave.

"I think I'll wait outside!"

But he'd already blocked her exit and shown her a pocketknife before pressing it to her neck and grabbing her by the shoulder.

"I rather you stay," he said.

He was still smiling, but looked less friendly than before.

"W–what do you want?" she shivered. "Money? I can give you money. It's in my handbag."

She reached into her handbag, but he snatched it away and threw it across the room. She dropped the folder of papers and tried to scream. Only a whimper came out.

"You think me stupid, no? You going for your weapon?"

"I–I don't have.... wh–why? What do you…?"

"Unbutton your shirt," he calmly whispered.

"Wh–what? No."

He pressed the knife against her neck with more pressure. "Don't make me hurt you. Take off your shirt. Now!"

She started to cry as she nervously unbuttoned her blouse.

"You don't have to do this," she tried reasoning with him.

He said nothing.

"Please. I–I'm... I can't. I'm on my period."

"Quit talking. Hurry up!"

She slid the shirt off of her arms and saw the collar dotted with blood from her neck.

"Oh, my god! Pl–please don't kill me!"

"You do what I say and I won't," he grimaced and snatched the blouse away from her.

"Turn around and shut up!" he shouted before flinging her around.

She closed her eyes tightly and felt the cold, flat side of the blade slide along the center of her spine. She jumped and muffled a scream from the sudden jerk and popping sound that her bra made when he cut the clasp with his knife.

"Please don't," she shuddered.

She felt a blunt thump against the back of her head before she lost consciousness.

When she dimly regained consciousness, she was lying face down on the floor. Loud music was blaring in the background and she felt the pressure of the man rocking back and forth on top of her, scrubbing her naked body in place against dirt and trash on the carpeted floor. She tried to sit up, but couldn't because he was leaning into her back with his weight, holding her in place.

She then became more aware that she was naked and what was happening to her.

She thrashed her arms and legs in desperation and screamed, "No no no! Nooo! Why are you doing this? No! Please stop! I have a baby and... and a husband. Please! Stop!"

And eventually, he did.

She wasn't certain how long she'd been screaming for him to stop or how long she'd been unconscious previously, but when she'd stopped screaming, any evidence of his threat and presence was gone.

She sat up in the vacant room, shuddering and in shock.

An eternity passed before she finally attempted to stand up and realized that her legs were weak. Her inner thighs were on fire and her crotch, stained with semen, was throbbing with pain.

Another eternity had passed before she was fully dressed and able to stop shaking long enough to drive home.

She didn't go to the hospital. Not at first. She took a scalding hot shower as soon as she got home, concealing any visible evidence of her rape from her husband, Brent. She followed with several more showers, but the hot water did little to soothe the fresh, open wounds of helplessness and being violated that would be engraved in her skin forever.

Eventually and three weeks later, she had to tell Brent. She had to explain to him why she was so withdrawn and would flinch whenever he attempted to touch her. She had to explain to him why she called in sick for four consecutive days after she'd had perfect attendance most of her career.

He took her to the hospital after she complained of feeling tired and sore with fever for several days. After several tests, it was confirmed that she had lupus. She also found out that she was pregnant. Ironically, she and Brent had been trying to have a baby so she was afraid to abort what may have been his.

It was very clear when Felona was born with pale skin, green eyes and a headful of curly, red hair, that she wasn't Brent's child. And blood tests later confirmed it.

Felona Mabel was the child and product of a rape. Conceived of a felony, what more appropriate and fitting name for a misbegotten child than "Felona" could there be?

33

With The End In Mind

"Ny, where's your mom?" Felona asks, looking around as she returns from the bathroom, joining Ny and her bridesmaids, Tierra, Mandy and June who are gathered around the table for a bachelorette brunch.

It was Felona's idea to bypass the traditional bachelorette party where the inevitable surprise stripper appears with some campy preamble of bad acting before disrobing of all but whatever hat compliments his theme.

Instead, she desired the warm alternative with the presence of friends, laughter, good food and, perhaps, salacious stories mingled with relationship advice. Ny volunteered to host with her mother assisting with the menu.

"She just left," Ny answers.

"Awwww."

"She and dad are having lunch. She was only here to help me put all of this together. She said that this was a brunch for the young'uns."

"Young'un?" June asks. "I resemble that remark."

Everyone laughs.

"Well, you both did an amazing job with this food.

It looks and smells wonderful," Felona says, inhaling deeply.

The long dining table is lined down the center with a colorful array of dishes and trays consisting of fresh fruit, slices of turkey bacon, prosciutto, tofu scramble, spinach quiche, hash browns, French toast, croissants, orange juice, coffee and the obligatory mimosas and white wine that no brunch is complete without.

Ny clasps her hands together, saying, "I'm sure all of you are starving by now so I won't delay any further with winded overtures, but we can't proceed without me first saying that we're here to celebrate our lovely friend, Felona, and encourage her in the new life that she's about to begin with her groom, Vincenzo. Cheers and blessings to you, Felo. We love you and God bless your marriage."

"And this food," June adds.

"Cheers," everyone says in unison as they raise their glasses and toast.

Ny continues, "Everyone grab a plate and let's eat!"

A distant cell phone rings.

"Oh, sorry. That sounds like mine," Felona says as she puts her plate down. "Let me put it on mute. Be right back."

She dashes to the room where she left her handbag and fumbles through it for her phone that is now ringing louder.

"Tobias? Why is he calling?" she mutters to herself as she disables the ringer.

A wave of realization suddenly washes over her and she gasps.

Has my mother already told him? Before I had the chance to?

Felona dismisses the thought and rejoins her friends who have already settled in to their places at the table.

"Mmmhmm," Tierra says enthusiastically, shoveling a forkful into her mouth.

"Ny, how long have your parents been together?" Felona asks.

"Thirty-five years this year."

"Wow!" Tierra says through a mouthful of egg.

"I know, right?" Mandy whines.

"Thirty-five years. That's a long time," June adds.

"What did she tell you when you and Mosi got married?"

"Begin with the end in mind," Ny says, smiling proudly.

After a brief silence, everyone laughs nervously.

"What? Begin with thinking of divorce?" Felona struggles to clarify.

"No, not divorce. Begin with the image and knowledge that you and Vin will grow old together. Know your purpose and what you both want – together."

"Ahhh," the women respond in an enlightened chorus.

"You need to make your marriage about each other; not your career, your house, your family, your vacations, or even your kids. That is if –"

Ny's voice cracks and she looks down thoughtfully, clearing her throat before continuing, "If you can have kids, they quickly will grow up and live their own lives. No one should start a marriage believing it will fail."

"Except for those who sign a prenup," Mandy says.

Everyone giggles.

"So what's the end? Since it's not divorce."

"The end is embracing the idea that you're living your happily ever after every day. You're growing old... together."

"Ohh! This is good stuff, even for us unmarried folk," Tierra says. "What other wisdom you got?"

"Okay. Umm - talk talk talk," Ny answers.

"Wait. Don't men hate that? I already do that," Mandy says.

"No. They hate it when we talk for the sake of talking," Ny laughs. "What I mean is to communicate. And half of communication is to listen listen listen while we encourage them to talk."

"Listen? Oh, now you're just being mean," Tierra teases. "I gotta listen to him talk talk talk too? That explains why I love being single. I ain't gotta do all that."

"Don't play, T. As soon as cuffing season comes around, you'll be talking about how you need someone to cuddle with and talk talk talk to."

"Ha! Whatever. Okay, maybe... but mind your own business."

After eating, the women migrate from the dining table to the living room to continue their conversations in a more casual and relaxed posture.

Mandy and Tierra are on an oversized couch. June and Ny are in separate recliners and Felona is seated on the floor where she is stroking Ny's cat, who welcomes the attention, sitting in her lap. On a side table, wine bottles and pitchers of mimosa accompany them.

"Gleaned from our own personal experiences with relationships, what advice do we have for our lovely bride-to-be to ensure that she has a happy marriage?" Ny asks.

"Keep your business, your business," Mandy says enthusiastically.

"Look good for each other," June follows.

"Get freaky every now and again," purrs Tierra.

"Take the time to talk about money. And save some!"

"Get freaky all the time!"

"Leave work at work."

"Wait to have kids."

"Choose your battles."

"And have makeup sex after the battles."

"Don't compare your marriage to others."

"Have babies and raise them as a team."

"Absolutely no third parties in your marriage. That includes in-laws."

"And sex! Have lots of sex!"

"Be honest with each other."

"And communicate."

"Don't keep secrets."

"What exactly are secrets in the context of marriage?" Felona asks. "I mean, everyone has some kind of secret, if they've lived long enough. Aren't some things best left in the past? What if that secret is an old one from a past life?"

Despite the mimosas and wine, everyone seems to sober at the slowed momentum and serious tone of the question.

"Could keeping that secret threaten the integrity of your marriage or hurt someone?" Ny asks.

"I don't think so."

"Does anyone else have a reason to bring that secret up down the line?"

"No?"

Felona ponders for a moment.

"I don't know. I guess it's possible."

"Look at it like this, whatever the secret is, you're reserving that part of yourself from your husband. If it's something that could hurt him, it's best to take that secret to your grave. But think about the affect that it might have on him if he found out from someone else."

She looks down thoughtfully.

"It's best to start your marriage off with no secrets," Ny says with an intensity. "You don't want to start trying to justify what's good to keep away and what isn't. Remember keeping the end in mind? What does that kept secret look like to your relationship twenty years from now? And isn't your husband supposed to be your best friend and love you unconditionally? Since that is so, you have to play a part by holding nothing back."

Felona looks up at Tierra, Mandy and June, pausing on each face before finally ending with Ny.

"I don't know how to tell Vin that I —"

A heavy silence interrupts.

"Felo, what's wrong? Tell Vin what?"

She frowns and looks around at the other women again before finally saying, "That I might not be able to have kids because I had an abortion."

Ny smiles nervously. Despite knowing Felona for five years, she's just as shocked as the other women.

"W-what? When?" she calmly asks, partially masking her surprise.

"I was seventeen. It was right before I came here to go to college. I got pregnant and my mother... she made me get rid of it."

Ny slides down from her chair to Felona, who is seated on the floor. Facing her, she clasps Felona's hands inside of hers.

"Felo, I didn't know, but it makes sense now. Your relationship with your mom... why you and she aren't close."

Felona intensely looks back at her and something in her eyes betrays her because Ny gasps quietly and returns, "So Tobias...?"

Felona nods her head, affirming the intuitive catch.

"That's nothing to be ashamed of, Felona. Not now. That was long ago. You were a child."

June chimes in, "Tierra's right. If anyone should feel guilty about having an abortion, it should be me. I had one three years ago, but I don't feel guilty."

"Who's Tobias?" Mandy asks.

"Wait. June, weren't you and Doug —?"

"It was right before we got married. Doug and I were split up before he proposed. I started messing around with this other guy – you know – to get over Doug. Well, Doug came back hard, professing his love for me, how he couldn't live without me and stuff like that. He proposed on the spot. I found out that I was pregnant a couple of days later."

"So you had the abortion?" Felona asks. "Why didn't you just tell Doug? Since he loved you so much, I'm sure he would've –"

"No man is going to take care of another man's child, let alone accept it," June whines, shaking her head back and forth. "Especially, if that child ain't even been born yet."

Felona shyly looks away.

"Vin wants kids. What if, because of what I did, I can't –"?

She looks at Ny.

Five years ago, Ny had a miscarriage after four months of pregnancy. As a means and an attempt to seek emotional healing and purpose past that tragedy, she started working with Dream Girls Mentoring, a volunteer program whose sole purpose is to uplift, empower and educate teen mothers.

Felona had been working with the program, on and off, for a couple of years, in her own attempt to bypass the lingering guilt and pain associated with her abortion.

When she and Ny met, she told Ny that she was working with Dream Girls because she had always wanted a little sister and this was her vicarious means of having several little sisters that she could impact in a positive way.

Tears flow down Felona's face.

"Oh no, Felo," Ny whines as she hugs Felona.

Tierra, Mandy and June join them on the floor, huddled around Felona who looks at each one of then again and asks, "What if I'm just broken beyond repair? What if I'm not good enough? I don't want to fail at this."

The consequence of good food and alcohol has already begun to sedate the remainder of the afternoon into a satisfied drowsiness. Tierra, Mandy and June have already gone home while Felona lingers.

The television is on, though barely audible, as she and Ny recline on opposite sides of the couch.

Ny is cycling through channels with a remote and a book is opened, face down, across her lap.

Felona isn't all that interested in what's on television or in the magazine, which she's absently flipping through, holding her attention.

She's often joked with Ny in saying that their only difference is, "five inches, a husband, and hope."

While the comment was meant to ridicule her dating faux pas before she met Vin, it would at times, to Felona, resonate beyond joking.

She sighs loudly.

"What's wrong, Felo."

"I'm sorry."

Ny returns a quizzical stare.

"For not telling you," Felona continues.

Ny shrugs and smiles softly.

"You know, while I would be lying by saying that I'm not a little hurt that you didn't trust me with that, I understand why you didn't share it."

"I should've told you about it before, but I was afraid that you'd judge me. I was afraid it would hurt you. Since you and Mosi are trying –"

"I would never judge you, Felo. You're my best friend. And I'm not fragile, you know. I deal with women and their reproductive issues all day long. Do you think I could do that if I was constantly having a pity party about why Mosi and I haven't gotten pregnant yet?"

"No. I guess I never thought about it from that perspective. I'm so fixated on not being judged, but then I turn around and judge you and what you might think or say."

"It's okay. Mosi and I are okay. I stay busy so that when those thoughts and feelings come that take me to a bad place, I can refocus by helping other people with problems that I can solve."

"You've been raw and revealing with me, while I've kept secrets of who I am and what I came from. You've opened your home and family up to me while I've barely talked about my mother. After five years of knowing me, you just met her. You deserve a better friend than I've been."

Ny sits up.

"Felo, you've been there for me and I'm proud to have you as my friend. You grieved with me when my mom and Mosi couldn't or didn't know how. You've endured my whining and random crying in the middle of the day."

"But your life seems so – together, while mine is so – not."

"Seems."

"What?"

"My life seems so together. But I assure you, it's not perfect. No one's is."

Felona nods.

Ny continues, "I wanted to ask when we were at the hotel –"

She hesitates.

"What? What is it?"

"Are you and Vin okay?"

"Why do you ask that?"

Ny twists her mouth, cocks her head sideways and says, "Come on, Felo. For real. Are you and Vin okay?"

Felona inhales deeply and exhales, dropping her head and shoulders.

"I thought we were, but right now, I don't know. I'm not sure if I'm simply nervous or if I should be heeding this hesitancy as something more real. I'm wondering if I'm doing the right thing."

"Have you and Vin talked about your fears?"

"No. Well… kind of."

"What do you mean, kind of?"

"Well, the last two or three weeks have been emotionally demanding. From losing out on that promotion at work to last–minute wedding stuff and then the drama with my mother… I feel like he's been absent through most of it. I've tried to initiate conversation about whether he realizes that marriage involves his presence. I've asked him if he's truly ready for the big changes that come with marriage."

"And he said?"

"He said that he loves me and that he's committed to me."

"But?"

"But I have this nagging tug that his idea of marriage is different from mine. I feel like I complete the set of things and successes that he's accumulated in life. I don't think he realizes that he has to give. I feel like I'm his — trophy."

"You shouldn't feel like a trophy or any object in the context of a healthy relationship, let alone marriage. You and he are supposed to be partners, forever. Did you truly forgive Vin for what he did? I mean, you accepted his proposal, but that doesn't mean that you've forgiven him."

Felona looks up thoughtfully.

"To be honest, I don't know. I think I have to some degree. I don't throw it in his face when he has to work late or when he's unavailable. That's evidence of me forgiving him, right?"

"It could be. Or it could be that you're just sweeping it all under the rug. Only you can answer that, love."

Ny smiles warmly at Felona and pauses thoughtfully before asking, "Why did you say yes?"

Felona exhales and looks away.

"A lot of women marry for money and security. But I already make my own money and have my own stuff. I didn't say yes because Vin has stuff or can buy me stuff. The security that I'm looking forward to with him is different. It's the security of belonging. I inherit a mom who adores me. I inherit a culture that accepts my mixed ethnicity. I get to start over. I would inherit all of that with marriage. That's why I said yes."

"Have you talked to Tobias?"

Felona masks her surprise at the question with a shrug and absently begins to thumb through the magazine.

"Wh… what? What does he have to do with what we're talking about? No. Why would I need to talk to Tobias?"

"It just seems like there's some unfinished business there. I mean, Felo… you kissed him. And you were very sober when you did it."

"I was emotionally overwhelmed in the moment with everything that was happening and we have a past. That's all."

"Hmmph. I don't think so. You said earlier that you were struggling with keeping secrets from Vin, but I don't think that you having an abortion is really the secret that's troubling you. I think you still have feelings for Tobias."

Felona laughs nervously.

"That's ridiculous."

"Is it? I think you're all twisted up because of what happened in Nathaniel. You and Tobias have a history and, that coupled with your mom's stuff, there's no wonder that you're a ball of nerves."

"Well, you're wrong," she scoffs.

"Fine. If I'm wrong, I'm wrong. I have no problem with that. I just want you to be happy. That's all."

"Happy? I'm working on it."

Ny smiles and stretches across the couch, pulling Felona into an embrace that is returned enthusiastically.

"So since I'm emptying my closet of skeletons..."

"Yeah?" Ny says as she returns to her side of the couch.

"Do you remember when we were mentoring those girls together in the beginning?"

"Yes, of course."

"And we were talking about how most of them didn't have a relationship with their fathers and, in some cases, didn't know who their fathers were?"

"Yeah. It's continuously heartbreaking because I encounter that common factor even when I minister to the camps in Africa. And those girls are caught in a vicious cycle. They don't know their fathers and then they mother children that end up in the same tragic scenario."

"Do you remember how you said that you couldn't think of anything that could be more potentially damaging to a young girl's psyche than to know that she was conceived through lust or a one-night stand? And how tragic it is in those circumstances where her origin isn't met with love and acceptance?"

"Yeah?"

"I do."

"You do, what?"

"I know what's worse."

Ny's look intensifies into a frown and her eyes search Felona's face, waiting for her to continue.

"The man who was my father was a total stranger

to my mother. He raped her and I'm the product of that. I'm what's worse."

34
Empty

2006

The bundle on the other side of the bed responded to her accidental elbow nudge and the covers were pulled back to reveal a man with mussed, blond hair, brown eyes and bad breath.

"Hey, babe," he yawned as the stench of stale alcohol greeted her.

He reached to caress Felona's face, but she blocked his hand with a feigned stretch before sitting up in the bed and gathering a sheet around her.

"We must've fallen asleep! It's morning already," she said, nudging to the opposite edge of the bed.

"Yeah, we did. We was going at it pretty hard last night. You wore my ass out. What you wanna do today?"

"What? Nothing. With you. You need to go."

"Don't you want some eggs or coffee or somethin'? Let's go get some breakfast."

"No. I don't want eggs. I have stuff I need to do today and you have to go."

The man sat up, drowsily.

"Chill out, babe. Do you usually wake up so tense? Geez."

No, I don't usually wake up so tense because I don't usually wake up with a man in my bed. Ever. We do what we do and he leaves before morning.

"I'm not tense," Felona said as she slid into a pair of jeans. "This can't happen again."

"I thought we had a good time. What's wrong? Why're you mad?"

I'm not mad. I just hate the obligatory compulsion after having sex with a guy. It's just sex. If I can go to sleep afterward and wake up like it never happened, I'm good.

She pulled a shirt on and yanked the cover off of him.

"I'm not mad, dude. I just have stuff to do. I got a test tomorrow and you need to go."

"Okay okay. Jesus! I don't know what the fuck your problem is, but I like you and I thought you liked me too. Just let me take a shower and I'll be –"

"No! You need to get on your clothes and go shower at your place!"

I don't want you feeling entitled to my space. Or to me. This was just sex.

He gathered his clothes with much mumbling protest and cursing, making sure to slam the door on his way out.

I long for the touch of a man, but I don't want what accompanies it – inevitable failure because I suck at relationships. And it seems that the more men I meet, the lonelier I feel. Will I always feel so – empty?

35

Broken

Tuesday morning, four days before her wedding, Felona's cell phone rings and it's Tobias on the other end.

"I talked to your mom. She told me everything. The pregnancy. The abortion. My child. Everything."

Felona waits for him to say more, but silence is all that trails his scant words.

She has often said that Tobias is a run–on sentence with a great smile and that he's not one to be economical with words. The fact that he isn't rambling or meticulously building to a point reveals to her that he might feel as betrayed by her as she did by her mother. And if that is the case, there are no words that can be offered to salve that wound.

I should have called him as soon as my mother left that voicemail threat, thinks Felona. *What happened between Tobias and I has always reminded me of my vulnerabilities, but I've never taken into consideration what he may have felt in all of this. I just ran away. I've been like the little girl hiding under her covers so that the monsters under her bed will disappear and worry her no more. But Tobias is no monster under my bed. He's been a true friend that I've discarded for misfortune's sake.*

"She probably didn't tell you everything," she finally responds to Tobias. "She probably told you her glorified manipulative version. I know you want clarity and I owe you that, but I'm not doing this over the phone. When're you free to meet up?"

"Now," is all he says, deliberately succinct.

Felona considers her obligations for the day and whether she has the bandwidth to meet while also realizing that she won't have another opportunity for a long while to meet with Tobias.

"Okay," she finally returns. "We need somewhere private to talk, but I'm not coming into the city."

"How about that café just outside Nathaniel off of 95. The Maple Teahouse?" he suggests.

"That works. I can be there around 3:00."

A current of fear warms through her, knowing that she will have to look into the eyes of the man who was once her best friend and finally confront what she ran away from.

By 2:45, Felona is parking her rental car in the parking lot of The Maple Teahouse, a café in the middle of nowhere. A grocery store and a couple of fast food restaurants are the only neighboring businesses for miles.

Despite its remote location and it being a Tuesday afternoon, the parking lot is filled to capacity.

Tobias is already there, wearing dark jeans, brown boots

and a white, pressed T–shirt that contrasts with his flawless dark skin. A thick, brown strap of leather garnishes his left wrist, lending attention to svelte, toned arms. Despite his casual dress, his appearance mimics that of a casual catalog model that just stepped from a location photo shoot.

He greets Felona with a tentative smile and an unfamiliar coolness.

They exchange polite greetings and agree to sit outside on the patio where they may have more privacy.

"Would you like anything to drink?" Felona offers.

"No, I'm good," he answers, still reserved with his words while studying her.

She looks away and at the ground for a few long seconds, waiting for her heart to stop thumping so rapidly. She forces a nervous smile, quietly amused with how ridiculous her silence is.

"I'm sorry," she finally exhales. "I'm not sure what all that my mother said to you, but the fact is... I found out that I was pregnant after graduation. I was terrified to tell you so I told my mother and then I had an abortion. I thought that I would eventually be okay, but I never was. And I couldn't tell you... I'm sorry, Tobias. I'm sorry you had to find out the way you did."

He nods his head, quietly staring back at her.

"Why didn't you tell me before?" he breaks, following a long silence.

She looks down again, searching for the answer in the stone tiles of the patio.

"I was afraid that... that you would be angry with me. I was afraid of what you would say or think of me. I was afraid you would reject me."

"So, you rejected me first?"

She looks up at him and pleads with hazel eyes for his understanding and forgiveness. He stares back, displaying no emotion.

"That wasn't my intention, but it's all I knew how to do at the time."

"All you knew was to run away? Forget about our friendship? Forget about me? Forget that I was the one that was always there for you?"

"I didn't run away. Well... I did, but that wasn't my intention. I was... wait. What exactly did my mother tell you?"

He sighs.

"She said... she said it was in June that you found out that you were pregnant. You got sick and that's how you found out. Or how she found out. She said you got scared that you wouldn't be able to start college in the fall. She said that you really wanted to leave... you really wanted to go away to college... and you were afraid that having a baby would force you to have to stay in Nathaniel."

"That's not –!"

He holds a finger up to shush her.

He continues, "She said she told you that you had choices. Your life wasn't over and if you'd kept... the baby, she would've helped you out with taking care of it and all. But you... you wanted a... an abortion. You wanted it out of you and you wanted out of Nathaniel. Regardless, she was afraid that the pregnancy put you at risk."

"Risk?"

"Health risk. She said she never had you tested for lupus, but was concerned that since she had it, there was a possibility that you had it too. She said detecting it is difficult enough, but with you being pregnant, your test results might not be conclusive. You were at a greater risk to bleed to death if the right nurse didn't tend to you properly. But she said you insisted on getting rid of it."

"But... she dropped me off and didn't tell me."

Felona's eyes widen and she puts her hand over her mouth as she gasps, "She thought I would die."

"What?"

"Oh my god! The abortion."

Felona looks around sheepishly and continues in a lower voice, "The abortion was her idea. If she'd suspected that I had lupus, too, she wouldn't have just dropped me off to let me go alone knowing.... unless... oh shit. If she thought I was at risk, why would she drop me off? Unless she knew something bad might happen to me. Unless she knew I could bleed to death."

Tobias shakes his head.

"That's a horrible thing to say and makes no sense. Your own mom wouldn't do that."

"What else did she tell you?" Felona whispers, kneading her temples with her knuckles.

Frowning, he looks at her and sighs.

"You had the abortion and afterward, you became extremely withdrawn. And after the car accident, it was like you and I were strangers. You were different... cold toward me. I knew something had changed with you, but I didn't know what it was. I didn't know what I'd done to make you cold toward me. All I knew is we weren't the same anymore and I didn't know why. My heart was broken."

Felona runs her hand over her face.

"My head is killing me," she mumbles.

"What?"

"She lied to you, Tobias. Okay? She made me have an abortion."

"It doesn't make sense. Why would she lie?"

"Because she's an abusive, hateful, unrepentant shell of a woman!" Felona exclaims. "At seventeen, what was I supposed to do? I was afraid. And I trusted her. A mother isn't supposed to be someone who lets you get hurt."

Tobias shakes his head, looking at the ground.

She continues, "And I didn't run away from you. I ran away from her. She carried on like everything was just supposed to return to normal for me. But it didn't. I felt dirty. I felt guilty. Every time I was on my period, I relived it. The blood meant something different and horrible. And my mother... she abandoned me."

Felona drops her head and covers her face. Tobias instinctively moves to console her, but he stops himself.

"So explain this to me. That kiss, the other day."

Felona looks up and wipes her eyes, shaking her head.

"I was out of line and disrespectful to my fiancé. And you. I'm sorry."

"Sorry? What? Sorry that you did it?"

"I'm saying it shouldn't have happened, regardless of whether it came from some latent feeling or not. I'm sorry for putting you in that awkward place."

He chuckles nervously.

"Awkward, huh? I didn't feel awkward. I felt confused. One minute you're telling me you're getting married to some dude and the next, you're trying to kiss me. Where was this knight in shining armor while you were in Nathaniel anyway? Where is he now? Does he even know you're here with me?"

Felona frowns and sits back in her chair.

"I'm not a child and I don't care for your tone, Tobias."

He shrugs.

"You put so much emphasis on your mom not being there for you then. He's not here for you now? And you're marrying this dude?"

She nods.

"So, when is the big day?"

Felona ponders for a moment before saying, "It's this Saturday."

"Congratulations," he says with sarcasm.

"You're welcome to come."

"Ha! That's rich," he blankly says.

"You should, Tobias," she repeats with more emphasis. "It would mean a lot to me if you did."

Tobias looks away, shaking his head back and forth.

"It would mean a lot, huh? I'm an afterthought, but it would mean a lot to you," he scoffs and continues, "I'm happy for you… if you're happy, but… I'm not… I can't be a part of that."

"What? Why?"

"Under the circumstances, I don't feel comfortable showing up at your wedding because of a half-hearted, last–minute, sympathy invite, Felona! I'm supposed to be your friend. Under the circumstances, I'm not sure that the man you're marrying is even the one for you."

She smiles uncomfortably.

"A–am I sensing a little jealousy, Tobias?"

He stands so abruptly that his chair almost topples over.

"Jealousy? You think this is a joke, don't you? You really don't get it, do you?"

"Tobias, what –?"

He forces a smirk.

"No, Felona, I'm not jealous. I actually want you to be happy. I actually want to share in your happiness. But I don't feel like someone you care much about anymore. I feel like I'm pretty much nothing to you. I agree with your mom. You've changed."

"That's not fair," she protests, shaking her head.

Tobias slowly backs away.

"I don't think your mom is lying. I think Nathaniel made you so bitter that you can't separate what is good from everything else. I know it wasn't a dream for you growing up in a close-minded, black or white town so different from the girls around you. I know you had identity issues being a mixed child. I know you often struggled with where you belonged, but everyone didn't reject you. I accepted you. I loved you... regardless. You disappeared for eight years and now you want me to act like everything is okay? Well, it's not and how you're trying to handle me is not. It's disrespectful and insulting. I thought that there was hope in us talking. I was encouraged that you wanted to talk face to face. I don't know what I was expecting, but I was sure that whatever transpired, it would restore us... whatever that looked like."

"Tobias, wait."

"What?"

"I... I'm... I don't."

Felona searches Tobias' face, looking for a trace of the friend who is unmarred by circumstance.

"Don't worry about it, Felona. I hope that he makes you happy and treats you better than you've treated me. I'm not trying to be nasty or rude, but I can't hang around and continue to be hurt by you," his voice cracks as he turns to walk away. "I wish you the best."

Once upon a time, Felona and Tobias were inseparable best friends but that was long ago and they were just kids then.

Now, they're just broken people who find forgetting more difficult than forgiving.

Felona rolls her car out of the driveway of The Maple Teahouse. Her eyes are red and burning from crying and her head is throbbing, but it doesn't stop her from making a most unlikely phone call.

The phone rings several times on the other end before going to voicemail.

"You've reached Dianne. Please leave a message and I'll call you back at my earliest convenience. Have a blessed day."

A tone briefly beeps.

"I can't believe your audacity!" Felona says sharply. "You intentionally misled Tobias to get him to side with you. Oh, but then I put two and two together with what you told him and what actually happened. What kind of mother would betray her own child in such a horrible way? I hate how you could never so much as mutter a kind word. And if a rare and seemingly nice thing did escape your lips, you immediately followed it up with an insulting or condescending thing. You're toxic. I'm done with you. Don't text me. Don't call me. Don't even think of me! You're done and dead to me."

Felona hangs up the phone and her jaws tighten as she plays back in her head other things that she should've said. She closes her eyes, rubbing her temples while paused at a traffic light.

"My head is about to explode!"

She fumbles through her handbag for pain reliever to no avail.

She drives a couple of miles before coming to a grocery store that looks like it might stock more than just car magazines, hunting gear and chewing tobacco.

As she walks through the automatic door, it convulses open and she's greeted with the aroma of bell peppers and bleach.

"What aisle is your headache medicine located?" she asks a clerk as she approaches one of the checkout counters.

"Hold on a second, please," he flatly remarks, as he's looking back and forth between a frozen package of something and the cash register.

"Now what is it you said that you needed?" he asks as he finishes keying in the price.

"Where is your headache medicine?"

He glances up at her and his scowl abruptly becomes a smile.

"Oh. Hellooo. How're you doing?" he sings.

"Hi. I have a really bad headache, thank you."

"Oh, now, that gorgeous head should not be hurting," he says, grinning widely. "Pain relievers are on aisle eight, on the right side."

He nods his head in the direction.

"Thank you," she mumbles as she makes her way around and past several shopping carts with mostly elderly attendants.

Today must be senior citizens discount day, she thinks.

On aisle eight, she browses through a vast selection of pain relievers muttering, "Let's see. Extra Strength, Maximum Strength, Nighttime, Cold & Flu, Allergy... goodness. All I want is something that's going to make my headache stop."

A screaming baby in the near distance prompts

her to make a hasty selection just as she also hears a woman loudly talking on the next aisle.

"I told you! Fool, they ain't got it!" the woman's voice barks. "What? I been to three stores already! Nawl! What's the deal then, Niles?"

"I know that voice."

Felona casually walks to the end of her aisle and briskly past where the familiar voice is coming from.

She captures a glimpse of a short woman with dark, spiked hair who is wearing a gray T–shirt with tattoos covering her arms.

Felona's breath quickens and she leans against one of the shelves to gather her composure.

"Oh my god," she gasps. *It's her! It's the woman who jacked me!*

36
Follow

Felona keeps a marginal distance behind the woman who is already making her purchases at the checkout line.

A middle-aged man is standing with a shopping cart full of groceries between Felona and the woman. As soon as the woman retrieves her belongings and change, Felona taps the shoulder of the man in front of her.

He turns around and Felona smiles sweetly at him.

"Excuse me, sir. May I go ahead of you?" She leans in to him and whispers, holding up the box of ibuprofen, "I'm cramping really bad and I need to take these as soon as possible."

He smiles uncertain and waves her to move in front of him, "Go 'head on, darlin'. I'm in no hurry. Do what you gotta do."

"Thank you so much," she says with syrupy enthusiasm as the clerk rings her up.

She hands the clerk a twenty-dollar bill for her $6.55 purchase saying, "Put the change toward his purchase," nodding toward the man behind her.

She turns and dashes off to catch up with her assailant.

As soon as she steps outside, she sees her getting into a small, white van with an orange ladder atop and lettering on the side that she can't decipher from the distance.

Felona keeps a safe distance behind her, as she makes her way toward Nathaniel, unsure if the woman might recognize her even though she's driving a Ford Mustang rental car.

The gas on this thing is powerful. I should just punch it and smash into her like she did me. But then what? I'm not sure that this little car would do much damage to that van.

The pursuit, which is essentially Felona staying three cars behind, continues for about twenty minutes.

She's tailed dangerous story leads before, but with less thoughtless compulsion than this one.

Maybe I should just call in the make, model and tag number of the car and let the police handle this, she ponders for a few seconds.

Nah, I can handle this chick. She's small. After all that I'm feeling right now, I need to take my frustration out on something. She picked the wrong one to carjack.

The woman pulls into an industrial area parking lot and parks on the side of a large, unmarked brick building that looks like a storage facility. There are no other cars or people in sight.

Felona continues past the building and parks down the street out of view. She sprints back to the building where the woman parked.

As she stealthily approaches, she notices that the back of the van is open near a metal door that leads into the building.

The woman reappears, gathering a few bags from the van. Afterward, she closes it and looks around before going inside. The metal door to the building yawns to close behind her.

Staying flush against the wall, Felona hastens to catch the door before it closes, uncertain if it will lock after doing so.

She slips in undetected and finds herself in a hallway that is almost pitch black. While her eyes slowly adjust to the dimness, she's met with the unpleasant odor of mildew and her steps crunch from dirt or sand on the floor.

Once she's able to make out soft shadows and form, she advances quietly down the hallway past several doors that look like they could be offices.

She listens intently.

A distant sound of voices and clattering beckons her. Once she gets nearer to the source of the sound, she sees movement of dancing light escaping through the opening of double doors that are askew. She leans close and listens.

There are at least two male voices talking, but she can't make out what they're saying because of an echo in an apparently vast opening.

She nudges the doors open slightly to listen better.

"… get back with the shit, we can patch up these last wires and we done, son. I'm starvin'!"

"Yeah, bruh. Me too. We been on this too long. My girl gone be callin' me in a minute, thinking I'm wit' some ho."

"I feel you, T, but this shit is big. We gotta do it right, you know. Our talent's been wasted on boostin' shit when we can engineer shit. This some ol' white collar crime shit right here."

"I hear you, bruh. Man, call Zoe. I'm tired o' waiting fo' her. I wanna get this shit done befo' it get dark. I ain't tryin' to get pinched."

"A'ight."

Felona pokes her head through the door to see to whom the voices belong. The door opens up into a large, windowless storage area. Muted, natural light casts ominous shadows on rows of giant, empty shelves from a tinted skylight above.

On the far side of the room, about fifty yards away from the doors, are the talking men. Their attention is fixated on whatever their flashlights are pointed to.

Suddenly, Felona is startled at the sound of her cell phone ringing.

She steps back from the opening of the door and pushes it closed. She shoves her hands into her pocket to silence her phone at the very moment that she realizes that she left it in the car.

The ringing continues behind her and she spins around to behold the woman that she was pursuing.

Felona gasps and something swings toward her before she can put her hands up in defense. She's struck across the face with such force that her head falls back against the metal doors. She slides down one door as it swings open and releases her onto the floor.

"Why the fuck did you follow me, bitch?" the woman barks as Felona loses consciousness.

37
Bang and Blame

"**O**pen yo' eyes, bitch!" a gravely voice barks from the darkness.

Felona blinks open to a blinding light. She squints past the brightness to see three blurry, shadowed forms standing over her.

A sharp pain streaks over her right eye and she reaches up to touch her forehead. She draws her hand back suddenly to discover that she's bleeding.

Her heart floods with panic and she begins to breathe rapidly as she wrestles to sit up from her crumpled position on the concrete floor.

She clenches her eyes tightly, but tears escape anyway.

"I said open yo' eyes, bitch!"

One of the men, leaning over her, lightly slaps her across the cheek.

Felona shrieks.

She brings her knees up to her chest with her arms folded, looking up at him.

"W–why are you –?"

The other man kneels down close to her and asks,

"You a cop?"

The stench coming from him is bitter and familiar. While she can barely make out his face, his teeth, white and wicked, gleam in the shadow as he glares at her.

"N–no," she whimpers.

His eyes widen.

"Wait a fuckin' minute. Zoe, we know this bitch," he exclaims, snapping his fingers as he stands, disappearing into the shadow.

The woman, Zoe, leans in over Felona who instinctively flinches away from her, tightening herself into a fetal ball against a nearby metal support beam.

"Yeah, you're right. I thought this redheaded bitch looked familiar. She followed me."

She kneels down and grabs Felona's chin between her fingers.

"What you come here for?"

She jerks her face away from Zoe, frowning.

"I… I don't know. My... my car. I came to get my car."

They explode into a cacophony of laughter.

"Your car? Are you fuckin' serious? You risked yo' pretty, little head for a fuckin' car?"

"Check her," Zoe commands as she steps back.

"Get yo ass up!" one of the men growls as he grabs her wrist and yanks her up.

Before he spins her around, Felona recognizes this as the same man who assisted Zoe in carjacking her. He grabs hold of the back of her neck, like before, and holds her against the support beam as he frisks and gropes her.

"Did ya miss me, pretty eyes? Tell the truth, you came back lookin' for me. I knew we had somethin' special."

He slides his hands up her stomach and gropes her breast while running his bearded chin along her neck. She whimpers quietly, waiting for the moment to pass.

"You smell nice. What shampoo you use? Your hair is sooo... smooth."

His hands slither underneath her blouse.

"Just like your skin."

Felona presses against the support beam and bucks backward, attempting to shove him from her.

"You a feisty bitch too. I like that shit."

But it does nothing to deter him.

"Niles! Quit playing!" Zoe shouts. "She wired?"

"She ain't got nothing but this," Niles turns and hands Zoe a set of car keys, before releasing his grip on Felona. "What we gone do 'bout her?"

Felona exhales and inhales repeatedly, trying to catch her breath.

Zoe steps in close to Felona, who flinches and puts her arm up to block whatever action is about to follow.

"Do you realize the position you put me in by followin' me?" she says calmly.

Zoe grasps Felona by the back of neck, snarling, "You stupid, fuckin' bitch. Gettin' rid of you is not part of the job."

She releases her grip and spins around, flailing her fists, exclaiming, "Shit! Fuck!"

Felona stutters, "W–wait. No. Get rid of me? Y–you don't have to kill me. I–I don't even know what's going on here. I just thought I could get my car back. Whatever it is that you're doing here... I won't tell. I won't! I don't care."

She leans forward and begins to hyperventilate.

An involuntary stream of saliva pours from her mouth and before she can wipe away the spittle, every muscle in her body hardens and she violently spews bile and chunks of undigested food.

Niles hops backward, away from the acidic, orange pool of vomit that splashes in front of him, narrowly missing him.

"The fuck?" he shouts.

Felona spits twice and wipes her mouth. She stands up and feigns a defiant stare even though her legs are still shaking.

"Bitch!" he shouts.

Unfazed, Zoe tips past the puddle of vomit, saying, "Bitch, I ain't as stupid as you. As soon as you left this buildin', you'd call the cops. By the way, yo' car is gone. You risked yo' dumb, skinny neck fo' that shit? You just straight stupid and fo' what? We chopped and boosted that shit soon as we got it."

She motions to Niles, "Bind this bitch! Let's finish settin' these charges and pullin' all the copper. She can go up with the rest of this piece of dump."

"W–wait. Go up? W–what do you mean? As in fire? Wait. No no! Please, just let me go."

Niles grabs Felona and shoves her toward the center of the large, darkened room, where the shelves are. Her legs buckle, so he drags her until she stumbles to her feet.

He flings her around and yanks her hands behind her back, tying them together with an electrical cord.

"That hurts!" she protests.

"What's wrong? You don't like a lil pain. Yo' fault for tryin' to play hero, stupid, yella, freckle-faced bitch."

"Why are you doing this?"

"Why anybody do what they do? We tryin'ta stack that paper."

"So this is about money? Because I can give you money."

"Shut up," he calmly says as he repeatedly loops the cord around her body and the iron support beam that she's pressed against.

"I can! Let me go. I–I can get you the money. Just tell me how much."

"Shut up! Ya think I'm stupid?"

"N–no. I don't think you're stupid. I'm serious. I won't say anything to anyone. If you let me go, I can give you more money."

"I said shut up!"

He pulls the cord so tautly that Felona briefly gasps for air.

"The fuck?" Zoe asks from across the room, where she's gathering items into a large crate.

"This bitch won't stop talking! She over here offerin' air and promises."

"I'm serious," Felona pleads. "I can get you money. That's why you're doing this, right? For money? You can make much more if you just let me go. Please."

Zoe returns and leans in.

"What money? Where?"

Felona smirks with a bit of newfound confidence that she has Zoe's attention.

"H–how much you getting paid here?"

She grabs Felona by the throat and shoves the back of her head against the support beam.

"You think I'm playin', bitch?"

Felona gurgles and gasps, twisting her head to loosen Zoe's grip from her since her hands are bound behind her back.

Zoe eventually releases her hold.

Felona coughs. "F–five... five thousand."

"Five thousand cash? To let you go?"

She gasps, "Yes."

"Where is it?"

"I don't have it on me. But I can get it. It's in the bank."

"The bank is closed, you dumb bitch." Zoe waves her hand to one of the men and says, "This bitch is tryin' to play us. Gag her. Hard!"

She turns to walk away.

"No! No no no. Wait! I can – I can get it! I can withdraw it. My bank has a cap on how much I can withdraw daily from their own ATMs, but if I go to other ATMs that aren't owned by my bank, I can temporarily bypass that and withdraw whatever their maximum amount is per teller."

"What's to keep me from taking everything that you got and then killin' you?" Zoe asks.

"Because you're a thief, but I don't think you're a killer. That would bring too much weight on you and your boys. If you kill me, what you're hoping looks like an accidental fire will suddenly become a suspicious fire when they find my body and realize that I don't live here. Things will get real complicated for you as they trace my steps backward to a closed-circuit camera in a grocery store where there is likely footage of me taking an interest in you."

Zoe raises her brow in surprise.

"You don't know shit about shit."

"Your guy is over there fidgeting with wires in the walls, you're collecting copper and you have some kind of liquid accelerant, so I'm guessing you're trying to create the appearance of a fire set by vandals. There're three of you so this isn't the amateur hour. I doubt that this building belongs to you so someone hired you. And I'm also guessing that your payday isn't as big as the payday of that person who probably owns this building. But you're taking the biggest risk."

"I thought you had no idea what we were doing here, you lyin' cunt. Well, congratulations, detective bitch. You cracked the case. Gag this bitch!"

"No no. Wait! My point is, we could both benefit by working together. I get to walk out of here and you get paid a bonus on top of whatever you're making here. I won't mention this to anyone and you'll never see me again."

Zoe stares at Felona for several moments in stark silence.

Niles pleads, "Zoe, I know you're not seriously listenin' to this shit. This yella, freckle-faced bitch is up to somethin'."

"Untie her," she finally says.

"What?!" Niles shrieks.

"You heard me. And give me a gun. I'm taking Freckles for a ride. Either she gives up five thousand dollars or she gives up breathing."

She tosses keys to Niles.

"When you and T get done, meet me at the spot."

For a few fleeting moments, Felona flirts with the thought of overpowering Zoe as soon as the opportunity presents itself. But the reality is, while she's spirited, temperamental and, perhaps daring to follow a thief into her den, she's no fighter.

And even if she were, it's unlikely that she would be a match for someone who's armed and appears to be extremely nervous. Despite her small size, Zoe is apt to be exceptionally dangerous with the gun that she's had trained on Felona ever since they got in the car.

Felona drives a few miles into downtown Nathaniel, but it's more like a ghost town. Investors and commercial developers have abandoned this part of town that was once the pulse of the city. All that remains are husks of abandoned buildings littered with a few scattered local businesses.

"So... are you from Nathaniel?" she asks in a clumsy attempt to mask her nervousness.

"We're not friends. Shut the fuck up and drive," Zoe flatly says as she rummages through Felona's handbag that only contains her temporary driver's license, cell phone, debit card, a credit card, some mints and hand lotion.

"You ain't got a lot in here. Scared someone might rob you?"

Zoe snickers.

Felona's cell phone rings.

"Vine—seen—o?" Zoe slowly enunciates, turning the screen toward Felona. "Who the fuck?"

"Vincenzo," she corrects her. "That's my fiancé."

"Whatever. You can talk to your dude when I get my money. Pull over there."

She points out an ATM next to a barbershop and a convenience store that has windows littered with lottery signs.

Felona sighs and pulls alongside the curb nearby.

Zoe backs out of the car, holding the gun low and out of the sight of passersby with it still pointed at Felona.

"Hurry up!" she says as she hands the debit card to her.

38
Simply Excuses To Hesitate

After ringing the doorbell several times to no avail, Tobias thumps on the door with the heel of his hand.

"Momma Mabel, it's Tobias!" he yells after hearing her moving inside.

Locks clack and the door finally swings open.

"Boy, why you beating on this door like you done lost your mind?" Dianne says. "You know it takes me a minute to get to the front of the house. Come on in here."

"I just met with your daughter," he says as she leads him to the living room.

"You want something to eat?"

"No ma'am. I'm not hungry."

Dianne plops down on the sofa.

"So what did that heifer have to say?"

Tobias nervously laughs.

"Why does she have to be a heifer, Momma Mabel?"

He sits as SoJo curiously sniffs him.

"That ungrateful heifer told me I was dead to her."

He sighs and a stern guise washes over his face.

"Both of you are hurting and both of you are saying hurtful

things that you don't really mean."

Dianne starts, "Well, I told you –"

"Momma Mabel!" Tobias says. "Please. Just listen to me."

She sits back and clasps her hands in her lap.

Tobias continues, "I've listened to both of you. There's your version of the story and her version of the story. Somewhere in there is the truth. But what good is the truth if neither one of you will acknowledge it. You were seconds away from death before God's intervention. Was it a coincidence that Felona's return happened at the same time as yours? I don't think so. Both of you have been given a huge second chance. Both of you are meant to reconcile, but both of you are too damn much alike to realize that you need each other."

"Now you know I don't like that kind of language," Dianne protests.

"You were just calling your daughter a heifer, Momma Mabel. And I've heard much worse come from your mouth. Now, please... hear me. All that's happened between you two is mired in anger, hurt, misunderstanding, distrust and unforgiveness. But you've been given a second chance that I didn't get. Mom and I had an argument while I was stationed in Afghanistan over money. I never had the chance to apologize about the ugly stuff I said to her in anger. You and Felona have different options. There's nothing to gain with being so stubborn, controlling and sensitive."

Dianne rolls her eyes. Seeing this, Tobias chuckles and takes her hand.

"See? You don't want to hear me."

He takes a deep breath and sighs before saying, "I know that you love me. I may have turned the blind eye to some of the stuff that went down between you and Felona while we grew up, but I know that you love me. I don't believe all of the stuff that Felona said. I don't believe all of the stuff you said. I know how I feel about both of you and you're important to me. I have nothing against you or her."

Dianne shakes her head and covers her face with her other hand as tears stream down.

"You just don't understand, Bias."

"I may not understand all of what's happened, but I understand enough to know that you need to reconcile with Felona. You love her. She loves you. Neither of you will express that beyond the hurtful things that you've said and done to each other. But you're the mom. You're the example. You're the queen. Reconcile."

"Reconcile, huh? Did you?"

Tobias shakes his head and smiles.

"This isn't about me. But no, we didn't fully reconcile. I didn't meet her for that purpose. But I will."

"Are you going to her wedding?"

He shakes his head again.

"No. I can't co-sign that. It doesn't feel right."

"So if you feel that way then why are you taking her side?"

"Momma Mabel, I'm not taking sides. Listen to me. That's what I'm saying. There shouldn't be sides at all."

"I sacrificed a lot with Felona. You just don't understand how it hurts a parent."

"No, Momma Mabel. I don't. But reasons and explanations are simply excuses to hesitate. Don't explain."

He grips her hand tighter and looks at her until she returns his silent stare.

"Reconcile with your daughter," he says slowly.

Dianne just shakes her head and looks away.

39

Faust

I *would've never been here in this foolish predicament if it weren't for my mother,* Felona thinks as she stares straight ahead, driving aimlessly, waiting for Zoe to direct her on where to stop next. Several stops have yielded four thousand, eight hundred dollars so far.

If she hadn't put my name on that form... if she hadn't lied to Tobias... if she hadn't tried to, once again, manipulate the course of my life, I wouldn't be in this mess of a life.

Now driving down Washington Street, Felona can't help but see the irony of the fact that she was driving on this same road in the opposite direction last week when Zoe smashed her from behind and stole her car.

I let my anger with her color my sensibility and here I am on the wrong side of a gun. Again. Because of her. I've been better off for the past few years not thinking of her... not being bothered with whether she accepts me or not.

Approaching the very place where it all happened, Felona slows and pulls into the gas station parking lot.

But no more. It doesn't matter now. It doesn't matter now.

"What the fuck?" Zoe excitably asks, thrusting the gun

in Felona's side.

"I remember seeing an ATM inside when I was here last. Remember this place? It's where we first met," she says with a smirk.

"Don't be a smart ass, bitch. It's too late in the game to do somethin' stupid. Keep it up and I will fuck you up."

"Sorry," she mumbles.

They get out of the car and Felona leads them into the gas station. Zoe shoves the gun and her hands in her pockets, as she follows closely behind her.

"I'm behind you. Don't try anything stupid," Zoe reminds her as they enter the store and walk all the way to the back where the ATM is located.

"Haven't I been cooperative? Why am I still getting such distrust and attitude from you?"

Zoe buffets Felona in the side of the ribs with such force that she drops the debit card just as she's sliding it into the slot.

"What the hell was that for?" Felona shouts.

"Keep your voice down and pick up the card. Or I will shoot you in your fuckin' face right here, bitch," Zoe forcibly whispers.

The attendant from the front of the store shouts from behind the counter, "Hey! What's going on back there?"

Zoe turns and laughs, "We just playin' around."

"Cut out that horseplay or leave now!"

"Sorry. We'll behave."

She chuckles again before turning back with a serious face

to Felona and mumbling, "Hurry up."

"I'm done. My little savings account is depleted now."

Zoe snatches the money away from her and rolls it in with the rest of her ill-gained fortune as they leave the store.

"You have a good day," Zoe sarcastically says as she passes the counter, walking closely behind Felona.

The attendant incoherently grumbles something back.

Once they return to the car, Felona turns to Zoe and asks, "Is life all about money to you?"

Zoe shoves Felona against the car.

"Here you go again wit' all your fuckin' questions! The fuck difference it make to you, bitch?"

Felona holds her hands up in surrender.

"I'm sorry. I'm just trying to understand. Is it all about 'getting that money,' putting everything at risk to do so?"

"I'm doin' what I got to do to make a livin', bitch. I got responsibilities. I can't ride around in my husband's SUV making salon appointments and whatnot. I do what I gotta do for mine."

"Why not just get a real job making honest money instead of taking from others who work hard for what they have?"

"Some o' us ain't win the birth lottery. Some o' us don't have a choice but to hustle hard and take control. Bitches like you are so protected from real shit that you think you controllin' shit, but you ain't. Let somethin' go sideways in yo' life and you fall apart."

Felona frowns, lowering her hands.

"You don't know me."

"I know enough, freckle-faced, white bitch."

Felona grimly stares back at Zoe.

If you didn't have that gun, I'd show you who was in control.

"Oh! Did I say something to make poor little rich girl mad? You don't scare me, bitch. Get in the fuckin' car."

But I'm not in control. For a long time now, I've been simply reacting... to everything. I'm tired of being out of control of my own life. I'm tired of reacting. I'm tired of being jostled about from the waves of the effect. It's time for me to be the one to create the waves. It's time for me to be in control. It's time for me to start being the cause.

A smile warms across Felona's face.

Zoe steps back, suspicious of this change in expression.

"How'd you like to make another five thousand dollars?" Felona calmly asks.

Zoe shoves her hands back in her pockets, gripping the gun.

"You ain't got another five thousand dollars. Or even another five hundred. Don't play me! I ain't stupid. I saw on the screen. You got one hundred thirty-six dollars and twelve cents left."

"Oh, I'm not playing you. Do you want another five thousand dollars?"

Zoe fidgets and looks around.

"How?"

"What you and your friends were doing... at that warehouse..." Felona looks around nervously and continues with a lowered voice, "I need your help with something like that... for me. This Saturday."

Zoe squints and tilts her head. She stares at her for several long seconds before blurting out in laughter.

"You need me to do a job?"

"Yeah. I do."

Felona steps toward Zoe who pulls her hand out of her pocket to reveal her grip on the gun.

She disregards the threat and leans in to whisper, "I need you to burn down a house and make it look like an accident."

Zoe looks at Felona skeptically.

"You? The prep school girl...the pretty, privileged chick from the house on the hill needs me to do a job for you? To burn down a house for you?"

Privileged? It's amazing what people assume from the outside looking in. There was nothing privileged about my life growing up in a house that never wanted me. There was nothing privileged growing up in a house with a woman who constantly reminded me that I was the consequence of a horrible thing and she often regretted having me. There was nothing privileged living in the care of that same woman who would have been happier had I bled to death on a cold, steel table during the procedure of an abortion that she forced me to have.

Felona looks around anxiously.

"Yeah. Five thousand. You interested?"

Zoe laughs.

"Your kind cracks me up."

"My kind?"

"You got that little dainty tattoo on your throat and you wanna make street deals? You ain't gangsta. You ain't hard. What kind of rich, white girl problems did you get yourself into that you tryin' to get out of now? You think you can buy your way out of anything? You think everything is for sale? Just make a deal with the devil and keep your hands clean, right?"

"White girl? I'm not...," Felona scoffs then asks flatly, "You interested or not?"

Without warning, Zoe pummels Felona across the face with so much ferocity that she falls back against the car.

"What the hell? What did you hit me for?" Felona gasps, holding her hand to the side of her face as she wrestles to correct her balance.

"That's just love tap, if you tryin' to play me. You don't wanna know what my punch feels like when I'm pissed off. Where's the money?"

"Jesus! What's wrong with you?"

Felona slides against the car and puts some distance between her and Zoe.

"Where's the money or do I need to smack you again?" Zoe advances.

Felona instinctively puts her arm up in front of her face.

"Okay okay. Do you remember that credit card? In my handbag?"

"Yeah."

"I can get a cash advance from it. Five thousand, right?"

Zoe contemplates while Felona rubs her face that is sore and caked with dried blood from the earlier assault in the warehouse.

"I got the gun. What's to say that I don't just take it?"

"Because you don't kill people. That tells me that you have some standard of morality. You have some good in you."

"Morality? This coming from the chick who wants me to burn down a house?"

The two women stare at each other in tense silence.

"Okay. Where is this house?"

"It's... it's on the west side. Barbaro Way... off of West Chatham Ferry."

Zoe frowns thoughtfully and then nods her head.

"I know where that is. That's over by the governor's mansion. Wait a fuckin' second. That's residential. People live in those houses. I ain't burnin' down no house where people live. You tryin' to play me into somethin'?"

"No. I'm not. The house is empty. The family member who used to live there is dead. But because there was no will, the house is tied up in probate court. Meanwhile, I have to pay out the ass to maintain this house that I can't even rent out. But the insurance money would bail me out."

Dianne taught me that bad memories could be purged with fire.

"Get in the car," Zoe bluntly says. "I need you to drop me

off somewhere."

"But you said –"

"Shut up, bitch! I need to hear myself think. Do what I said. Get in the car and drive!"

As Zoe sits in silence, Felona drives to their next unknown destination as her thoughts wander.

"Right here. Right here," Zoe hurriedly says as Felona pulls to a random curb.

Zoe gets out of the car and digs in her pockets for a disposable cell phone that she tosses on the seat.

"Alright. There's one number on that burner. If you change your mind, you call it and you'll never see my face again. You try to play me, I and my guys know who you are, where you work and where you live."

She holds up Felona's temporary license before tucking it into her jacket pocket.

Zoe slams the door closed.

Felona looks in the rearview mirror to steal a hint of what direction she might be headed, but she's gone as if she were never there.

She looks around, unsure of what part of town she's in. Her car is idling alongside a row of boarded up storefronts. A few parked or abandoned cars dot the curb in front of and behind her.

Some men walk past her with curiosity that slows them.

To them, she's likely a cop or someone waiting to buy drugs.

Whereas she might typically be nervous in scenarios like this, Felona's experience has conceived a strange boldness replacing fear.

She tilts the mirror at her face and, even in the dimness of night with scant streetlight, she can see that her eyes are tired and sunken while the side of her face is swollen and red.

She jerks the car into gear and rolls out into the otherwise vacant street.

Her heartbeat quickens as she resides in the thought of what she's done – emptying her checking account and paying an unstable stranger to burn down her mother's house.

She was supposed to die, Felona mulls. *I'd accepted it and prepared for it like a sneeze that never happened.*

As she merges onto the highway, she abandons such thoughts and, instead, allows herself to be allayed by the hum of the tires against the road, content with not thinking or considering what she's set in motion.

40
Releasing Grip

Felona pushes the button on a remote that is tucked in the visor of her rental car as she approaches the gated parking lot across the street from her loft.

She notices a familiar car parked on the side of the street near her parking lot and though it's dark outside, streetlights expose the car and identity of the blonde woman inside.

"Danielle? What's she doing here?" Felona exclaims as the gate's magnetic lock clicks just before sliding open to allow her entry.

Though still sore from her encounter with Zoe, she springs from the car and darts toward the pedestrian gate that exits onto the street. As she approaches the waiting car, the cabin light inside turns on as Danielle steps out.

Danielle tosses her head, pulling her hair into a ponytail. She's wearing oversized sweat pants and a T-shirt, giving the appearance that she's just left the gym.

"What the hell are you doing here, Danielle?"

"Oh! You startled me. I wasn't expecting you to come up behind me."

Felona, veiled in shadow by a planted tree on the sidewalk,

stops a few yards from Danielle.

"You weren't expecting me to come up from behind you in front of my house? What the hell are you doing here at 10:45?"

"I saw you at the station the other day, but I didn't really get a chance to talk to you."

Felona frowns, looking at Danielle's car.

"Wait a second. Did I see you out here the other night?"

Danielle, smiling wryly, leans against the trunk of her car. "I'm not stalking you, if that's what you're asking."

Felona sighs heavily, maintaining distance between them. "I've had a hell of a day so I'm going to ask you one more time and then I'm simply going to call the police. Why are you sitting outside my building late at night?"

"What do you... why're you standing way over there?"

Felona reaches inside her handbag for her phone.

Danielle raises her hands in surrender.

"Okay okay. I wanted to ask you... about your wedding. It's this weekend, right? When I saw you the other day, I thought what I wanted to say to you was too personal of a matter to discuss at work, but I wanted to give you a bit of advice."

"You? The chick that cheated with my fiancé wants to give me advice? No, thank you. Please leave with this foolishness now."

"If you would just listen to me, I'm trying to help you."

"You can help me by leaving. And stop trying to talk to me about my business."

"Well, I'm trying to warn you because... there are things

you don't know. It seems he's got you fooled."

"Who are you talking about?"

"Your fiancé."

"Fooled?"

"Yeah. Fooled. Do you think he's been totally loyal to you all of a sudden?"

"Well, other than that time he slept with this whore that I work with, yeah, I'd say he's totally loyal to me."

"Oh, wow. So I'm a whore now? Well, you're stupid if you believe for a second that we were a one-time fling. You're stupid if you think Vin just up and got religion when he got caught and, with seeing the light from heaven, he decided to be forever faithful and make you his wife. Happily ever after, right? You're starting to believe your own make-believe stories."

"I'm well aware of my fiancé's shortcomings, but what happened between you two has been done for a long while now. I trust him."

"I'm just trying to tell you before you make the mistake I made when I was twenty. I married a cheating douche bag who continued to disrespect me, even after he got caught."

"Danielle, I don't care about your past life choices. I'm not you and we're not about to start exchanging stories like old friends. You're sneaky and conniving and I don't know what you expected to result from this late night ambush, but you need to tuck your fake blond ponytail between your legs and leave. This is the wrong night."

Danielle smirks.

"Okay. Just so you know, Vincenzo and I have been together several times since you got engaged. But I'm done with him. I just wanted to let you know. Woman to woman. Do with that what you want."

"Woman to woman, huh?" Felona scoffs. "You know what? This is low, even for you. You stay away from Vin and you stay the fuck away from me."

"You two deserve each other," Danielle laughs. "Vincenzo with his money, big dick and disloyalty, and you... you're just stupid. You have no idea what I could do to upset your planned, little life of matrimony. But I'm not going to be petty like that."

Felona steps closer as she retrieves her phone from her handbag and dials.

She stares at Danielle as she says, "Yes, I'm calling to report a trespasser on my property. I think she might be a danger."

"Fine!" Danielle says throwing up her hands. "You don't have to call the police on me. Don't say I didn't try to warn you, you fake, freckle-faced bitch."

Felona hangs up the phone and lets it fall back into her handbag.

"What did you call me?" she snarls, stepping even closer from the shadows into the glow of the streetlight.

She lunges at Danielle and before she can spin out of the way, Felona is bearing down on her, forcing her body backward onto the trunk of the car.

"What did you call me?" she repeats in a maniacal whisper as she holds Danielle by the neck.

Barely able to speak, Danielle wheezes, "Let me... go."

Felona complies, flinging her to the sidewalk.

"Get in your car and never come back here," she says tersely.

Danielle crawls backward, putting distance between her and Felona before she struggles up from the ground.

"You're crazy!"

"I'm not the one stalking someone."

"I'm only trying to help you!"

"Help me? You steal my promotion by setting me up and you sleep with my boyfriend just for spite. I don't need your kind of help."

"You don't have to listen to me. But before you walk down that aisle, you need to talk to your man. And you might want to keep him out of my bed."

Felona closes her eyes, takes a deep breath and exhales. She smiles, saying nothing, and turns to walk away, pausing only to let three cars pass before crossing the street to her building.

Danielle shakes her head and opens the car door.

She mumbles, "Fine. Walk away from the truth. Stupid bitch," and plops into the driver's seat.

She fumbles her key into the ignition and the engine turns. The radio blares at the volume it was last when the car was running. She lowers it and flicks on the headlights.

Still shaking her head and mumbling incoherently, she turns her attention to her handbag, which is on the seat next to her. She retrieves her cell phone and scrolls through her call history while reaching to close the door.

But before she can close the door, a force slams it shut and she's startled in her seat by the suddenness of the sound.

She whips around to see Felona leaning on the car door with one hand and reaching for her collar with the other.

Danielle shrieks and leans away in surprise, but not before Felona can firmly grasp her by her neck.

Danielle pulls away, attempting to free herself from Felona's hold.

Felona doesn't relent as she leans further into the car, now choking Danielle with both hands.

In tense silence, the two women squirm and struggle as if in some tightly choreographed death dance.

Felona braces her thighs against the outside of the car for leverage as the rest of her reaches almost fully into the car and is on top of Danielle, who is trying desperately to wrestle from the adamant grip around her neck.

Unable to speak, Danielle searches Felona's blood-caked and swollen face for meaning or mercy.

Felona sternly stares back, yielding nothing.

Danielle's struggle weakens as she begins to lose oxygen.

Illuminated by the streetlight outside the car, her quizzical expression turns to fear.

Then regret.

And then pleading.

Images flash before Felona, as she has been here before, but she was on the other end of being choked while her mother held her down countless times before.

Danielle's faint sounds of desperation remind her of

the car accident where she tried to end her own life and the tattoo that covered the scar that bore the resemblance of so many abuses.

She remembers being on the other end of violence just hours ago and how she responded in kind by perpetuating further calamity at her own behest.

She is no better than Zoe or the memories that torment her.

Felona releases her grip from Danielle, who is seconds away from losing consciousness.

She backs out of the car, staring in disbelief at what she almost did, as Danielle coughs and wheezes for air.

41

Nothing

The outside sounds of dawn awaken Felona who is still fully dressed and atop her made up bed.

She stretches into a seated position and runs her hands through her hair. Her fingers discover a painful lump on the back of her head.

Suddenly, she recalls the violent night and falling backward into the metal door when Zoe slugged her from behind.

She touches her face, but quickly withdraws from the pain there as well.

She jumps from the bed and runs to the bathroom mirror where she discovers that the side of her face looks worse than it did in the dimness last night. It's swollen and caked with blood.

"Shit! My face looks like Quasimodo. I'm going to need a lot of makeup and a miracle to cover this."

She splashes cold water over her face, rinsing away the dried blood and thinking that it will make the swelling go down immediately.

It doesn't.

As she stares into the mirror, she twists her body and

sees that her arms and neck bear evidence of last night's struggle with Danielle.

My life, and perhaps my wedding, is falling apart. I thought that I could at least hold on to the idea of marriage, but after last night, I'm not sure about that either. What was the real reason that Danielle showed up last night? What was she trying to say that I wouldn't hear?

Her phone rings. She glances at it to see that it's her mother.

What more could she possibly have to say to me at this point?

Felona ignores the call and falls back onto her bed, looking up at the ceiling.

What do I do? I thought I was regaining control of my life. Of my thoughts. But last night... the thing with Danielle has me wondering if... I'm losing grip of what reality is. Or isn't.

Her phone rings again.

Ugh! I need to block her number. Oh, it's Vin.

I can't talk to him right now. Not the way I'm feeling. I need to get it together before I talk to him. At this point, I'm convinced that there is a much greater conversation that we need to have. But I'm not in a chatty or confronting mood right now. I just want to take some more medicine and go back to sleep.

She lets out a loud, deep sigh.

Maybe I should call Ny.

She sighs again.

No, I need to do more than whine about my problems and that's all she would get from me at this point.

Felona glances over at her wedding dress hanging

in the corner.

I should be feeling anxious, excited, nervous, or something about my wedding. But I don't. I feel numb. At this stage, I'm not even sure whether I should be getting married. Am I fooling myself? I'm so messed up and all over the place, putting myself in danger like I've lost all sense of reality.

I should be feeling resolved, content, pleased, or something about deciding to burn what memories remain of a past that's been haunting me. But I don't. I feel indifferent.

I should be feeling ashamed, disgusted, or at the least, tinges of guilt with delving into such a devious conspiracy. But I don't. I feel paralyzed to continue or correct what I've set in motion.

Felona continues to stare blankly at the ceiling, as if she can see past it and well into the black night. She fingers the tattoo on her neck, reminding herself of its intended meaning and significance that it might tether her to something hopeful again so that she doesn't float away into the cold void, alone and murderous, feeling nothing.

42
Enfant Mauvais Souvenirs

A wedding is allegedly one of the most wondrous experiences in a woman's life. All attending her presence are to make the occasion completely about her. Her beauty in that sliver of time is to be suspended in eternity so that ten years, thirty pounds and two kids later, she may sigh at the princess she once was.

With her wedding only two days away, Felona is uncertain that she will attain that level of grandeur or, for that matter, if happily ever after is meant for her.

Yesterday, she spent much of the day in thought, in solitude and in bed.

Today, she can't afford that same luxury nor use the same excuse of suffering a migraine that kept Vin away.

Her phone rings, as it has been doing a lot for the last twenty-four hours. From her wedding planner to the bridesmaids to the coordinator, everyone has been calling her with some concern or last–minute change.

This time it's Vin.

"Hey."

"Are you feeling any better this morning, bella?

I'm concerned that you're letting stress of the wedding get to you."

"I'm still a little groggy, but I needed the day to rest. I'm sorry I was so short with you yesterday, but –"

"It's okay. Don't worry about it. I just got a call from the photographer. She called me about her deposit. She said she reached out to you, but couldn't get you. She said that the check that you gave her last week came back."

"What?"

"She that said she deposited the check a couple of days ago, but when she got her balance online yesterday, it didn't reflect the amount. After talking to the bank, they told her that your account had insufficient funds to honor it."

"But I –" *Oh... shit.*

It suddenly dawns on Felona that the events of two days ago where she emptied her checking account in exchange for freedom have affected previously pending transactions.

"Bella?"

"Yeah. I'm here. Sorry. I was just trying to... I'm not sure what happened, but I'll look into it. What did you tell her?"

"You'll look into it? What does that mean, bella? We're getting married in a couple of days. We need this photographer, but she's not going to show up if we don't pay her."

"Vin, I told you... I'd take care of it. I'll call her back and straighten it all out. Don't worry about it."

"I'm not worried about it. I already took care of it."

"W–what? You already...?"

Felona sighs, annoyed.

"So why all the drama if you already took care of it?"

"Drama? Why do you call it drama when it's something that you don't want to deal with? Bella, you've been irresponsible with money in the past and it's starting to become a problem."

"Irresponsible? What makes you think I've been irresponsible with my money? You apparently don't know all of my expenses with this wedding. And maybe if you were more involved in what's going on with me, you would recall that I had my car stolen, along with my ID and credit cards. While I called to make sure that everything was cancelled, that doesn't mean there wouldn't be some damage. And again, it's my money."

"It's our money since we're getting married and I don't want money management to become an issue for us, bella. I work too hard and make too much to argue about money."

Her phone beeps to alert her to an incoming call. She glances at it long enough to see that it's her mother. She doesn't answer it.

Felona's voice rises, synonymous with her irritation.

"You're not the only one that works hard or earns good money, Vin! And while you're concerned about money management, I'm concerned about more important things like if you're really ready."

A knock at the door defuses an inevitable argument.

"Vin, Ny is here. I gotta go. I'm not trying to have an argument. We can finish this later. Thanks for handling that.

Love you."

She pauses for a moment, expecting him to return with, "I love you too," but he doesn't, so she hangs up.

"What the hell happened to your face?" Ny bellows, closing the door behind her.

"I ran into a wall," Felona dismisses, stepping back and looking away. "It's nothing."

"The fuck, you say! Come here."

Felona flinches as Ny leads her into the kitchen and tilts her head while she leans in close, inspecting her wounds.

"Felo, what the hell really happened? Did Vin do this?"

"No!" she protests, jerking away. "Why would you even think that Vin would put his hands on me?"

"What happened then?" she persists.

Felona sighs, abandoning her secrecy, "I met up with Tobias."

Ny's eyes widen and she quietly gasps, with her hands over her mouth.

"No, Tobias didn't do this either."

She exhales deeply, looking at her best friend whose eyes plead with her for inclusion of the truth.

"I went to talk with him. You know? Resolve some things, end chapters, and so on. It didn't really go all that well. While I was there, just north of Nathaniel, I spotted the woman who carjacked me, so... I kind of followed her."

"You did what? Felo! What the hell? You could've been killed!"

Felona shakes her head, acknowledging Ny's concern, and forces a nervous smile.

"She ended up at this warehouse and I followed her in. I was like the dog chasing the car with no plan of what I would do once I caught up to it."

Ny gently touches her face.

"Evidently, the car slowed down, but you didn't."

Felona looks away, embarrassed with her appearance.

"Not exactly. Once she realized she was being followed, she turned the tables and ambushed me. I got roughed up by her and her accomplices."

"Have you lost you mind?" Ny shrieks. "What were you thinking?"

"To be honest, I wasn't. My temper and adrenaline kind of took over at that point."

"How did you get away?"

"Money. I gave her all that I had."

"Felona Mabel! She could've taken your money and killed you anyway. I know that you're accustomed to some degree of danger with your job, but do you have some kind of a death wish?"

"No," her voice trembles, looking away as a tear trails down her cheek.

Ny relents from her stance.

"Oh no... oh, sweetie."

Ny pulls her into an embrace and Felona feels her legs

weaken as if they can no longer hold her weight or her sadness.

Sensing her sudden lapse in balance, Ny guides Felona to the couch to sit down.

"What's really going on with you, love? You can talk to me."

Felona smears quiet tears from her face.

"I don't know, Ny. I feel like I'm losing control."

"Of what? Is this about your mom? The wedding?"

Felona shakes her head, sniffling.

"My mother... seeing her just dredged up all of the ugly stuff about me. I feel conflicted and unsure all over the place."

"Maybe you need time, sweetie. Maybe you need to postpone the wedding until you're in a better place."

Felona vigorously shakes her head.

"No, I can't. Vin and all the people we invited... and the food. Everything's ready."

"Everything except for you. You don't owe anyone anything. This is your life."

Felona collapses her face into the soft pillows on her couch and cries.

She feels Ny nudge toward her and rub her shoulder and back as a loving mother might.

"Let it out, sweetie. It's okay. Let it out."

Moments of silence lapse with Ny asking, "Have you ever considered talking to a counselor or therapist?"

Felona smirks and sits up.

"Ny, are you insinuating that I'm crazy?"

"Aren't we all?" she laughs.

"I guess so."

"Yeah, I tried to talk to a counselor. I went my junior year of college when I realized that promiscuity wasn't the road to recovery or any degree of acceptance."

"How was it? Did anything come of it?"

"I only went a few sessions, but the therapist made me uncomfortable."

"Uncomfortable?"

"Have you ever looked at the word, therapist, and noticed that it can also read, the rapist?"

"Uncomfortable how, Felo?" she persists, undeterred by Felona's distraction attempt.

"Umm... he would stare at me a certain way whenever I would talk. Like he was seeing through me. Or seeing through my clothes, more specifically."

"Are you serious?"

"Oh yeah. At first, it was very subtle and I thought maybe it was just my suspicions with men coming at me from a superficial angle. He was an older guy and he had the fatherly thing going on with the balding, gray head, the professor glasses hanging on the end of his nose and the cardigan sweater. The first two sessions were innocent enough. I did most of the talking, sharing some of the details of the fractured relationship between my mother and I. I told him about the abortion. I told him how I had no problem drawing people, especially men, to me, but I struggled in maintaining any semblance of a fruitful relationship. I told him about how sex was a temporal form of acceptance, but sexual encounters left me even more empty and alone. I struggled with trusting people, you know."

Ny nods intently.

"Well, like I said, he was more of the listener type in the beginning. Creepy in how he stared at me, but still the listener type. I figured that was just what therapists do. He would just nod his head as I talked and occasionally coach me to keep talking whenever emotion would give me pause. This was the first two sessions, but by the third session, I started getting impatient and discouraged at going any further without some kind of professional advice or opinion on what to do and how to deal with all of the stuff I was revealing to him."

"What did he say?"

"He said that it seemed that I didn't allow myself to be fully engaged in intimate relationships. At the end of that session, I got every impression that he was trying to become one of those intimate relationships."

"What do you mean? How?"

"When my hour was up, he offered to continue to counsel me over drinks."

Ny leans in excitably.

"What? No way! He just came out and asked you out?"

"He wasn't blatant with it, but he was direct enough that I didn't mistake his advances as anything less than professional. I felt betrayed because I trusted this total stranger with personal and vulnerable details about me simply because he had a door plaque with PhD following his name."

"Oh no. What did you do?"

"I called him on what he was doing and made no qualms about threatening to report his behavior if it continued. He said that I misunderstood his intentions and that therapy is a relationship of trust. He said that he was trying to address me in a more casual way since I was still very guarded. I, of course, called bullshit on his story and he saw that as an opportunity to dig into me. He told me that, from what he surmised, I avoided any real personal connections because deep down I didn't think that I was good enough to be loved."

"Wow."

"Yeah. Exactly. Let me see. How exactly did his psychobabble go?"

Felona keenly ponders for a few silent moments and then explodes with, "Oh! Oooh ooh! I remember now – 'Obsessive thoughts of your fate are a demonstration of your own padded egotism and narcissism that's made more intricate by your struggles with insecurity.'"

"Wow. You remembered the exact words?"

"Give or take an adverb or two. Needless to say, that was my last appointment or attempt at seeking so-called, clinical help."

"That's crazy. I'm sorry that that was your experience. I've had much more success with my therapist. I should share her with you."

"Wait. You go to therapy?"

"Oh, of course. There's no way I could begin to help other women deal with their issues if I didn't have my own head together."

"I don't need a therapist now. I got you," Felona beams, raising her arms out to welcome a hug.

"Oh, you –"

Ny pulls her into yet another embrace, but there are no tears this time.

"I meant what I said, Felo. You don't have to rush to get married until you're ready. It's normal to feel anxiety, but if that's overcoming your excitement, maybe you should listen to it."

"I'll be fine. Besides, if I wait until my life is perfectly put together, I won't get married until I'm menopausal and have nine cats."

"Do you love Vin?"

Felona searches Ny's face for motive before answering, "Yes."

"Does he love you?"

She raises her left hand in front of Ny, displaying her engagement ring.

"We're getting married in two days. Of course."

Ny sighs, but relents.

"Have you talked to your mom?"

Felona scowls.

"Why would I do that?"

"Well, if you're clearing things up with Tobias, I figure you might as well go for broke."

"No. I'm not doing that. I don't have anything to say to her."

"So she's not coming to the wedding?"

"Kinaya Odoyo! I thought you were my friend. Where is this coming from?"

"It's coming from a place of love, sweetie. I want you to be happy. Thoroughly."

Felona pokes her lips out, squinting, "Yeah, okay."

"I'm your therapist now, right? So you have to listen to me. I promise I won't invite you out for drinks or touch you inappropriately."

They both laugh, but the mere mention of her mother brings with it a latent sadness and regret that Felona can't ignore.

"Felo, I've been thinking about this ever since we talked the other day."

"Thinking about what?" she asks, getting up from the couch.

"I think I have a solution for you," she answers, trailing behind Felona as she walks to the bathroom mirror. "One that can help you and help others at the same time. I've never really gone into detail about the organization that I work with in Africa, but the women that I see all have one thing in common."

"What's that?"

Felona taps the light on to study the swelling on her face, touching the raised skin and flinching from the pain that's still there along with the swelling.

"They were all raped."

Felona pauses as in suspended animation, looking at Ny in the mirror.

"Raped?"

"Yes. All of these women were systematically raped by military hostiles during a longstanding civil war. Afterward, they're either forced into sexual servitude or they're exiled from their own communities."

Felona turns to face her.

"But... they're the victims. Why would they be exiled?"

"That's not how the men see them. They see them as tainted or ruined by the enemy. And to add insult, their own government refuses to intervene because the rapes, as widespread and frequent as they are, aren't considered to be war crimes. It happened in Rwanda; it's happening in Darfur; it's happening in several smaller regions, yet on the same broad scale."

"And you go to these places? Isn't it dangerous?"

"It's dangerous, but I never travel alone. Because of the civil war, we usually travel with a unit of at least fifteen and our driver. Some of the medics are armed. I go because I'm needed. Sadly, most of the women I administer medical care to are HIV positive and have much deeper scars than are physically apparent."

"Wow," Felona exhales. "And here I am whining about my life."

"I'm not telling you this to make you feel bad. This is the world we live in. I'm telling you because, after what you told me, I think your presence can help."

"My presence?"

"Yeah. These women aren't the only victims. There are children that are born from and into these circumstances. Some of the children, who aren't sold, abandoned or aborted, know of their origins... like you. During the Rwandan genocide, the term was coined enfants mauvais souvenirs – children of bad memories. Next time I go, I'd like for you to consider going with me. I know the women would benefit from your presence and I think you could benefit as well. You may even decide to do a documentary about the experience."

Felona starts to shake her head, but Ny says, "Don't answer now. You have your wedding to concern yourself with. I'm not planning another trip until late fall at the earliest. Take time to think about it."

In that instant, Felona does take time to think about it and she's already convinced that Ny's passions are not her own.

I'm no hero. I'm much less and, perhaps, on the opposite side of hero. Ny may be a soother, a nurturer and champion for a better world, but I'm none of those things.

Felona turns to look in the mirror again.

"I'll think about it," she sighs.

"Good. Now let's fix your face up. We have a mani-pedi appointment in an hour."

Felona leans in closely to her reflection.

"This looks bad. Can makeup cover this?"

"Yep. I can work miracles, sweetie. A wise man once wrote, 'It's not what you look at that matters. It's what you see.'"

43
Amends

Felona paces back and forth in her bedroom, from the closet to the bed and back again, gathering attire for her honeymoon in Venice, Italy.

Spread across her bed are several leather handbags that she's collected over the years – Yves Saint Laurent, Fendi, Rochas and Moreschi, among others.

Also, littered across her bed are her traveling essentials – lip-gloss, concealer, mirror, passport, yet another temporary driver's license, insurance card, ibuprofen, birth control, mints, comb, and a few other trinkets and perceived necessities.

She glances at the burner, among the articles on the bed, that Zoe gave her and deeply sighs.

As she's staring at it and mulling over the significance of it, her own cell phone beside it suddenly vibrates.

She jumps at the unexpected interruption of silence.

It's her mother calling. Again.

"Think of the devil," she mumbles.

Feeling a sense of control in the moment or for no discernible reason, she answers it this time.

"What can you possibly have to say that is so important

to keep calling?" Felona says flatly. "I made it quite clear that I was done."

"Lona, I'm so glad you finally answered," Dianne brightly says.

"Haven't you done enough? Or do you have a couple more 'bitches' or 'fake white girls' to throw at me?"

"No, Lona," she says softly. "I don't want to continue to say or do hurtful things at all. I called... I been calling desperately... because I wanna say I'm sorry. For everything."

Felona drops the phone to her side and stares across the room.

She toggles the phone to speaker and tosses it back on the bed.

Her mother continues to talk.

"I been angry for a long time, Lona. And I had no right to take it out on you all these years, but I did. You got every right to hate me right now 'cause I didn't know how to tell you... it's not your fault. It never was your fault."

Felona falls onto the edge of the bed, putting things into a beige Louis Vuitton handbag as her mother continues talking.

"You never met your granddaddy, but you woulda loved him. I lost my daddy when I was thirteen. I loved that man so. He was both momma and daddy to me. My momma was always high. She drank too much. Smoked too much. Cursed too much. Most of my memories of her were of her passed out on the couch. So I was always with daddy. He took me wherever he went. Even when he was fidgetin' around with his car, I was right there handin' him greasy tools, just a proud, daddy's little girl."

Dianne continues, "And then one day, he had a heart attack. He just passed out while he was working. I never thought when I went to school that day, that I would never see him smiling back at me again. I think he died of a broken heart. My momma was so mean to him. She would get high and say all kinds of things that make a man not feel like a man anymore."

Felona sighs loudly and then impatiently blurts out, "I'm in no mood for stories about ghosts and alcoholic apparitions. What does this have to do with –?"

"Just listen. Please," Dianne calmly responds. "I think momma was jealous of how much daddy loved me. She drank even more after he died. And nothin' I did was good enough. She wasn't like daddy. With him I felt like I could do no wrong. With her, I felt like all I did was wrong. She died a few years later while I was away in college. Liver cancer. Around the same time, I met Brent. He was kind, just like daddy. I never met a man like him. And he accepted me for me. Past my dark skin and short, nappy hair, he loved me. He made me feel like God was proud that he made me."

Her voice trembles as she continues, "That is until you happened. He tried to stay. But I think every time he looked at you, he felt like my daddy musta felt when my momma would call him them ugly names. He didn't feel like a man should because another man had ruined his wife. And then..." She inhales deeply. "And then Iris... his little girl... our little girl... was killed right in front of him. And he couldn't stop it. He was too far away and the car was so fast. By the time he got to her, she was lifeless and limp. He couldn't stop his wife from bein' raped and he couldn't save his little girl from bein' killed. He left me. Unlike daddy though, he chose to leave me. I was unacceptable to him. And God... wasn't proud of me no more."

A sudden silence causes Felona to pause filing articles in her handbag to look at her phone, unsure if the connection has been lost, but Dianne's voice returns.

"When you got pregnant, I failed you. I failed you in so many ways as a parent. And I let my fear push you away when you needed me most. I don't blame you for being angry with me. I can't blame you for feeling abandoned. You have every right to never ever want to speak to me again. I know what it's like to be afraid and alone. I know what it's like to feel like no one cares."

Felona freezes and stares at the phone and Dianne continues, "I been thinking about you and how I been unfair to you all these years; how I've been like momma in my cruelty toward you. I been blaming you... for everything. I made you feel like you weren't good enough. I made you feel unacceptable. But we just alike, Lona. We just alike. We been chasin' the same thing this whole time – acceptance. I coulda gave it to you, but I didn't. And I'm so sorry, baby. I'm so sorry for hurtin' you."

"Is that all? Are you done? Because I am," Felona says.

Dianne goes on, "My biggest sin was that I didn't know how to tell you before. When I would look at you, I just saw my failures. I didn't see the miracle that you are. It wasn't until you went away to school that I realized it. Everything flooded to the front of my conscience about all the wrong that I'd done to you. I did so little to encourage you and you tried so hard to find encouragement from me anyway."

"Yeah, well we both know how that turned out so no point in crying over it now. I survived. Barely."

"Lona, I didn't die when I was raped. I didn't die when that car killed Iris. I didn't die when Brent left me. But when you left... when you left for all those years and I was certain that you were gone... I almost did. My lupus got worse and I almost died of a broken heart... until you came back. As soon as you came back, life came back to me."

Dianne's voice quivers, but she persists to continue, "Well, in two days, you getting married. I've missed eight years of your life, but that don't mean that I can't give you my blessing. That don't mean you and I can't reconcile with each other. And Tobias... that man loves you 'cause as soon as he saw you the other day, he came back over here. I never seen this man so serious in my life. And do you know what he told me? He told me about myself. It took his broken heart to see how I broke yours."

"Is that it?" Felona returns flatly, despite wrestling back a deluge of emotion.

"Baby, I–I don't expect you to forgive me on the spot. But I just wanted you to know. It's going to take time for you to trust what I'm sayin', but I never been more sincere than I am now. I love you and I'm sorry that I hurt you so deeply. I accept you for who you are and –"

Felona abruptly hangs up the phone just as tears threaten to come forth.

44

Mens Rea

It's Friday and the day before Felona is to become Mrs. Vincenzo Alonzo Ricci, but her conscience is not good company right now. She's allowed the wound of unforgiveness to fester and infect everything.

The idea of matrimony has failed to shift from reverie to reality for her. Where she should be elated and giddy with anticipation, her thoughts are laden with guilt, anger and indecision.

And she has the audacity to make it all about her, Felona thinks as she frowns, unaware of her appearance at the moment. *We're just alike? No. We're nothing alike. I'm not chasing acceptance. I have acceptance. And I have love. Don't I?*

"Are you nervous, honey?"

"What?" Felona dimly asks, startled from her thoughtful trance.

"Are you nervous about tomorrow, honey?" June, Felona's hairdresser and friend, asks while removing clips from Felona's hair.

"Not really," she lies.

"That's good. Unless you're lying."

"Well, we've been together long enough to know that this

is what we both want."

"Yeah? Marriage is such a big deal. I think less people are doing it these days though. The few that still brave the tradition to walk down the aisle and publicly declare their love for one another intrigue me."

"How long were you married, June?"

"Were? I'm still married, honey."

"But... I thought you and Trevor –?"

"Trevor's my man, but he's not my husband."

"O–okay?"

June laughs, "Don't hurt yourself, child. It's not that complicated. My husband ran off two years ago and refuses to give me a divorce or pay child support. It's his passive aggressive way of punishing me for cheating on him."

"You cheated on him? With Trevor?"

"No. I didn't know Trevor at the time. I messed around with some young, boy toy that worked next door as a barber."

"Oh."

"I love Trevor, but I think I'm afraid of marriage at this point. Besides, I'm forty-seven. I'm too old to be walking down somebody's aisle in some church wearing white like my ass is a virgin."

She leans in close and says, "No offense if you're wearing white tomorrow, honey."

"No, my dress is off-white. Kind of creamish."

"Well, you're braver than me and that's the truth."

She teases Felona's tightened curls with a comb.

"I've been meaning to ask you, what happened here?"

June gestures at the discolored skin across Felona's cheek.

"I got into a scuffle with a piece of furniture," she dismisses.

"Mmmm. I hope that furniture looks worse than you," June chuckles. "It's not too bad though. Some makeup should cover that up. You're going to look so beautiful. And I know you're going to love your hair. So tell me, honey... you happy?"

"What? You mean, in general?"

"Why you acting brand new to this conversation, honey? Are you happy with the man that you're going to marry tomorrow?"

Felona frowns.

"Of course. Why would I be getting married if I wasn't happy?"

"Come on now. You know plenty of people get married for the wrong reasons. Money, kids, attention, you name it. Some people actually think that getting married will make them happy. Shiiiiit. Not if they knew what I know. They running they ass in the wrong direction to find happiness."

As she sits and listens to June wax on about the woes of modern society and togetherness, a sudden sadness washes over Felona – a sadness in the realization that happiness is far from her.

"Now, I know how your memory is so I also want to remind you that the rehearsal dinner is at six," Felona says to Ny.

"Girl, I may have Swiss cheese memory sometimes, but I'm not that forgetful. I haven't forgotten your rehearsal dinner at all. Mosi and I will be pulling double duty tonight though. We'll be there, but we may be a little late because he's hosting that fundraiser."

"Don't worry. Tierra volunteered to stand in for you, in case you can't make it."

"Is that all you called for? To tell me about your hairdo and remind me about tonight? You sound weird. Are you okay?"

"Not really. I talked to my mom. That is... she talked to me. I mostly just listened."

"You talked to her? That's progress, right? I'm surprised that you took her call. I'm proud of you. I figured you would eventually talk to her, but I didn't think it would be until after you got back from your honeymoon and you'd had time to think about everything."

"Yeah, well I kind of needed to go ahead and get it out of the way. That whole starting a new chapter thing?"

"Yes. That," Ny chuckles. "So what did she have to say?"

"Nothing. Lies. Fake sentiments. Nothing that I haven't heard before. I'm not getting sucker-punched this time. But I did let her talk. I can't return back to that place."

"But?"

"What do you mean? That's it."

"Felona, while you're a part-time woman of mystery, I still know you. There's an edge to your voice. What else is there?"

"Well, some of the things that she said... she went back into her past and tried to explain her actions. She even seemed sincere, but –"

"But you don't trust her?"

"Hell, no. I've been there before. And every time I'm mistaken about her sentiment, it kills a little bit of hope within me. And every time I've returned, there was less of me. And now, there's nothing. I'm just done with the emotional roller coaster. I'm done with being disappointed."

"I'm sorry, sweetie. You and she have years and years of bad blood. It's not going to be resolved overnight or in one well-meaning conversation. In truth, only counseling and willingness will get you where you want to be."

"Wanted. I don't want that anymore. Past tense. I'm moving forward."

"Okay. Forward. Meaning another time when you don't already have enough on your plate. You're getting married tomorrow. Your focus should be there. You should be occupied with thoughts of excitement and being happy."

"There's that word again."

"What word?"

"Happy. I want to be, but my doubts are becoming more dominant than my excitement."

"Doubt? Wedding day jitters? Or change of heart?"

"Right now, I'm not sure. I don't think –"

As Felona pulls into her parking lot, she notices Vin's car is parked outside on the curb.

"What is he doing here?" she mumbles.

"What's that?" Ny responds.

"Ny, let me call you back. Okay?"

Felona opens the door to find Vin inside watching television and drinking wine.

"Hey. What're you doing here?" she greets him with a peck on the cheek before putting her things down.

He turns to get up.

"Bella, my bride-to-be, I haven't seen you in – what the hell happened?"

She instinctively puts her hand over the bruise on the side of her face.

"I had an accident a couple of days ago while I was moving some things around."

He moves in closer to inspect, but Felona pulls back, turning her wounded side away.

"What the hell? Did you get this looked at? Because it looks bad. And why didn't you tell me?"

"I didn't want to worry you. Besides, Ny took a look at it. I'm fine. It looks worse than what it is."

"But it looks bad, bella," he insists. "We have the rehearsal tonight. And the wedding tomorrow. The pictures and all."

"Vin, relax. No one will be able to see it. I'll put on makeup."

He sighs sharply.

"What the hell? Why are you so careless? With money and your appearance?"

"My appearance? Are you kidding me? What are you

talking about?"

"It seems that for the last couple of weeks, you've just let yourself go. I don't want to be that couple, you know?"

"Are you listening to yourself right now? You're constantly talking about not being that couple. Who is that couple, Vin? And why do you care? Shouldn't our love be the only thing that matters? Fuck other couples!"

"There you go with that mouth. You didn't always have that mouth. It's not very ladylike."

"Ladylike? Are superficial things all that are important to you? Have you once asked me how I feel about anything that's going on with me? With my mother? With the wedding?"

"You know, you should be thankful that I'm interested in your appearance... that I find you beautiful."

"Is that so? I should bow down to you for thinking me attractive? Fuck! Do you know how many men comment on my looks on a daily basis? That doesn't carry a whole lot of weight with me in the grand scheme of so many other things that will last well beyond wrinkles and weight gain. What's important is that you love me for me."

She sighs loudly and says, "You know what, I'm going to pretend that you haven't said any of this and dismiss you until rehearsal tonight. You're upsetting me and we really shouldn't be doing this on the eve of our wedding."

Vin scoffs.

"Fine!"

"What did you mean the other night when you called me your bitch?"

"What? What are you talking about?"

"When we were together. You said I was your bitch."

He looks up to the ceiling with his eyes closed for a few moments before smiling and then laughing.

"Oh! That. Bella, you know what I meant. We were in the moment."

"I hate that word though. How can you call your wife-to-be that word?"

"Oh, my god. You're serious. I'm going to go before this turns into something."

Vin gets up and walks toward the door, but Felona stops him with, "Vin? Do you still love me?"

He turns, scowling.

"We're getting married tomorrow. What kind of question is that? Of course I do. But I don't know what's going on with you right now. You seem like you want to fight. I don't. I'll see you tonight."

He leaves, closing the door behind him.

Felona stands in his stead feeling less alone now that he's gone.

She falls onto the couch, shaking her head back and forth.

"I don't know if I can do this. I don't know if this is for me."

She grabs a pillow and holds it over her face, muffling a scream.

I feel like I've suspended one forlorn relationship for another.

I'm supposed to be veering foolishly toward marital bliss, but I feel like the only one foolish here. I thought I was done reacting. I thought I was getting control back.

Right now, all I want to do is to just lie down in that colorful field of flowers in full bloom and let velvet ribbons flow from my wrists.

"I think I've made a terrible mistake," she sighs, breathlessly..

45
Something Blue

For centuries since ancient Rome, brides have worn some manner of blue on their wedding day to symbolize love, modesty and fidelity. Even the Virgin Mary has been depicted in blue as evidence of purity being associated with the color.

Accents of blue run throughout the St. Camillus de Lellis Sacred Heart cathedral in honor of Felona and Vin's wedding that is scheduled to commence in forty-five minutes.

The intricate facade of the building is overwhelming at first sight and it's known to attract tourists and onlookers from all over for its aesthetic grandeur and harmony alone. It's easily one of Admah City's landmark buildings.

A rare 1936 black and cream painted Daimler Limousine is parked in front of the cathedral. Its vintage design is no less majestic as it awaits the bride and groom once they exchange vows. A large blue bow on the grill appears fitting for the occasion.

People are still migrating into the cathedral from the side parking lot, but their progression is slowed by a slow fascination with all that is to behold.

Inside, stained glass windows reach all the way to the

frescoed ceilings while the edifice is filled with brilliant color and light. The air is crisp as a fall morning.

An organist plays 18th-century hymnals that could easily be mistaken for old love sonnets due to the slow tempo and major key. Blue hydrangeas line the aisle and provide a stark contrast to the dark oak of the pews and the red carpet that runs along the floor.

Tucked away in the basement, the wedding party has begun to gather in the order in which they will proceed into the sanctuary within the hour. Last–minute fittings, tucks and adjustments are being made to the groomsmen and bridesmaids' ensembles.

The wedding planner, Arcadia Wyatt, is an energetic, mature, small, blonde woman with large ears and red horn-rimmed glasses. She darts from person to person, checking to ensure that every detail is consistent and pleasing.

She abruptly pauses, removes her glasses and scans the room. Agitation washes over her face and she asks in a raised voice, "Has anyone seen the bride?"

The black constellation of thoughts that accompanies Felona is as random and varied as the freckles on her face. Her life has been a series of cul-de-sacs, twists and last–minute left turns that have ultimately led her to the same destination.

The queasiness that she's felt for the past forty-five minutes is not subsiding, but getting worse.

She hovers over a toilet in one of the bathrooms on the other side of the basement, wearing her wedding dress. She's dry heaved twice and nothing has come up... probably because she hasn't eaten anything.

A booming knock on the door startles her.

"Felona! Are you in there?"

"Y—yes. I'll be out in a minute," she weakly answers.

The doorknob rattles furiously.

"Open the door now, Felona!"

She unlocks the door and Arcadia shoves her way into the bathroom that is barely the size of a broom closet.

"I said I would be out in a minute! Can't a woman have some privacy?" she whines.

"No, you can't today. It's my job to know where you are at all times so that things run smoothly. Now let's get –"

Arcadia gasps.

"My word! You look as pale as your dress."

"I'm just a little nauseous. Give me a minute. It'll pass."

Arcadia crouches down and looks at her with a concerned scowl as Felona leans her weight against the wall in front of the toilet.

"You don't look so good. Can I get you some water?"

The door thrusts open and thumps Arcadia in the back.

"Oh my Jesus!" she yelps.

"Knock knock. Felona? Are you in here?" Ny asks, peeking in.

"Can I get some privacy, please," Felona wails just before spitting in the toilet.

"Are you okay? What's wrong, love?"

Ny nudges past Arcadia.

"I just feel nauseous and I'm waiting for it to pass."

"Is she pregnant?" Arcadia asks Ny.

"No," Ny turns and barks. "Why would you ask that?"

She turns and leans in to Felona, whispering, "You're not pregnant are you?"

"No, ladies. I'm not pregnant!"

"Oh, honey, that's good news. Because you can catch a lot of stuff out there, but babies are the worst kind of STD."

"Arcadia?" Ny says calmly.

"Yes, darling?"

"Please get out."

Ny gently shoves her into the hallway.

"You have five minutes!" she shouts as Ny slams and locks the door.

"Okay, sweetie. What's really going on? What do you need me to do?"

"I–I don't think I can go through with this. You know how you asked me if Vin loves me?"

"Yeah?"

"Well, I know he does. But not like I want him to. Not like I need him to."

Felona straightens her back against the wall and points to her wedding dress.

"This is important to him. The church, the elaborate décor, and the guests... I didn't know half of the people at the rehearsal dinner last night... this is all his world. You and the girls are the only hint of me in this. Everything else is him. This is his day. Not our day."

"Have you talked to Vin about your feelings?"

Felona shakes her head.

"I tried. Several times. I've known for some time that Vin loves me for what I can become, not for who I am. I'm another symbol of accomplishment for him. He loves me as someone who can make him look a certain way. For a while, him simply loving me at all felt like acceptance. But that's not good enough. He's okay with me not having family because it doesn't compete with him. He's never questioned much about my relationship with my mother or my past. He doesn't care. I thought that was a good thing for a while. I didn't want him to know where I came from. I wanted to forget. But my past is a part of me. And this stuff that I've been going through lately... I should be able to talk to him about that, but he's emotionally removed."

"You're right. You have to know that he loves you... unconditionally. If you don't feel certain about that –"

"I'm certain of one thing. One day, Vin will become bored with me and I'll just be another expensive purchase that he'll pawn off for something younger, fitter and more beautiful. I've been 'not good enough' my whole life. It took me putting on this dress to realize and declare that I'm not playing that role anymore."

Ny's eyes dart back and forth across Felona's pale face.

"Ny... my mother," Felona's voice trembles. "I've done something... something –"

"Don't do this, Felo," Ny interrupts.

"W–what?"

"You will only be more miserable if you go through with this. You don't have to do this… now. Or at all."

Felona scoffs.

"I'm wearing a wedding dress, Ny. I'm minutes away from matrimony. And Vin will hate me if –"

"If Vin loves you, he can never hate you. He'll be pissed off, he'll be angry, he'll be embarrassed… and then he'll eventually understand."

Felona shifts her weight and folds her arms across her chest.

"I just want to be happy. I just want to be loved."

"I love you," Ny reminds her.

"I know, but… you know what I mean."

"I do. And I wasn't saying that as a substitute or to be insensitive to what you're going through. I say it as a reminder that you're not alone. So what do you want me to do?"

Felona searches her face.

"I've done something and I need to go try to fix it. Now."

Ny frowns, confused, but she resolves to be supportive and ask questions another time. She nods her head.

"You should go then." She points at Felona's dress. "This isn't you today. You have other things that need to take place before this happens."

"Really? I'm leaving Vin at the altar. He'll be embarrassed. The media and my peers are here. I'm sure that even my own network will have a ratings field day with labeling one of their own as the runaway bride."

"So. That's not your problem right now. Your concern is to finally put things in the proper order… no matter how last minute it is. What's most important is most important."

"This is what every girl dreams about and I'm throwing it away."

"Felo, I don't think this is what you dream about, sweetie. Stop trying to fit in when you were made to stand out. Be who you are without apology. If it's meant to be, you'll get married to the right guy… some day… but I don't think today is your day, love."

Felona nods her head gently.

Ny studies her for a few moments, clasping Felona's hands tightly.

"How're you feeling?"

"My head hurts and I'm still a little nauseous. I'll live."

"It's all nerves. You'll be okay."

"Thank you. I love you."

"I know, sweetie. Now, go," she says, nudging her toward the door. "I got your back. Always."

Felona reaches to open the door, but hesitates and turns to Ny.

"I need my handbag. Can you get it for me?"

"I'll meet you in the back lot in two minutes. I'll run interference. Now hurry. Run."

46

Run

Adrenaline and panic radiate through Felona. There may still be time to get to Nathaniel before her few good memories are reduced to ash and regret alongside the bad ones. There may still be time to save her mother from the horrible act and inevitable consequence that she initiated.

At the first stoplight that she arrives down the street from the church, she fumbles through her handbag for the disposable cell phone that Zoe gave her.

She flips open the lightweight, plastic phone to see one number programmed in. She calls it.

The phone rings several times until she's convinced that no one will answer.

But then someone does.

"Who this?" a woman's voice flatly asks.

"Hello? Zoe?"

"Yeah? This you, Fiona?"

"Felona."

"Yeah, whatever."

"I was calling to see if you already did the... the thing?"

"We already –"

The line goes dead.

"No no no. No!"

The light turns green and Felona resumes her hasty retreat to the highway.

She looks down at the phone to see if there are any minutes left on it before she redials.

"Pick up pick up pick up!" she says excitedly.

The phone rings incessantly, but this time when a connection is made, the return is a busy signal.

"Fuck!" she screams, looking at the screen on the phone as she begins to drift into another lane.

Before she realizes that she's straddling two lanes, a car coming from behind her barely avoids colliding with her. The driver blasts his horn, startling Felona.

She jerks her steering wheel to the right as the vehicle whizzes past, still blaring its horn.

She exhales sharply.

She blindly fumbles through her handbag for her own phone, keeping her eye on the road this time.

She dials the number and it rings.

"Come on. Pick up, Zoe," she shouts, beating on the steering wheel.

But the incessant ringing finally culminates with a busy signal again.

What did she say before we lost the connection? We already? We already what? Have they already set fire to the house? Was my mother there, weakened by smoke inhalation so much that she couldn't escape the flames?

I feel powerless not knowing what's happened and not being able to prevent the inevitable. I feel like I'm stuck between before and after.

47

Burn

Today was supposed to be one of the happiest days of Felona's life, but all she's experienced is disaster in her wake. And she only has herself to blame.

When she finally turns onto her mother's street, she sees no billowing smoke on the horizon. As she gets closer to the end of the street where her house is, she sees no commotion of the emergency vehicles camped about. When she whips her car into her mother's driveway, she finds that the house and the memories within are still intact.

She smiles, relieved. And in that instance, she feels as if this day has suddenly taken a turn for the better.

Unlike the last time she was parked in the driveway, she doesn't linger nor procrastinate. She's ready to be wed to the life that hope promised long ago. She springs out of the car with the excitement of true reconciliation.

She imagines that her mother will initially be startled when she sees her at the front door in her wedding dress, standing on her porch. But few words will have to be exchanged for her to realize that all is forgiven.

She rings the doorbell and waits a few moments.

She doesn't hear any rustling or voices so she knocks on the door.

Still her mother doesn't come to the door.

Then it dawns on Felona that her mother has always kept a spare key hidden in the garden. She hurriedly combs her fingers through the dirt in the flowerbed in search of it.

As she's bent over, she chuckles.

I wonder what a passerby might think at the sight of a woman gardening with a wedding dress on.

She eventually finds the key in a hollowed out rock in front of a row of marigolds.

"Mom?" Felona calls as she walks inside. SoJo greets her ankles with purring.

Felona continues to call for her mother as she walks through the house. After checking the bedroom, bathroom and kitchen, it dawns on her to check the garage for her car. It's gone. She's not there.

She walks back inside and to her mother's room. Her bed is made up and the room smells of freshly sprayed perfume.

She didn't just go to the grocery store, Felona deduces. *She got dolled up and went somewhere special.*

Felona walks back into the hallway and runs her fingers along the wall leading to her room. The door is closed. She grasps the doorknob, but learned fear gives her pause. So many bad memories were born here. She's afraid what truths the other side will reveal or remind her of.

So many memories.

She twists the knob and pushes the door open.

Hues of pink pour into the hallway.

Walking into her old bedroom is like stepping back into the eighties. Everything is just as she remembered – the big window with the pink sheer curtains; the white lacquer bed with purple polka dots all over; the oversized stuffed elephant that she named FeFe; the glow-in-the-dark constellation stickers on the ceiling; the giant dollhouse in the corner.

She kneels down beside the dollhouse and runs her fingers over the aged wood. She composed so many scenes of the perfect family with her dolls, hoping that she would one day have that same life where she and her mother were best friends and traveled the globe solving mysteries.

SoJo nudges her head against Felona, purring and she suddenly remembers BookerT, her cat from long ago and how he did the same thing when she would sit on the floor and play with her dollhouse.

So many memories. Some of them are good ones.

Felona looks across the room and something snares her glance that causes her to gasp.

The door has swung closed and on the back of it is a collage of cards that she made for her mother over the years. Birthday, Mother's Day, Christmas, Thanksgiving and even Halloween.

"How long have these been here?" she mutters with astonishment.

Look at my tiny hand outline that made a turkey. And this birthday card where my mom has on a cape and is flying with Wonder Woman and Super Girl. She saved all of these?

And there's more of them? They're all tacked, one on top of another. Some of these I don't even remember, but there's my distinctive, little signature right there... on all of these.

Felona feels her cheeks tautly smiling as she flips through to new discoveries or histories that she vaguely remembers.

And then, as if the emotional trip down memory lane isn't enough, she happens upon a felt bouquet of yellow, pink and white flowers with green stems and leaves – the same bouquet that she gave to her mother for Mother's Day – the day that she first got her period.

"I thought she threw this away. I didn't even know she saw it."

Felona smiles.

"She was so angry with me that day."

And underneath the flattened bouquet is the card that she gave with it. It's torn on the bottom right and around the edges.

Happy Mother's Day to the best mom ever.

Felona's eyes sting as tears rush forth. She sniffles and clears her face, but more tears take their place.

Then, a loud pop startles her followed immediately by a resounding thump that vibrates the books and trinkets on the bookshelf. SoJo darts out of the room.

"What was that?"

Felona looks around and realizes that smoke is spilling from the vents in the ceiling. She swings the door open and the hallway is black with smoke that parts just enough to reveal long flickers of flames.

"Oh my god! I can't see – where did SoJo go? Oh my god. I gotta call 911!"

Felona pats herself where her front and back pockets would be, forgetting in the moment that she's wearing a wedding dress.

"I left my phone in the car! Fuck!"

She slams the door and immediately goes to the window, but when she flings the curtains back, security bars discourage her hopes of exiting that way.

"Bars? When did these happen? Shit!"

After futilely trying to pull the bars loose, she turns her attention to the smoke detector that never went off and recalls how her mother disconnected all of them long ago so they wouldn't go off whenever she would have her rituals of burning scraps of paper in the bathroom sink.

"Wait. The bathroom! It's right across the hallway. If I can dart across into the bathroom, I can soak some towels and –"

She reaches to open the door, but now the doorknob is hot to the touch and smoke is wafting in under the door.

"Dammit!"

She snatches the blanket from the bed and tucks it in the crevice to prevent more smoke from seeping into the room.

Needles of heat tingle down her leg and Felona violently flinches, thinking that she's on fire, but she isn't. The hot sensation is urine trickling down her leg.

She hears what sounds like another muffled explosion on the other side of the door.

"This is my fault. I deserve this," she whimpers.

She retreats into the farthest corner where the dollhouse is and crouches on the floor away from the smoke holding a sheet over her mouth and nose.

Another loud crack and the ceiling above her opens. She rolls out of the way just as burning timbers fall where she was crouched.

The hem of her dress is ignited by a spark from stray embers and begins to burn. The flames quickly overtake the lace as if they were doused in gasoline, but she beats the flames out with the sheet, creating more smoke. Her eyes sting with tears.

She rocks back and forth, crying.

"Somebody help!" she shrieks. And coughs.

As she cowers on the floor as low as she can, away from the smoke and flames, embers and falling debris rain from the gutted ceiling as the room collapses piece by piece.

Hot needles burn her skin and ignite her dress in random places and all she can do is pat the flames out as soon as they appear.

"I can't smell the flowers in my mother's garden anymore –"

A jolt of electricity sears through the top of her head and she grasps it in response to the excruciating pain.

"My hair!" she screams, covering her burning hair with the smoldering, tattered sheet.

"H–help!" she gasps quietly, until she can't breathe or talk anymore.

She falls forward, face down, curled in a fetal position, tightly closing her eyes waiting for the burning, stinging, loud noise and her breathing to stop.

A vibrating thud, the tinkling of glass and a rush of air stirs Felona from darkness.

She struggles to open her eyes, but everything is blurry.

"I'm… I'm too weak… to fight… my skin feels like it's on fire."

"Felona? Felona? Felona!" a faint voice calls repeatedly.

And then she hears a loud commotion.

"Felona!" the voice shouts again, closer. "Felona, I got you! Don't worry. I got you! It's gonna be okay. Just stay with me. I'm gonna get you out of here."

Something covers her nose and mouth while gentle hands cradle the back of her head.

"Breathe in. Come on. Breathe deep."

She coughs from the cold air that fills her lungs.

"Yeah, that's it. Good. Good. Breathe."

A heavy, icy weight covers her and she feels herself become weightless as someone lifts her.

Her eyes flutter open for a moment, but darkness greets her again.

"Felona?" the voice beckons her again.

She opens her eyes and bright, blinding light floods in. She blinks tears away until she can barely make out the blurred edges of trees, clouds, sky, black smoke and…

"Tob–Tobias?" she wheezes.

A cool tear rolls down the side of her face as he cradles

her in his arms, rocking her back and forth.

"Shhh. Don't try to talk, Curlytop. Help is on the way."

Sirens sing in the background, getting closer and louder.

And Felona's ears start ringing in chorus with the sirens just before everything fades.

48

Reporting Live

Hours later, 1865 Barbaro Way is no more than billowing, dark smoke and rubble as fire investigators move in to sift through the charred remains for clues as to what prompted the fire.

Danielle Dashley returns to the WADM news van that is situated a safe distance from the smoldering remains.

"What'd he say?" the cameraman asks her as he lifts the camera on his shoulder.

"The fire chief won't go on camera to comment until they have more details so we're just going to roll with what we have right now. We can't wait for these slack-jawed yokels anymore."

She adjusts her appearance and establishes where she wants to stand to capture both the post-fire activity and good lighting. Her cameraman sets up a large spotlight that will bring greater focus to her and cast out any blemishes.

"Are we ready?" he asks.

She fixes her earpiece to hear her cues from the station and nods.

"This is Danielle Dashley for WADM reporting live in Nathaniel on Barbaro Way where Felona Mabel, one of our very own, was seriously injured in a fire that broke out in her childhood home."

"When firefighters first arrived on the scene, the house was already consumed in flames. Additional agencies were called in to assist in containing the fire to ensure that embers did not extend damage to neighboring homes and property."

"Chief Howell has declined comment while fire investigators are searching through rubble to ensure that there are no victims in the debris and for the cause of the fire."

"We don't yet have details on Felona Mabel's condition other than that she is in critical condition at Mercy General Hospital in Admah City. We will keep you informed on her status as this story develops. This is Danielle Dashley for WADM reporting live in Nathaniel. Back to you, Ross."

Danielle waits a few seconds before dropping her microphone to her side after her cameraman lowers the camera from his shoulder.

"You alright?" he asks her.

Visibly shaken, Danielle shakes her head.

"No."

"Every act of creation is first an act of destruction."
— Pablo Picasso

49
Act of Creation

Light flutters in and the outline of the figure of an angel hovers over Felona. As the figure comes into soft focus, she can see that the heavenly apparition is wearing a tunic of white and her skin is like black porcelain. Her crown is made of leaves and large brown curls. She smiles at her with dimples etched deeply on either side of her cheeks.

"Are... are you an angel?" Felona slurs.

"No, Ms. Mabel. I'm not an angel and you are very much alive. My name is Sydney and you're in the hospital. We've given you a little something to make sure that you're as comfortable as possible so you may feel a little floaty."

"The... the hospital? What happened? Where –?"

"There was a fire and you were burned, but you're going to be okay."

Felona tries to raise her head to sit up, but nothing happens. She can't move.

"No no, Felona. Don't try to move. I need you to lie still and relax. You're in Admah City and your family is here. They'll be able to see you shortly."

"My family? Who?"

"Try to lay still and quiet, darling. The doctor is on the way."

"Ny?"

Muffled conversation and a commotion of beeps awaken Felona.

But her eyes are closed.

Or, perhaps, she's dreaming.

Where am I? I can't see. I can't move. Am I paralyzed? My head hurts. I can't remember... anything. And I'm floating. Like a bird. With a migraine.

Yet no one answers or responds to her voice.

No one hears her.

She is dreaming.

The voices and beeping continue, ebbing in and out of focus.

I hurt. I just want to go back to sleep.

"Can you feel this, Ms. Mabel?"

Felona opens her eyes, still groggy.

"Ughh! Oushhh. Y–yessss... sssstop that... now."

"Good. Very good," says a small man with an emotionless expression and a head full of dark hair. "Your feeling is coming back nicely. How're you feeling?"

"I feel like... like I have a mouth... a mouth full of cotton and head full of horses. Who are you? What are you doing to me?"

"Ms. Mabel, I'm Dr. William Godin and I'm the head of surgery here at Mercy General Hospital in Admah City."

"Hospital? I thought I dreamed that."

"You were airlifted here three days ago after suffering third-degree burns to your right leg, second-degree burns to your hands and arms and a concussion."

Burns? The house! The house burned. Where is my —?

Felona struggles to sit up, but instantly realizes that moving is painful.

"Owww."

"Ms. Mabel, calm down. You can't move around just yet. I'm certain you're in a lot of pain. We had to perform a skin graft on your leg, borrowing tissue from your left thigh to restore some of the tissue damage. The good news is that there was no damage to the muscle, tendons or bones. You, also, suffered some hair loss and first-degree burns to your head. Your hair follicles were not damaged though, so your hair should grow back at its normal rate."

"Three days? I–I've been here three days?"

"Yes. You've been in and out of consciousness because we had to sedate you until the swelling on your brain went down. You endured a severe concussion. But you're out of the woods now and, based upon your head injury, you're very fortunate that you didn't suffer any fractures or neck damage."

"I don't feel very fortunate in the moment. I hurt all over."

She lifts her arm and sees that it's covered in gauze with an IV tube leading from it. A concerned look of fear washes over her face and she looks up at Dr. Godin.

"Have you talked to Dr. Odoyo or my mom?"

"I'm right here, Lona," a distant voice says.

Felona's eyes widen and again she scrambles to sit up.

"Careful now, Ms. Mabel!" Dr Godin interrupts. "You don't want to disturb your stitches. Let me adjust the bed."

As the motor whirs on the bed, Felona sees her mother rising from a nearby chair.

"Mom!" she says, reaching for her like infants reach for their mother to pick them up.

"I'm here, Lona."

Dianne steps closer and leans over to kiss her daughter's forehead, while gently hugging her.

She sits on the edge of the bed.

"I'll leave you two," Dr. Godin says. "Mom, don't get her too excited. She needs her rest."

"Thank you, doctor," Dianne says as he leaves.

Felona stares at her mother who takes hold of one of her gauzed hands.

"You're here," she says, smiling.

"Of course I am. Why wouldn't I be?"

"I mean, you're not gone. You're here."

Dianne's forehead furrows as she tries to understand.

"I went to see you. But you weren't there."

"I was at your wedding. I know I wasn't invited, but I wanted you to know that I meant what I said over the phone.

I'm sorry for all the wasted years and for how I treated you. I want my daughter back and I'm willing to do whatever it takes to have her."

Felona faintly smiles.

"You know how you said that we're the same? We are. While you were rushing to see me, I was rushing to see you. And I almost lost you."

"I almost lost you. That fire was horrible. It's a miracle you made it out alive."

She gently touches Felona's cheek and continues, "But Tobias was your guardian angel."

"He always has been."

Felona smiles, but it fades as quickly as it appears and she looks away.

"He said he looked for SoJo, but couldn't find her," Dianne's voice trembles.

"I'm sorry, mom. She'll turn up... I'm sure. You know how cats are."

Dianne nods and continues to stroke her hand.

"The fire... does anyone know what happened?" Felona asks.

"They said that they're still investigating what exactly happened. They said it might have been electrical."

"I had no idea. I was there and then all of a sudden, there was fire everywhere."

"I'm so sorry, baby. That house has been falling apart for a while now and I just haven't... I'm sorry."

Tears stream down Dianne's cheek at the moment that

she reaches to hug Felona again.

A long moment passes and she pulls back to wipe her face. She then notices that Felona is crying too. She wipes her face as well.

"You get some rest," she whispers. "I'll be right here."

Medication conceals the true nature of pain and passage of time for Felona as she succumbs to the routine and confinement of a hospital bed.

Yet the lapse of seven days concedes to a truer reality.

"It feels as if a million tiny needles are stabbing me in the thighs. And my head is about to explode," she moans to the nurse who is wheeling her back to her room after her initial physical therapy consultation.

"We'll get you some relief for that," the nurse says to Felona whose eyes are shut tightly as she winces from the pain. "But considering that your surgery was a week ago, you did amazingly well."

The wheelchair comes to a stop.

The nurse then says with distinction, "Good afternoon, Dr. Odoyo."

Felona opens her eyes and towering before them is Mosi, Ny's husband. He's a dark, broad man with a stern glare that is easily softened by his smile. He's dressed in light blue scrubs and a white lab coat.

"Good afternoon, Anne," he nods to the nurse with

a thick accent and booming voice.

He then turns his attention to Felona.

"What are you doing sitting in that chair, young lady? Get up from there and stop lazing around."

"If I could stand and run out of this place, I would. You have no idea how much I hurt right now."

He leans down and swallows her in a hug, pecking her on the cheek.

"We'll take care of you. Your sister is in your room waiting for you. She'll help you get comfortable."

She faintly smiles, past her pain.

"I got her. Thank you," Mosi says to the nurse as he assumes the duty of wheeling her back to her room.

Mosi turns his attention back to Felona.

"Kinaya and I just got here a few minutes ago. I was just stopping by to see you before I head to surgery."

Ny's smiling face greets them as soon as they open the door into Felona's room.

Felona excitedly attempts to get up to greet Ny, forgetting for a split second that it's poor judgment to stand on her own, but the stabbing pain reminds her as she falls back into the wheelchair.

"Oh, sweetie, be careful!"

Ny kisses Felona on the bandaged head and gently rubs her back, while helping her into the bed.

"Your mom was just here," she says. "She must've just missed you in the elevator. She was going to try to meet you on your way back from PT. How was it?"

"Excruciating. Painful. Embarrassing. And those are the good points."

"I'm sorry, sweetie. Let me get some pain meds in you now."

Felona collapses on her pillow.

"I'm so ready for this painful stage to pass," she exhales.

With the advent of scar tissue, the influence and intensity of physical pain decreases, but the mind never forgets the ache that has given it new nightmares to ponder.

With Ny's help, Felona returns to her bed from the bathroom. She looks down at her bandaged hands and realizes that her engagement ring has been removed.

A melancholy swells within her.

"Has Vin been by?" she asks.

Ny studies Felona for the intent of her question before shaking her head.

"No. Well, he did stop by when you first got here, but he didn't stay long. He was initially worried about what had happened to you. And then he had a lot of questions as to why you were in Nathaniel and not at your own wedding."

"Oh... yeah," Felona replies, disappointed.

"Sweetie, he's hurt. You left him standing at the altar. He's embarrassed. You know Vin. He's all about appearances. Give him some space and some time. Like I said before, if he truly loves you, you both will work this out. If he doesn't..."

well... fuck him."

They laugh.

Ny instinctively checks the integrity of Felona's bandages for bleeding before she begins to reconnect the vital signs monitors back to her.

"You should be feeling the pain subside a little bit about ten minutes after I hook you back up."

Ny pauses for a moment and sits on the edge of the bed, looking at Felona with a concerned expression.

"Felona?"

"Yeah, Ny?"

"Before the fire, you said that you had done something terrible and needed to go fix it. Did you have anything to do with what happened?"

Felona sobers at the question, but a knock at the door interrupts.

Ny says, "Come in," but the door has already begun to open and a man wearing dark slacks and a pressed, white shirt enters. An official-looking badge hangs from his neck on a lanyard. He's a clean-cut, middle-aged man with white hair and worry lines.

"Good afternoon, ladies. Are you Felona Mabel?" he asks as he approaches.

"I am."

He presents his badge.

"Ma'am, I'm Lieutenant James Cronin with the Nathaniel Fire Department and I'm conducting the investigation on the fire that you were injured in at 1728 Cardinal Lane.

Are you lucid enough to make a statement or answer a few questions?"

"I guess so. I don't remember a whole lot though."

"She suffered a concussion," Ny speaks up defensively, extending her hand to the investigator. "I'm Dr. Odoyo and I'll allow you the opportunity to ask her a few questions as long as they aren't too upsetting. She did almost lose her life where her childhood home was completely destroyed."

Felona looks at Ny and smirks at her assertiveness despite the fact that she's not her doctor.

"I understand and I'll try to be sensitive to that, Doctor."

Lt. Cronin turns his attention to Felona and looks at her with intensity.

"Ms. Mabel, I've already gotten a statement from your mother who said that she wasn't home when the fire started. She said that she was en route to attend your wedding here in Admah City. But when emergency services found you, they said you were wearing a wedding dress and –"

"Let me stop you right there, Lieutenant. You're to ask simple questions only. This exploration route that you're on will stop now. My patient is glad to help you with your investigation and be cooperative, but she's not going to help you solve it. Again, please be brief and more sensitive in your questioning," she says with a smile. "Or leave."

He nods apologetically, "I'm sorry. Let me try a different approach."

He pauses and reaches in his pocket for a small notebook that he flips through before directing his attention back to Felona.

"Ms. Mabel, do you know a... let's see here... Zoe Cooper?"

50
Where You Belong

Felona's heart thumps.

If Ny had already reconnected her to the monitors, the machines would betray her with excited beeps and elevated LED readings.

"No. I–I don't know that name. Why?"

"She was in the area around the time that the fire was initially reported," Lt. Cronin responds.

Felona looks at Ny and back at him.

"What does that have to do with me?"

"The officer that cited her for speeding noted that she had materials in plain sight in her vehicle that might have been consistent with arson."

"Are you saying that she set the fire?"

"No. Not that one. We didn't find any of those materials consistent with the fire at your mother's house. In your mother's case, it appears that old wiring set off an explosion in the attic and the aged insulation acted as an accelerant, which is why it spread so fast. At first, we were suspicious of the disconnected smoke alarms that we found, but your mother has already cleared that up."

Felona's pulse sighs back to normal just as Ny is restoring the blood pressure cuffs to her arms and fingers.

She frowns, "So, I still don't understand then why you're asking me about this other person."

"Ms. Cooper is now a suspect in two previous fires that were deemed as arson. Like I said, the fire at your mother's house is inconsistent with her involvement, but if you know her personally, you might be able to assist us with our investigation."

"So this isn't the investigation that involves the fire at my mother's?"

He furrows his brow and shakes his head.

"No ma'am. This is a separate investigation."

Felona looks at Ny again, shrugging.

"I'm going to have to ask you to leave now, Lt. Cronin," Ny finally says. "She's already answered your questions. If you would like her to make an official statement, she can do so after she has been released and is capable without the influence of pain medication."

Felona's mind darts from possibility to possibility.

Was the fire truly accidental? Did Zoe have nothing to do with it? Or is she just that good? If so, why would she allow herself to be caught?

"Are you okay, sweetie?" Ny asks, returning from ushering Lt. Cronin into the hall.

"Oh. No, I'm fine. I'm just… feeling a little… exhausted."

She sinks into her pillow, exhaling.

The toilet in the temporary holding cell at Nathaniel Detention Center sings and Zoe Cooper can't sleep.

She isn't alone with her thoughts though. Three other women are crowded into the space of a 10x16 concrete room with a view of a dim hallway through iron bars.

One of them is passed out on a temporary cot while the other two argue back and forth about sharing their last cigarette.

Zoe has isolated herself on a bench in a corner near a puddle of vomit on the floor.

She's been in and out of institutions most of her life, and it seems that she finds more solace confined inside concrete walls than with the bondage that freedom offers her.

Her thoughts drift and float like dandelion seeds through the dank halls of hopelessness. Among those thoughts, she imagines her son. Three years ago, she gave birth and had to surrender him to the state because she was deemed unfit as a parent.

Guilt isn't a luxury that she's been able to afford during her short stints of freedom, yet now she mulls over how she has repeated the cycle. Her own mother lost her when she was only four.

Unlike her mother who was an addict, Zoe's latest compulsion to make money was for nobler means as she has been trying to earn enough money to pay a private investigator to locate the foster family that has her son.

Once he finds them and ascertains that her son is in a suitable place, she would anonymously funnel money to the family to assist in her son's future, albeit, from afar.

"I guess I won't be able to call you Curlytop for a while now," Tobias says as he sits near Felona, smiling at her.

"Tobias Coles, if the word 'bald' comes out of your mouth in any way referring to me, I will miraculously heal just long enough to get up and pound you senseless," Felona returns, mildly sedated.

"I'm so very scared," he mocks. "Besides, being bald isn't too bad. I think it brings out your other lovely features like your freckles. And you know what they say. A girl without freckles is like a night without stars."

She smiles, weakly.

"I bet you say that to all the girls."

"Only the ones without freckles."

"Cute. And lame at the same time."

Her smile fades into a serious expression.

"What is it?" he leans in. "You need something? You okay?"

She shakes her head.

"I'm good, thank you," she slurs. "I was just thinking that I didn't thank you."

"Actually, you have. Several hundred times in drug-induced hilarity at times."

"Well, I don't think I've ever thanked you for saving me

from myself."

Tobias returns a perplexed expression. Felona has already begun to fade.

He takes her hand, smiling as she drifts off to sleep.

"How is she?" a voice from behind Tobias timidly asks.

He turns and answers, "She's getting better. Sleeping a lot."

Tobias stands and extends his hand. "And you are?"

"Oh, I'm a friend and we work together. Guy Greatstorm."

"Tobias Coles," he responds, shaking Guy's hand." Nice to meet you. Please, have a seat."

Another day yawns into night and Felona has been left alone for a couple of hours to be allowed time to rest, although her mind is far from inactive.

Images dance on a silenced television in the dim hospital room as she dwells in thoughts of resolution.

I'd been so fixated on adopting a perfect life that I didn't take the time to define what perfect was for me. I don't know every detail of what's perfect, but I know family is a big component of it.

Felona sighs loudly.

I've always envied Ny's relationship with her parents and Mosi and, even though they welcomed me in as one of their own, I still felt like an orphan... longing for my own family.

I haven't seen Brent, my mom's ex-husband, since I was little. I don't think he and mom even talk anymore. And Iris died long before we could ever argue over petty things that sisters do.

All that's left is my mom. Without her, I felt like an orphan and I almost killed her.

 But, ironically, her love for me saved her life. And, deserving or not, I was spared. God gave me a second chance. Again.

She sighs again, scanning the room and the emptiness that still accompanies her.

 I was looking for Vin to save me, but I was right to walk away. I regret that I waited so long to do so. I know I hurt him and knowing him, he won't forgive that for a long time... if ever.

 He didn't love me. Not like I needed – deserved – to be loved. He even struggled to say the words. But he played the role that I wanted to believe in so well. I wanted him to be my prince charming so much that, for a moment, he was. But he isn't the man for me.

 No man can be the man for me until I get myself together. That unfamiliar face that stares back at me from the mirror... I need to learn how to love her. I need to love her whether anyone else does or not.

Felona shifts from her back to her side, struggling to find a more comfortable position. She rolls a pillow under her neck so that her bandaged head isn't aggravated by pressure of lying flat. Now facing the door, she sees light dance from the crack underneath the door. Her focus begins to diminish.

 Sometimes you have to leave where you came from to know where you belong.

As she drifts off into a drug-induced slumber, Felona glimpses her mother and Tobias come through the door together.

51

Other Exiles

A hot, dry autumn wind greets Felona as she steps outside into the airport shuttle area. She runs her hands across the top of her stubbly head, stretching after sitting on a flight for several hours.

She breathes in deeply and exhales. The air is a mixture of car exhaust, cut grass, livestock and perfume.

"Just wait until we get to the hotel," Ny says excitedly as she hugs her from behind. "How're you doing, Ms. Mabel?"

Felona turns to say, "I'm so elated," before realizing that Ny isn't addressing her.

She's talking to Felona's mother, who she insisted experience this trip with them.

"I'm happy to be off that plane!" Dianne answers. "Ooh, child, when we landed I thought we were gonna crash with all that noise and shakin'."

Seven other people flew in with them with the intention of meeting with the rest of Ny's entourage, who came in on a separate flight, in the morning.

Aza, one of the nurses with them, says something in Swahili to a uniformed man. He studies them before smiling widely.

"Karibu! This way. This way," he gestures them to a small bus parked a few yards away.

Another uniformed attendant, who looks young enough to be a teenager, appears from out of nowhere and smiles at them saying, "Karibu. Karibu," before putting their luggage on the bus.

Ny whispers, "Karibu means welcome."

"I've been here fifteen minutes and I'm already in love with Africa," Felona says, beaming.

The scenery changes dramatically as the airport landscape melts in the background. Soon the cluster of hotels and restaurants is replaced with a scattering of smaller buildings, houses, and farmland littered with animals.

As the landscape becomes a more lush, green, rural view, the bus finds smooth travel increasingly difficult as it jerks and bumps over potholes, rocks, and dead animals.

A flock of gazelles whisk away in unison as the vehicle startles them from the roadside.

Excited to share, Felona squeezes her mother's hand to get her attention, but she's fast asleep and snoring.

Upon looking around, Felona sees that Ny and the rest of the group is also quiet and sleeping too. They've done this trip several times before and, perhaps, it's now routine for them.

Felona notices the bus driver stealing glances at her in the rearview mirror. Apparently, he's amused with her childlike wonderment as she presses her face against the window.

Felona is still energized with discovery the following morning, despite very little rest.

Before they head to the village, they eat ugali – which has the consistency and taste of mashed potatoes and glue – and roasted goat meat with tomatoes and spinach.

Previous to the trip, Ny attempted to mentally prepare Felona and her mother for the cultural differences there, but there's nothing equal to experience – especially when it comes to food.

After breakfast, they meet up with the rest of the team and head to the village in several off-road vehicles. Once they get there, several native women and children greet them with smiles and intrigue.

There is an obvious interest in Felona, in particular, as she stands out from the group with her pale skin, freckles, buzz-cut red hair and throat tattoo.

As they walk through the village, the increasing number of children following behind her in curiosity is akin to her being the pied piper leading children out of Hamelin – although this particular scenario is nothing like the sixteenth century tale.

The township consists of houses made of brick and concrete, as opposed to the clichéd straw huts and tents that are popularly depicted in fictional mediums.

There are no sidewalks or paved roadways, while goats and small monkeys wander among the people. In the immediate area, there are a few jeeps and trucks, but most people are walking to wherever they're going.

They make their way to a white building that looks like an abandoned church. Ny leads in introducing all of the newcomers to the women that begin to gather inside. Some of them speak broken English, but most of them rely on translators to communicate for them.

One of the trucks that accompanied Ny's party is filled with medical supplies, dry goods and clothing. Two heavily armed men guard it.

The bounty is an incentive for the women to bring their children to have medical and dental checkups. The adults and children are tested for many diseases and viruses, including HIV and Hepatitis A. Once they receive the proper exams, they're given supplies and goods to take home.

"Their lives are so basic here. They seem happy... thankful... with the little things," Felona whispers to Ny.

"They're exiles. The basics are all they can get most times, if even that. Yet they choose to be happy, despite the circumstances that put them here. I love this energy. Do you see why I keep coming back?"

Felona nods enthusiastically.

"Josie," Ny calls to one of the younger women, tending to the stray children.

She runs over and some of the children follow her like little ducks. She appears as young as a teenager.

"Josie, tell Felona how you came to be here."

Josie looks at her sadly before saying in carefully practiced English, "Last year, uncle find that I was pregnant and he told me that I could not live in his house anymore."

She pauses and looks away, embarrassed.

"He ask me who father was and I told him I not know. Many men from the militia raped me on the way to school one day. He told me that I carry the child of the enemy and the only way I would be welcome in his house was if I got rid of baby. I could do no such thing. I had nowhere to go. When I collapsed in the wilderness with child, ready to give birth, one of the women from here found me and brought me here. My baby is over there."

She points to an older lady sitting with one of the doctors holding a six-month old baby.

"Josie is very educated and wants to be a doctor someday," Ny proudly says.

"Wow. And you will one day be a great doctor," Felona says to Josie, hugging her.

"Everyone will gather in a couple of hours to hear your story, Felo," Ny says. "No pressure though."

She walks away, giggling.

The temperature begins to fall as evening approaches and all still in attendance begin to gather outside in the center of the village around a bonfire.

Women, young and old, share their various stories with the common thread being that they now live in poverty and fear after being ostracized by their own families because of the stigmas attached to rape and bearing the evidence of it.

One of the younger voices shares, "Ever since I was little girl, all I know is war in our region. Men have fought so long, I do not know what they fight for. And women do not matter to men. We no different than coins or livestock or land to be taken and burned. Men armed with machetes find us hiding in the places that our husbands and fathers instruct us to run to when fires start. They tell us that they will kill us, but they will rape us first. Many women are killed, but some are not."

An older woman joins in with, "It would be better that they kill us than what they infect us with. We have been exiled because of fears of HIV. We are shunned because many of the rapes are so violent, we can no longer control our bodily functions."

This congregation of consequential sisters nods their head or mumbles agreements in support of whoever is speaking. And it continues, from one heartbreaking testimony, told with transparent candor, to the next.

The testimonies are soon replaced by questions directed at the medical professionals and volunteers in attendance.

"Are there women in America like us?" "Why do you come and help us?" "Can your government stop these bad men from returning?"

Ny and her colleagues take turns answering the questions, but then a timid woman, who looks to be barely beyond her teens, raises her hand. All attention turns to her as she hesitantly stutters to speak, cradling a one-year old.

She directs her question to Dianne as the translator trails, "Can you tell me how to love my son more? I want to love him and I try my best, but when I look at him I remember what happened to me and it's hard."

Tears flow down her face as she looks at her son who is sleeping.

Her timid question becomes a fierce challenge as she asks, "Can you help me love my son?"

A few other women follow with their own confessions of an inability to feel any degree of affection for the children that they carry and deliver because they're reminders of the atrocities they've endured. They struggle to accept the children as their own.

Others say that the children they bear are a source of hope that has instilled within them the will to survive and forge forward.

Felona rocks back and forth in her seat, thankful for the many tragedies that have led her to this place. She has spent a number of years feeling like a leftover, like these women are expressing.

She has felt abandoned and exiled for a long time and, despite the evil that has spawned the atrocities she's hearing, she's reminded that she's not alone.

There are other exiles, just like her.

52
Nimefurahi

Felona's voice quivers as she nervously stands. "I never thought that I would hear or experience such profound strength that was born of the effects of malice, hate and evil. But... all... all of you are... I am overwhelmed with how extraordinary all of you are."

She looks around slowly, scanning the faces of almost two hundred and twenty faces that are present.

"My name is Felona Mabel. I am a product of rape. I, too, was born of the consequence of malice and evil. The man who raped my mom didn't know her. He was just a hateful man who did hateful things. At the time, my mom was married to a man who loved her. They even had a child together. When she chose to give birth to me, it was an amazing testimony of how strong of a woman she really was. Every one of you reminds me of her in some way. She put all of her security at risk to bring me into the world."

Felona briefly looks over to her mom who is wiping back tears as Ny rubs her back.

She returns to the crowd listening to the echo of her words leaving a translator's lips in a language that the non-English-speaking audience can understand.

"Her life was very difficult following my birth. As if dealing with shame and doubt wasn't enough, my big sister was killed in an accident. And shortly after that, my mom's husband left her. I thought for a long time that my mom possessed an inability to love or feel affection for me because she always seemed so angry with me... and so sad."

"But I learned more recently, that she was more like me than I knew. She was hurting because she felt like she was unlovable. She felt like she wasn't good enough. She felt unacceptable."

Felona pauses again and walks through the crowd of women and children, touching each of them as she passes. Once the translators finish, she continues louder with more confidence.

"But she is acceptable and lovable and good enough! As all of you are! Despite your broken hearts and scarred, battered bodies, you have proven through your acts of love and sacrifice for one another that you are strong and good women who instill hope in your children no matter how those children were conceived. You give me courage and confidence that I, as a woman, can do anything. I live in a man's world, but every man is born of us. Every man draws life from our womb. Some of them may regard us as less than starving cattle, but they would be no more than semen on the ground if we were so insignificant."

"Let me tell you about strength. My mom's house burned down over four months ago and I was hurt badly in the fire.

She took a leave of absence from her job and moved to the city, where I live, to care for me until I was better. Just as if I were a little girl again, she took care of me – despite the fact that I had thought, did and said so many hurtful things to her. Now that's strength through love. And that's what I see here."

"There is this old saying about strength and struggle that I'll never forget," her voice trembles. "We're not strong because we struggle, we struggle because we're strong."

She stops where her mother is seated.

"Now, we're not strong alone. We need each other. We need outside help. My mom and I are strong, yes, but we can also be stubborn. Just like you submit to the doctors here to help you, we submit to a doctor, too. He's a therapist and he's going to help my mom and I work through our pain. He's going to help us love each other more."

Dianne stands and hugs Felona tightly before turning to the crowd and saying, "I talked to a few of you and it has blessed me to meet you and hear your amazin' testimonies. Even though I live far from here in another country, we share similar experiences. We can't do this without help. We need each other. Don't go away from here thinkin' you can make it on your own strength. Don't think that you can't love yourself or your children. I'm proud of my daughter. It don't matter how she got here, I love her. Once upon a time, I couldn't admit that and I lost her… almost for good. But God brought us back together and gave us a second chance."

She pauses, choking back tears before continuing, "We go to counselin' to talk to a therapist and that helps a lot. Because, accordin' to him, there's some stuff that we have to unlearn. There's some stuff that we can't just know how to do on our own. We need help."

Dianne pauses and shakes her head, closing her eyes.

Encouraging chants spill from the audience of women, many of whom are wiping tears from their own faces.

Dianne continues, "We all need each other. Let me tell you a funny story before I start cryin' again. I always loved having animals around when Lona was growin' up."

She places her hand on Felona's shoulder.

"Now I love my history. My daddy taught me to love where I came from so I always named my pets after African–American revolutionaries. Well, when my house burned down, I lost my pet cat, SoJo. She ran away and we never found her. Last month, I come home – I call Lona's place home now – I come home and she leaves this big box with a bow and a card addressed to me on the counter. I already know what's in it because it's makin' a ruckus and meowin' like crazy to get out so I open the box and this little black kitten sticks her head up."

Dianne pauses for the translator to catch up.

A few staggered moments later, laughter breaks out.

"Around her neck is a card that reads, 'My name is Harriet Tubman. Thank you for setting me free.'"

Some of the women in the crowd understand the story while others mumble amongst each other wondering of the significance of the name, Harriet Tubman, to the story.

One woman in the audience asks a question in her native tongue while one of the translators articulates to Felona, "She wants to know if other relationships are hard for you. With men."

Felona chuckles and a few people in the audience laugh as well.

"Romantic relationships have been very hard for me most of my life. How can you expect someone to love you if you don't know how to love yourself? When I was in my twenties, I was promiscuous. That is, I had sex with many different men that I wasn't in a relationship with. I was looking for acceptance yet none of those encounters gave me what I was looking for. I left each one feeling less than before."

"But there is one man who I've known since we were children... he has demonstrated to me what love looks like. He has been consistently loving me even when I didn't love him back. He taught me unconditional love. And lately, I refer to him as my hero."

Felona cranes her neck, looking over the audience.

The crowd returns a sentimental "Awww," as the translator echoes Felona's words.

"My story isn't told completely unless I include my rafiki, my friend, Tobias. Tobias where are you?"

A commotion of translators talking and people shifting finally culminates with Tobias clearing the crowd and joining Felona in the front.

He's grinning widely and as he hugs her, turns to face the audience.

Felona continues, "I asked him to come with me and he agreed to, without hesitation. I knew that I would be sharing my story with you and, quite frankly, it's incomplete without him."

A voice from the crowd in stuttered English asks, "Will he be your husband now?"

Laughter from the audience crescendos while Felona blushes.

Tobias speaks, his quiet demeanor betrayed by his booming voice.

"You know what? I love this woman. We're really good friends. Best friends, actually. We've been through a lot and I'm not going anywhere. Unless she comes with me. So... yeah... that's all I got."

He laughs hardily and others join in.

Once the laughter wanes a bit, Felona says loudly, "Someone once asked me if I was happy and I said no."

Her voice shakes and a tear rushes forth.

"But that was like a lifetime ago, it seems. Because now, my mom, Doctor Odoyo and Tobias make me smile on the inside and the outside. They make me happy. I feel like I belong somewhere and with someone."

Felona smiles tightly, as more tears trickle from her eyes. Her mother, Ny and a few small children come and hug her.

"I believe that in your native tongue you say it best with – nee-muh-fry? Yes, that's it! Nimefurahi. I am happy."

53

Elation

Months meld into a progression of seasons and there is no truer exposition of metamorphosis than the passage of time.

"Your hair is gettin' so long," Dianne says as she strokes her daughter's hair.

Felona turns and smiles at her, while sitting on the floor with several textbooks sprawled in front of her.

A few months ago, she concluded that she no longer had fervor for being a reporter and weekend anchor, so she went on an extended sabbatical, supporting herself from savings with assistance from her mother's retirement and disability payments.

Apparently the trip to Africa had such a lasting impact on her, she decided that she wanted to commit her energy and passion to helping troubled young girls. As a result, she applied to the Clinical Psychology PhD program at Edison State University and finds herself absorbed in recreational study while waiting for her acceptance letter.

"I always wondered what it would look like long. My hairdresser, June, keeps wanting to cut it," she says.

"It makes you look taller. Like a model. I like it. But I like it short too. Oh, I don't know which way I like it better."

A black cat darts across the room and lands sprawled with its front claws dug into the side of the couch.

"Harriet! Stop!" Felona shouts, clapping her hands together.

Harriet is startled into a playful stance, before scampering away.

Dianne chuckles.

"Mom, we need to break her of using the furniture as her personal scratching post."

"That's what kittens do, Lona."

"Mom. She's not a kitten anymore."

Dianne nudges Felona lightly.

"Well, she thinks she is. And she thinks your couch is the Underground Railroad the way she was diggin'."

"Well, she'd better straighten up or she'll be shouting, 'To freedom! To freedom!' without her front claws."

They both laugh in chorus.

Dianne sighs into a comfortable silence for a few moments.

"Don't get so caught up in studyin' that you forget about our appointment tomorrow," she finally says.

"I won't. I actually look forward to it. I like this new therapist a lot better than the last one we saw."

"Me too. She's fair. And very thorough. That other therapist though… please! A man can't tell two women how to be."

They both quietly smile.

"I feel like we're making real progress. We should have

done this years ago."

"Hmmmph. Child, everything happens at the perfect time it's s'posed to."

"Is that the door?"

The knock comes again.

"That must be Ny," she says, getting up to answer it.

"Hey!"

Felona and Ny hug tightly at the door.

"Hello hello hello," announces a booming voice from behind Ny.

"Look who else came. Mosi! Come on in."

"There's that beautiful couple," Dianne says as she stands to greet them while Harriet curiously inspects.

"Felo, I wanted to talk to you about the trip we were planning for November."

Felona looks at her mom and back at Ny.

"The Kenya trip?"

"Yes. I know you already made arrangements with your studies to allow you to go for two weeks, but we're going to have to postpone it until next year because I won't be able to travel around that time."

Felona frowns, concerned.

"Why? Is everything okay?"

Ny sighs and looks at Mosi, who looks at the floor. She turns back to Felona with a serious expression before taking her by the arm and leading her to the living room.

"Come sit down."

Everyone gathers in the living room.

"It is so hard keeping anything from you. All of our conversations as of late... I have been bursting at the seams, literally, for three months, wanting to tell you."

"Tell me what?" Felona asks with agitation in her voice.

A smile warms across Ny's face and she's blurts out, "We just got confirmation from the doctor that I've made it past my first trimester. We're pregnant!"

Screams and shrieks of elation fill Felona's home as the women jump up and down and Mosi smiles proudly in the background.

54

And So It Is

Inconsolable cries of a baby echo down the hallway to the ears of his mother who is fighting the urge to console him.

The wailing has been going on for thirty minutes now, but she's hoping that he will wear himself out and eventually go to sleep so that she can also.

Though she's still on maternity leave from work, she's been trying to adapt to a consistent schedule so that when she returns to work in less than a week, it won't be upsetting to him.

The crying stops.

It stops so suddenly that she gets up to check on him just as Vin enters the bedroom holding him.

"Vin! What are you doing?" Danielle whines.

"My little man just wanted his daddy. I'll put him down in a moment."

He cuddles the baby to him as he sits on the edge of the bed.

"That's the problem. He needs to learn how to go to sleep on his own. I thought you were working downstairs."

"I couldn't really focus with Alessandro crying."

Danielle sighs and falls back into bed.

"You know I have to go back to work next week. I'm trying to make that transition easy on him."

"My ma offered to help out, Danielle."

"Your mom hates me and criticizes everything I do that concerns our child, Vin. I'd rather not deal with her and her constant comparisons of me to your ex. I'm not Felona."

Vin turns and glares at her for a moment.

"No, Danielle. No, you're not."

He stands, lovingly nestling the baby to him.

"Get some rest," he flatly says. "I'll get Alessandro to sleep."

"Okay. Love you," she says with a tinge of doubt as Vin leaves the bedroom.

Vin doesn't answer.

Felona's phone rings while she's in her usual position as of late – studying at the dining table.

"Hey, Curlytop. I'm just checking in to see how you and your mom are doing?"

"Oh she's good. We're good. I'm studying my butt off, of course, and she's living the big city life, still helping out."

"Tell her that I miss her."

Felona talks aside from the phone to her mother who is in the kitchen preparing dinner for the both of them.

"Tobias said hey and he misses your cooking."

Dianne smiles.

"What's up, Smartypants?" she says as she returns to the phone.

"Have you ever heard of Jacob Lawrence?"

"Umm... duh. Of course. You know anything that has to do with art or history, I'm into it. Jacob Lawrence was one of the painters that became popular during the Harlem Renaissance. Why?"

"Well, I'll be in town next weekend and there's this exhibit of about forty gouache paintings of his."

"Yeah! I know about that. There's also going to be a few pieces by his wife, Gwendolyn Knight. My mom wanted to go to that. We were thinking about going."

"Well, can you hold off on taking her before I come?"

"Why? You want to ask her out?"

"No. I want you and I to go. And I want you to experience it for the first time with me. After that, you can take her."

"Oh."

"Yeah."

"Okay, I can... wait a minute. Are you asking me out on a date, Tobias?" Felona smiles.

Immediate silence follows for a few long seconds and then, "Yes, Felona. Yes, I'm asking you out on a date. Will you wait for me?"

She smiles and says, "Then, yes, Tobias. I'll wait for you before I go. And, yes... I will gladly be your date. Whatever we do... wherever we go... yes."

And so it is.

Afterword

What you're born into doesn't define what becomes of you. While I'm not a woman nor am I of mixed heritage nor was I born of rape, I've had to struggle with feeling like I didn't belong or fit in, based on where I was from, how I looked or what I wasn't.

The truth is we all have our own insecurities. Unbridled, those insecurities have the potential to become lifelong burdens that hinder healthy relationships and future endeavors, as seen in *the Wedding & Disaster of Felona Mabel*

The "wedding" in the title isn't about the impending matrimony of Felona and Vin. It actually refers to the relationship between Felona and her mother. Until their relationship had been resolved and repaired, everything else for Felona would inevitably end in disaster.

Another aspect of "disaster" for Felona was her struggle with fitting in. She'd heard during all her impressionable years that she was a, "fake white girl, an accidental baby and a bitch." Unfortunately, her tragedy is not isolated to fiction.

Many women (and men) carry the burden of verbal abuse imposed by a parent or caregiver. Although this burden can be lifted and removed through proper counseling, the first step toward that healing is to acknowledge that it exists and where it was born.

While this story is tragic in that it addresses rape, abortion, euthanasia, infidelity and infertility, I wanted to end it with a smile and hope.

Regardless of your past circumstances, know that you can fall into the arms of hope. You matter. You were created intentionally by the Creator who loves you.

I hope that you've enjoyed reading *the Wedding & Disaster of Felona Mabel*. So much so that you'll read it again. And again. It's likely you'll discover hidden nuggets that you didn't see before.

Thank you for reading.

~ Kenn Bivins

Acknowledgments

To the One who is the Creator of all, my Dad and the God of my life: thank you for the redemption story that is my life because of your undying grace.

To Cindy, Lisa, Pamela, Jennifer, Katherine, Patricia and Aunt Mary: your influence in my life from childhood to now helped me create this story. I salute you as examples of the strength that makes up amazing women.

To Kenn II and Spencer: I hope to make you as proud of me as I am of you.

To the friends that have endured my absences, unavailability and reclusiveness while this novel was being produced: I love you for being and for still being here.

To my beta readers: Lyn Thomas, Damali Noel, Karen Nicole Smith, Courtney Dry, Denitria Lewis, Jaime Lincoln, Samara Barks, Karen Marshall, Pamela Johnson, Kinah Lindsay, Geanina Bullock, Tierra Andrews, Geanina Bullock, Katina Ferguson, Raegan Burden, Shana Nunnelly, and Molly Kott. Thank you for your input, critique and invaluable guidance from a woman's point of view.

To Richard Wright, Jonathan Tropper, Ralph Ellison, James Patterson, Chuck Palahniuk, Paul Auster, Andrew Vachss, William Shakespeare and Mary Shelley: thank you for the continuous inspiration to be a better storyteller as a result of your amazing body of work.

To you, my readers: I am especially grateful that you see fit to spend some time with my words and support me. I am fortunate to have you in my life.

To the generations of people affected by atrocities carried out by cowards who see fit to control others through barbaric means: your suffering is not in vain.

Special Acknowledgments

The following people have gone above and beyond offering their finances, time, influence and resources to the production of this novel. I'm thankful for each and every one of them.

Jonathan Chaffin
Karen Nicole Smith
Guy Wyatt
Tiffany Arnold
Denitria Lewis
James & Linda Bivins
Dr. Thelma Dillard
Jennifer Price
Renate Joseph
Craig Brimm
Brooke Hull Brimm
Livia McKenzie
Shawn Jones
Reiko Jordan Brown
Chris De La Rosa
Rhonda Ware
Jane Wong Shing
Josanne Wong Shing
Tammy Kelly
Judy Khamphiphone
Anitra Favors

Chanté LaGon
Lisa Alburquerque
Karen Marshall
Bianca Walker
Lisa Zunzanyika
Lauren Daniel Loden
Carolyn Rogers
LaSheka Payne
Helen Cox
Gabbie McGee
Tierra Miles
Aileen Barrameda
Elaine Drennon Little
Evonna Summers
James Tomasino
MiSook Kim
Joy Bala
Tracy Hall
Damali Noel
Aisha Waller
Curtis Glenn

Micheline Jean Louis
Malaika
Cindy Bivins Coleman
Michelle Ross Okwandu
Jami Nowak
Charlotte Hicks Todd
Lisa Stover
Crystal L. Lowe
Shaton Winston
Fajr Strong
Lynda Meador Wicker
LaNiece Morgan
Rhonda Yelder Ware
Lyn Marie Thomas
I-am Yeti
Sara
Jynxx Johnson
Kim Bright
Asabi Olaniye Beal

Sara Alloy
Kendra Livingston
Yolanda Williams
Jia Gayles
Ebony Glover
Elisha Alford
Courtenay Dry
Darnie Glover
Katina Ferguson
Erica Whiteside
Valerie Sue Love
Pamela Johnson
Luam Fessehazion
Ronald LaGon
Menelik Pope
Clay
Todd Pullen
Aaron Westerman

Resources

SUICIDE

No matter what problems you're dealing with, you have a reason to keep living. Talk to a skilled, trained counselor at a crisis center in your area, anytime (24 hours, 7 days a week)

National Suicide Prevention Lifeline

1.800.273.8255

http://www.suicidepreventionlifeline.org

DEPRESSION

Depression is not just a problem that women encounter. Kristin Brooks Hope Center offers help and hope during crisis for men, elderly and veterans, as well as women.

Kristin Brooks Hope Center

1.800.442.HOPE

http://www.hopeline.com

LUPUS

Through programs of research, education and support services, the Lupus Foundation of America provides help and hope to people with lupus and their families.

Lupus Foundation of America

http://www.lupus.org

SEXUAL ASSAULT

RAINN is the nation's largest anti-sexual violence organization. It created and operates the National Sexual Assault Hotline and carries out programs that prevent sexual violence, helps victims and ensures that rapists are brought to justice.
RAINN (Rape, Abuse & Incest National Network)
1.800.656.HOPE
http://online.rainn.org

COUNSELING HELP

Sometimes we need help working through issues or we need a third party to assist us in staying on the path of a healthy mind and relationships. No matter where you are in the United States or Canada, you can find professional listings for Psychologists, Psychiatrists, Therapists, Counselors, Group Therapy and Treatment Centers.
Psychology Today
https://therapists.psychologytoday.com

or

National Board for Certified Counselors
http://www.nbcc.org/counselorfind

Jonathan Torgovnik's documentary, *Intended Consequences,* was a catalyst and inspiration for this novel.

Visit http://www.foundationrwanda.org to learn more about how **Foundation Rwanda** was born of that documentary and how you can help build a brighter future for the survivors and second generation survivors of the 1994 genocidal mass slaughter in that region.

You've already helped with the purchase of this novel. For every book sold, Invisible Ennk Press is donating a percentage of the proceeds to Foundation Rwanda to help raise funds for bicycles and school fees, which will assist the children on the road to success. One bike helps 5-10 people in a village access clean water, food, school, medical treatment and jobs.

Book Club Guide

1. Acceptance, despite origin, lies at the heart of the novel. How has acceptance or lack thereof played a role in your own life experience? How prominently has it shaped your life?

2. If Felona's mother, Dianne, had succumbed to her coma and died, do you think the overall outcome would have been different for Felona? Why?

3. Fire is a constant element throughout the story. What did it represent in regards to Dianne? Tobias? Felona?

4. What was Felona really afraid of?

5. The cities, Nathaniel and Admah City, are both backgrounds and characters. What do they represent?

6. Every woman is representative of a kind of strength. How did Dianne display fortitude? Felona? Ny? Zoe?

7. Was Felona wrong to leave Vin at the altar?

8. A significant character from Kenn Bivins' *Pious* makes an appearance. Who is that person and when does he/she appear?

9. Tobias and Felona clearly love one another. Do you think that their relationship will mature into a romantic relationship or will they always be platonic best friends?

10. How do you envision Felona and her mother's relationship five years from now?